MW00586087

The Aluminum Turtle

© 2013
Cover © CanStockPhoto/JensKlingebiel

Black Curtain Press
PO Box 632
Floyd VA 24091

ISBN 13: 978-1627553599

First Edition
10 9 8 7 6 5 4 3 2 1

The Aluminum Turtle

Baynard Kendrick

Ronnie Dayland, Jr., just turned nineteen in February, less than two months before, gave the appearance of having everything in the world to live for.

He had light brown hair, intelligent blue eyes, and a serious, mature, and pleasing face. Even though not yet twenty, his body was tall and lithe, muscular and strong. He had known scarcely a day of childhood illness. His family was kindly and wealthy. Reared in the quiet environment of a growing Florida city, Mandalay, on the Gulf of Mexico, Ronnie was an expert swimmer and skin-diver, almost as much at home in the water as he was on shore.

Yet, inside of Ronnie there was a rotten spot that had already spread beyond his control. The outward ravages of a habit that would eventually consume him if left unchecked were still not too readily apparent, as they were bound to be in a few years more. Neither Ronnie, himself, nor his doting parents could rightfully be tagged with all the blame.

Years before a competent psychiatrist might have steered the boy onto another path that would have saved him. Assuming always that Ronald and Celeste Dayland, his father and mother, had sensed the fact that all the high-priced tutors, nurses, and private schools could not supply the young child's craving for security. Security exemplified in Ronnie's preadolescent mind by two things he had never known—discipline and affectionate interest.

From as far back as he could remember he could buy anything he wanted from his parents, or gratify his silliest whim for the very cheap price of keeping out of their way.

He'd found out just as early that there was one thing he couldn't buy at any price—their undivided attention.

God only knows, he'd tried! And Ronnie Dayland, Jr., had a fertile brain from the day he was born.

He wasn't quite six when he added a bucket of beach sand to the oil intended for the motors of his father's fifty-foot Diesel cruiser, the *Kalua*. As an abrasive it was very successful in burning out both main bearings, but it produced no abrasions on Ronnie's rear, a fatherly attention that he had unconsciously hoped for.

It merely produced a pontifical statement from Dayland, Sr., that "Boys will be boys! Some day he'll have a boat of his own and learn how to take care of it!"

The motors had been replaced with new ones. Otis Marble, the *Kalua's* skipper, had been cautioned not to let Ronnie play on board, and the *Kalua* was still the winner—ahead of Ronnie in his father's interest, along with golf, the horses at the Sunshine track, the Day-land orange groves, and the mysterious refrigeration plant where juice was frozen.

Ronnie was eight when he turned his attention to his mother's infatuation with contract bridge. He set the house on fire on the Thursday that she was to entertain her monthly bridge club. It was a workmanlike job, and burned up most of the living room and dining room.

Celeste was very provoked, and blamed Miss Lederer, his governess at the time, for not keeping closer watch on Ronnie. Miss Lederer had a few things to say and eagerly quit, or was fired, according to the point of view.

Celeste moved the party to the Yacht Club, and to teach Ronnie a lesson had the whole sumptuous house redecorated from stem to stern. Later she had a private talk with her husband and both agreed that some day in the indeterminate future Ronnie would have to be sent away to school.

At the age of ten, still fighting his losing struggle for parental recognition, Ronnie preempted Mr. Ross Hubbard's high-speed outboard fishing boat from the Yacht Club slip, where Mr. Hubbard had left it, motor idling, in temporary custody of his eight-year-old daughter, Betty, while he went into the clubhouse to get some cigars.

Less than five minutes and one mile later, Ronnie crashed the boat at twenty miles per hour into the heavy pilings of Red Flasher Two C in Little Pass and reduced the boat to kindling.

By some miracle he and the screaming, clawing Betty, whose antics Ronnie stoutly maintained had caused him to lose control, were tossed free. Both expert swimmers, they were picked up by an outbound charter boat and delivered back to the Yacht Club, little the worse for wear.

For a year the incident had been a local *cause celebre.* Celeste Dayland, running true to form, had denounced Ross Hubbard for leaving his boat and daughter unattended and thereby jeopardizing Ronnie's life by putting temptation in his way.

Ross Hubbard, backed up staunchly by Carolyn, his wife, had declaimed publicly, where all might hear, that the Daylands, pere et mere, were a couple of jellyfish who had unwittingly spawned a two-headed Portuguese man-of-war in the shape of a boy.

In rebuttal the Daylands had resigned from the Yacht Club and moved the *Kalua* to a berth at the local marina at the Mandalay Beach end of the Garden Causeway. Realizing that this serious step might wreck Ronnie's life and career, his remorseful father had tempered the harshness by buying Ronnie a rowboat with a three-and-a-half horsepower outboard that was all Ronnie's own.

Two years later, when Ronnie was twelve, his father was brutally murdered.

Presumably the crime was committed by a hitchhiker whom Mr. Dayland had picked up either at Drew Field, the Tampa Airport, or at some point on State Road 60 between the airport and the place about eight miles west on the Courtney Campbell Parkway where Mr. Dayland's body was found.

His head had been battered in with almost maniacal ferocity, and robbery was undoubtedly the motive, but the facts that Sheriff Dave Riker, of Poinsettia County, had to work on were meager.

Ronald Dayland was an ex-all-American, an athlete of some standing and he hadn't let himself go to seed. He was forty-eight the year he was killed, and still a man to be reckoned with in a free-for-all, a victim not to be easily taken.

Secure in his own strength, plus the fact that he was kindly, generous, and open-hearted, he had the reputation of being afraid of nothing. In spite of warnings from Celeste, who was inwardly timid to a fault, Ronald Dayland seldom passed a hitchhiker by.Early on the day he was killed, he had driven to the Tampa airport, left his Buick there, and caught a flight for Jacksonville. There, his business completed, he had dined with Judge Marston, a lawyer friend, who had driven him to the airport where Dayland boarded a flight due in Tampa at 11:20 p.m.

According to Judge Marston, Dayland had insisted on paying for the dinner from a full wallet. The Judge hadn't looked closely, but his opinion was that Dayland must have had a couple of hundred dollars with him, maybe even more.

His body was found the following day behind one of the picnic fireplaces that bordered the Courtney Campbell Parkway, a ten-mile-long causeway that runs east and west across Old Tampa Bay.

Dayland's wallet, the money gone, had been tossed away in the ashes of the picnic fireplace. The next day his Buick, the gas tank empty, was found abandoned on the outskirts of Ocala about a hundred miles north of Tampa on U.S. Highway 301.

There were discrepancies in the hitchhiker robbery theory that Sheriff Dave Riker's police-trained mind refused to accept, and that seven years later with Ronald Dayland's killer still at large, the sheriff was still unable to explain to his own satisfaction.

The money had been taken, but the robber had left a solid gold wrist watch worth five hundred dollars, a gift from Celeste to her husband. Even more out of character, to Riker's mind, the robber had failed to remove from Dayland's finger a ring with a perfect blue-white diamond of two carats or more that had belonged to Ronald Dayland's father.

Sheriff Riker couldn't picture a greedy murderous thief astute enough to figure, in the heat of a crime, that the watch and ring might be traced, nor a killer with enough self-control to take just the money and leave two such valuable pieces of loot behind.

The sheriff became still more puzzled when the Buick was found near Ocala.

There had been bloodstains on the Courtney Campbell Parkway at the spot where Dayland was bludgeoned, and more on the ground marking a trail where his body was dragged from the road to its place of concealment in back of the picnic fireplace.

But there had been no trace of bloodstains in Ronald Dayland's Buick!

Trying to reconstruct the crime with Ralph Toland, an

investigator for the State's Attorney's Office at the time, both men considered the evidence irrefutable that Dayland had been struck five lethal blows from behind as he stepped out of the left-hand side of his car. Any one of the skull-crushing blows could have killed him.

Then why had he been dealt so many, and why had he gotten out of his car?

The more they tossed it around the clearer it became to Riker and Toland that no mere knockout and robbery was intended. The assassin wanted his victim dead, not just unconscious.

Why dead?

Why risk a murder rap if the robbery could have been committed by merely sapping the luckless victim and stealing his money and car?

Again it seemed obvious to the two officers that the crime had been committed by someone Dayland knew. He had been killed to avoid the certainty of identification.

Then there was the matter of the empty gas tank on the Buick. A check by the sheriff determined that Dayland had filled the tank at the Esso station in Mandalay the morning he drove to the airport. He had charged twelve gallons on his credit card.

Twenty miles from the Esso station to the airport.

Eight miles back to the spot where his body was found.

Twenty miles back from the murder scene through Tampa to the juncture of U.S. Highway 301.

One hundred miles north to Ocala where the abandoned Buick was found, out of gas.

A liberal one hundred and fifty miles—and the twenty gallon tank was empty.

That didn't prove anything, except that the killer had driven all over the state before abandoning the car—or tried to make the police believe that he had.

The sheriff and Toland had painstakingly figured half-a-dozen alternate routes—up U.S. 19, or U.S. 41—and crossing east on various State Roads to U.S. 301. Even the most roundabout route figured less than two hundred miles of traveling.

When the Buick was returned, Sheriff Riker filled the tank in Mandalay and drove the car to Ocala and back without refilling. Two gallons of gas remained in the tank on his return.

Over a period of seven years Dave Riker had built a mental picture of what had happened—a picture so firmly branded on his perceptions that it would never be changed until he put his hands on Ronald Dayland's killer.

Or killers?

He had finally convinced himself that there were two or more.

The picture was this:

Dayland, who was known to carry a lot of cash, had been spotted at the airport by someone who knew him and followed by another car with two men in it.

The robbery car had passed him on the causeway, then pulled to one side, pretending a breakdown.

One of the killers carrying the lethal weapon, probably a jack handle, had walked back a short distance and hidden among the trees bordering the road.

The one who stayed with the car had flagged Dayland down.

As Dayland got out from his car he had signed his own death warrant by calling the man who stopped him by name.

Hearing this the thug behind Dayland had realized instantly that his companion, who thought Dayland didn't know him, had goofed. Dayland did know him! Maybe knew them both! Instead of striking just hard enough to knock Dayland out, the man with the jack handle had struck to kill. And followed up the first blow with others to make doubly sure.

What had started as a hold-up was suddenly a murder.

From there, Riker figured, both cars had been driven to Ocala— an easy six hours, or less, round trip from either Tampa or Mandalay. The sheriff favored Mandalay since he was convinced that Day-land knew the man who flagged him down.

Ronald Dayland knew a great many people in Mandalay—men who had worked in his groves and freezing plant, as well as hundreds of residents. But then he had lived his whole life in Mandalay, as had his father and grandfather.

It was less likely that Dayland had recognized someone from Tampa, a city of a quarter of a million—at that time ten times the population of Mandalay.

The Buick's empty gas tank could be explained if Sheriff Riker's reconstruction of the crime held water: the hold-up car had run low on gas. So the gas was siphoned from the Buick into the hold-up car to avoid the danger of a stop at some all-night filling station. In the hold-up car the two, or more, occupants had sped back to Mandalay to arrive home in plenty of time for work in the morning.

"Or in time for school?" Dave Riker hated himself for allowing such a question to enter his mind. The very thought gave him chills. He had two children of his own. Still, as much as it revolted him, it was an angle that couldn't be overlooked.

Tampa was already faced with the problem of some dangerous teen-age gangs that stopped at nothing. The poison of rumbles and zip guns was spreading worse than atomic fallout. Mandalay turning overnight from town to thriving city was like every other town in the United States receiving its share.

Maybe more than its share, the Sheriff felt—and the local police department, too. A teen-age club that called itself the Water Rovers had sprouted like some toxic mushroom a few years before. Ostensibly devoted to racing rowboats with outboard motors, sailing, and skin-diving, it had grown apace and broadened its activities into drinking parties, and drag racing with the family car.

It wasn't long before the Water Rovers received the opprobrious name of the "Wharf Rats"—and from then on they began to constitute not only a problem, but a real menace to the peace of the town.

Rowboats and outboards began to disappear from private docks. Some of the boats were traced and found repainted and sold in Tampa and St. Petersburg, but most of the outboard motors vanished forever. It became foolhardy to leave a cruiser or sailboat, or anything else around the waterfront unprotected. Anchors, tools and other gear were slickly stolen.

There were those who said that Sheriff Dave Riker developed a morbid prejudice toward members of the Wharf Rats, and parents who defended them, after the murder of Ronald Dayland.

Boys grew older and went in the army. Girls grew up and got married. Finally the sheriff admitted defeat. If any of the Wharf Rat gang had been connected with Dayland's killing, the sheriff, who had investigated every member through long dreary months, had failed to unearth a single tangible clue.

So the members grew older, and new ones came to take their places, and along with Mandalay the Wharf Rats grew. Shortly after his father's death, Ronnie Jr., trying to find excitement enough to revive some spark that had died inside of him along with his father, joined up with the gang. Two years later, Betty Hubbard, firmly established as Ronnie's gal, joined up with them, too.

It was doubtful that Celeste ever knew of her son's connection with the local gang. Certainly, if she did, its implications made little or no impression on her.

Ronnie was her only child, all she had left. He was a good boy, even if he was inclined to be an introvert, and too self-willed for a woman, tragically widowed at the early age of thirty-five, to handle alone.

Other and more important problems were driving her crazy and interfering with her regular routine—the management of the Day-land groves and freezing plant, plus the unpleasant necessity of keeping up a very full social life without a husband in attendance. As to groves and plant—she knew nothing of business, and didn't want to. Her place on the Board of Directors of Dayland Fruits, Inc., a closed corporation, had been merely a nominal one, rubber stamping anything her husband and Jack Manning, the general manager, who comprised the other two Board members, had to say.

Now with Ronald gone, lonesome and distracted, she found herself being constantly heckled by Jack Manning to make decisions on matters that she was not only utterly unqualified to pass on, but matters that she found unutterably boring.

Jack Manning, two years younger than Celeste, was in matters of business, as in everything else, immeasurably more mature. He was quiet and unassuming, over six feet tall and well built, with jet black hair and quick intelligent black eyes. Cast in a rougher mold than Ronald Dayland, he still had all the social graces that Celeste was missing so badly. Topping it all, Jack and Ronnie got along famously, and with a minimum of the friction that Celeste so dreaded.

In less than two years of almost daily contact, Celeste began to realize that she was dependent on Jack Manning not only for his advice on nearly everything she did, and his help in handling Ronnie, but also for his bolstering and sympathetic company.

With Ronnie's full approval his mother and Jack Manning were married when Ronnie Dayland, Jr., was fifteen.

If Celeste had hoped that a stepfather would make a change in Ronnie's life, she couldn't have been more wrong.

It was far too late to save Ronnie.

Within four more years Ronnie was an expert snow-bird and doomed entirely.

Events were to prove that no one could have saved him—not even his father's lifetime friend, Captain Duncan Maclain.

TWO

On a sparkling morning in early April, Ronnie Dayland, Jr., turned over wearily in bed and shut off the buzzer of the electric alarm that had disturbed him.

It was half past five. It was already warm, but not warm enough to make him sweat the way he had all during a restless night. He lit a cigarette, annoyed by his trembling fingers, and took a long drag. It did nothing but parch his throat and make his dry mouth taste worse. The cigarette wasn't going to satisfy him first thing in the morning and he knew it.

Yet, every morning now, for how long was it? Six months? No, more than a year. Let's see! He'd talked Celeste and Jack into fixing up this part of the guest house for him as an apartment more than two years ago. That had been a pushover. He wanted to live his own life. That was the pitch. Have a sitting room where he could play his hi-fi, or watch TV, and set up his own chemical lab without smelling everybody out of the big house. A place where he could entertain Betty or other girl-friends without having parents in his hair.

Sometimes he thought Jack Manning was on to him. Jack had a look in those sharp black eyes and a quirk to his mouth that was pretty keen.

But Ronnie could handle him through Celeste. Jack knew where the greens came from that fed the cats in the Dayland machine. All Celeste ever needed to do was blow a few flat notes on the stick and Jack would roll over with his four paws up in the air.

Ronnie loved his mother after his fashion, but you had to admit that she was something of a square. He wished she wouldn't act like a nitwit, too. But what was there was there. Face her with a fact of life and she fluttered worse than that actress had in that TV show.

So he wanted to live his life alone in a place of his own. Cats, this was the show! Celeste must have known that he'd flunked everything in school, and never finished his senior year.

Or did she know? That or anything?

Experiments in chemistry. Big boff! She never took the trouble to see for herself that the chemical lab in her darling boy's apartment was a front for a well-stocked bar. God, she wouldn't even believe that he'd been stoned when he'd run his MG off the Garden Causeway into two feet of water in Mandalay Harbor. Nice for him the tide was low. That was the year before.

Quarter to six and he needed a fix!

The music goes in here and comes out in the same routine. Starting the same losing battle that he'd been through every morning for longer than he could remember now.

Happy talk! This was the day he'd make the break. Leave one off. The next time skip two days. Then three. Then four. Until finally an entire month would pass without the craving. Then a year and he'd be free forever more.

He got out of bed, the matting hot against his feet, and went to the window to stare out over the water of Mandalay Harbor.

The Dayland estate occupied the whole end of Bayside Drive, one of four ringers of land that extended due east at the southernmost end of Mandalay Beach out into the waters of Mandalay Harbor.

A mile across the green and blue water the rising sun had already touched the houses in Mandalay and turned them into glistening white with a sprinkling of red tiled roofs among them.

Ronnie's sixteen-foot fishing boat, the *A-bomb*, powered by a thirty-five horsepower Johnson Sea Horse, lay bumping gently against its fenders at the Daylands' private dock.

The water was too shallow and the dock too small to accommodate the Daylands'—now the Mannings', Ronnie thought a bit sulkily—fifty-foot Diesel cruiser, the *Kalua*.

She was berthed at the Mandalay Marina, where Otis Marble, the taciturn hard-bitten skipper, who had captained her for more than ten years, lived on board.

Ronnie flashed a glance at the sky. Just a few fair-weather cumulus clouds. Maybe just this morning he could skip the shot. He was taking his father's blind friend, Captain Duncan Maclain, out fishing. Crazy, taking a blink out fishing, but it was going to be a beautiful day.

Ronnie drew in a long deep breath of the cool morning air.

Captain Duncan Maclain had been blinded in the war. He was godfather to the late Ronald Dayland, Sr. The Captain, with the help of his partner, Spud Savage, had beaten blindness by becoming a private investigator, and defeating crooks with such success that his fame had spread around the world.

He had shown that with help and friendship, courage and persistence, there was no goal too difficult for a blind man to attain, and very few things in the sighted world that a blind man couldn't do.

Every year since Ronnie could remember, up to seven years before—the year his father was murdered, Maclain and his wife, Sybella; Spud Savage and his wife, Rena; accompanied always by Maclain's two dogs, Schnucke and Dreist, had been welcome visitors for a week or two in the Dayland home at the end of the winter.

For the past seven years, although Celeste and the Maclains had corresponded frequently, circumstances had interfered with their visits. Three times Maclain and Sybella had flown abroad and toured the Riviera. Then the Captain, aiding the New York police and the FBI, had been shot and seriously wounded by an international criminal.

Convalescing, and slightly crippled, he had foregone two annual winter visits to Florida.

It was certainly not Celeste's second marriage that had kept them away, for all of them knew and liked Jack Manning. Anyhow, now they were back again and settled for ten days, or a couple of weeks, in the big two-bedroom apartment that adjoined Ronnie's in the spacious guest-house.

With their coming, Ronnie, desperately lonely and nursing a secret vice that was far too torturous for any boy to bear, conceived a plan.

Maclain loved to fish. Jack and Celeste had taken out their four visitors on the *Kalua* the second day of their arrival, but they had caught practically nothing.

Ronnie had grinned quietly at this fiasco, and persuaded the Captain to come with him on a lone expedition. He claimed he knew every set of grouper rocks in the Gulf of Mexico within a radius of twenty miles of Mandalay. It wasn't too much of an exaggeration at that, for he'd prowled the Gulf every single day he could get away, too often at the expense of his school.

The Captain was blind. Maybe if he got him out in the boat alone, Ronnie could muster sufficient nerve to ask for help from a man who couldn't see the terror in his face, and read the truth of his weakness. Yes, if he could ever bring himself to talk, Captain Maclain might help him. Any step he'd be able to take to pry that monkey off of his back would make it a really doubly glorious day.

Crazy!

The sun was a little higher now, flashing off the harbor water, and the scintillating glare sat heavy on his eyelids. He was playing a solo. He couldn't ask Maclain, or anyone else, to sit in with that combo while he was taking a ride any more than he could ask his mother. When you started the ride that he was on, you tootled the stick alone without any maestro to stomp the beat, or signal quitting time.

Still, it was always nice to think you were going to make a try. Hell, these beautiful days were becoming a source of annoyance. He'd fought the good fight and gone down for the count as usual.

He tore his eyes away from the shining water and looked down at his naked body. His skin was black as mahogany except for the stark white from navel to thighs where his trunks had protected him from the sun.

For an instant he stared almost professionally at the parallel row of red dots that marched across his belly below his navel.

Crazy!

Dragging his feet across the matting he walked to his clothes closet, pushed hanging slacks and jackets aside on the rod and dug into a back corner for his tackle box.

He set the tackle box on a table and opened it. He took out the top tray where a dozen or more plugs lay in their separate compartments. From under a clutter of hand-lines, gigs, and leader wire in the bottom he fished out an oblong metal box that might have contained fishhooks, but didn't.

Walking rather awkwardly, he took the small box into the tiny kitchenette that Celeste had had built on for him when he moved in. He set the metal box on the drainboard of the sink.

Taking a white enamel saucepan from the oven of the stove, he ran a couple of inches of hot water in it from the faucet, set it on one of the burners and turned on the gas.

Ronnie opened the metal box on the sink and took out a 2

cc. hypodermic, deftly twisted a slender #25 needle onto it, and gingerly lowered it into the saucepan of water which had started to boil.

For five minutes that dragged past with somnambulistic slowness, he watched it boil before he picked it out, using a couple of forks like tongs.

Sterile technique! That was the trick you had to learn if you were going to pop yourself sub-cue—just under the skin. Mainliners, who used a vein in their arm, didn't have to be so careful. If there were bugs on the needle, the flowing blood in the vein would carry them away and disperse them. But then you had to wear a shirt all the time or advertise yourself as the tattooed man, and even the mainliners got infections if they grew too sloppy. So far he'd been lucky because he was careful to keep the shots in his precious belly nice and clean.

He took a teaspoon from the cabinet drawer and a small white capsule from the box, then broke the capsule and emptied its white powder into the spoon.

"Ride a white horse to Banbury Cross!" he muttered as he flicked out the last few grains.

Barely cracking the faucet he allowed a few drops of water to trickle into the spoon. Turning the burner low, he briefly held the spoon over the flame, watching half hypnotized as the contents turned into a milky fluid.

Skillfully he sucked it up into the hypodermic and went into the bathroom.

There was absorbent cotton and alcohol in the medicine cabinet. Soaking a piece of cotton with the alcohol he wiped off the needle and picked a fresh spot to the right of the double row of dots on his belly. Using the moistened cotton he vigorously rubbed clean a place the size of a quarter.

He didn't even wince as he deftly inserted the needle and pressed the plunger down with his thumb, careful not to lose a drop of the precious fluid.

Man, he felt better already, just thinking of the sense of well-being and joyful buoyancy and the delightful euphoria that would shortly take possession of him, turn him into a superman and sustain him all day.

He returned to the kitchen, cleaned up his kit and put it back in his tackle box after checking his supply.

Ten more shots. He didn't intend to run out again as he had a couple of times in the past. He'd have to ask Otis Marble, the skipper of the *Kalua*, to go into Tampa and make another buy. He was lucky to have old Otis as a steady source of supply.

Meantime today was what counted. He showered, put on trunks, a sports shirt and sandals, and drank two cups of instant coffee. He was feeling better every minute. He could catch all the fish in the Gulf for Maclain. He was really the mostest! Maybe he'd be happier just to keep his mouth shut and stay where he was in Endsville, living with the horse and the monkey.

What about it?

Sooner or later didn't everybody have to die!

THREE

The *A-bomb* was a sixteen-foot fiberglass craft with an eight-foot beam. She seated two up forward, back of the rakish windshield, and two in the stern just forward of the powerful thirty-five horsepower Johnson Sea Horse that was mounted on the transom. She carried a six-gallon fuel tank, inboard, that fed to the motor with a fuel pump. She had an electric self-starter and steered from the left-hand front seat like an automobile. A nice two-thousand-dollar plaything for any boy.

Ronnie got the Captain settled in his seat, admiring the confidence with which Maclain stepped from the dock into the boat guided only by a word from Ronnie, and a light touch on his arm. It was more trouble loading his mother in, when she would get in.

There were lots of things he admired about Maclain. According to Ronnie's quick figuring he must be older than God, but his clipped black mustache didn't show it, nor the quickness of his step. The only indications Ronnie could see were the touches of white at his temples, and the few threads of gray in his crisp dark hair.

The old boy was wearing khaki slacks, a tan pair of topsiders, and a white terry-lined zipper jacket with a hood that hung down back of his neck. The jacket was decorated with tiny colorful prints of yacht-club pennants. Really keen!

Nice tackle he had, too. Ronnie sized up the rod and reel stowed amidships behind the front seat: a Shakespeare glass rod six foot five, heavy duty; a German silver star drag reel and not too heavy a line. You could get real daddy grouper on that outfit, but you couldn't exactly horse them in. They'd give you plenty of fun.

Ronnie eased the *A-bomb* out toward Flasher Six and turned her right inside the marker. He opened her up a little more for the short run between the can and nun buoys to where the channel turned at Flasher Two C.

There was a straightaway from there for about three-quarters of a mile where you kept three red markers and another red flasher to port on the way out. It was early and no other boats were in sight to be bothered by his wash.

In a spirit of quick bravado, feeling that he was master of everything, and partly to see if he could get a rise out of the Captain sitting so relaxed beside him, he gunned the Johnson wide open.

Water surged under them as the *A-bomb* lifted to meet the gentle incoming roll from the Gulf. Thirty miles per hour! Not too much on land but on water you were flying.

Less than two minutes later they were close to the black pilings of Green Flasher Three that marked the end of Little Pass.

Ronnie went around it without slackening speed, dipping the *A-bomb* recklessly to starboard. There were a group of shallow spots straight ahead, but not shallow enough to ground the *A-bomb*. Larger boats with deeper draft when coming out of Little Pass usually held a coarse due west to Number One Bell Flasher, nearly a mile offshore. A six-foot channel meandered along closer in to shore—if you knew how to follow it.

Ronnie took it, running past beautiful beach-front homes, some with their own private docks. He glanced at Maclain to find the Captain's mobile face set in a smile of tolerant amusement.

"Cool, isn't she? Thirty miles per hour!"

"I thought you brought lunch, Ronnie." The Captain's smile turned into a grin.

"I did. Sandwiches, hard-boiled eggs, and a dozen cans of beer. You hungry already?"

"No. I just thought from the way you were pushing her that you wanted to get to the fishing grounds and be back home by noon."

So he had gotten a rise out of the old boy! It was Ronnie's turn to grin. "Too fast for you?"

Maclain shook his head. "Too fast for the motor, and you know it. Your stepfather says you're one of the best boatmen in Mandalay. I got that from Otis Marble, too. So, I'm impressed! Now you can bring her down to three-quarter throttle. You don't need to prove anything to me by scraping the barnacles off of a marker and nearly dumping us into the bay."

A trifle crestfallen, but inwardly feeling much relieved,

Ronnie throttled the *A-bomb* down and settled her at a steady twenty miles per hour.

For a while he was silent, then he said disgustedly: "I don't know what got into me back there. It's getting so that I have to prove to everybody that I'm a big shot of some kind. Impress them, like you said. Drink a lot of liquor, just to show the world I can get it when I'm too young to go into a bar. Drive my MG faster than anyone else—off the causeway into the harbor. Let everyone know I've got a car. Smash up a boat—like I did Mr. Hubbard's when I was ten years old—"

"I remember that," the Captain said quietly.

"What am I trying to prove? That I'm still ten—by taking a chance on cracking us up before we get started today? Or maybe that I'm a hep-cat when I'm really a square from Endsville. Or that—"

"What?"

Ronnie turned to look into the sightless dark eyes, so perfect you'd think they could see. There was suffering in the Captain's rugged face, but much more than that—deep sympathy.

Why not tell the old boy now? Give him the lowdown on the big deal. The Wharf Rats. Their club house in the old shed in the abandoned grove, where the trees were so thick that even the sheriff couldn't find it, and where parties went on that the Yacht Club members couldn't imagine.

Why not tell him?

The goof-balls! The Red Devils! The Yellow Perils! The Green Dragons! And the acrid smoke of the marihuana—the bitter beautiful tea that put your feet to sleep and speeded up your brain so fast that it slowed the music down until you could pick each note of the jive apart and study it in its entity.

Wouldn't this man who had lived so long with blindness know the answers? Know how to beat most anything?

Why not tell him about the horse that you rode day and night, and the hat full of rain, and the monkey that rode you? But first get his promise to keep it away from his parents, Jack and Celeste, then finish quite simply by saying: "For God's sake take me away from all of this. Away from myself. I'll do anything. Go any place. If you'll only help me!"

He couldn't right now. The time wasn't ripe. The very

thought was bringing on those nervous yawns, starting him to sweat again. It was far too early in the day for that. He'd go to pieces and crumple up like an empty scarecrow if he let himself go on thinking this way.

Suddenly he blurted out: "I wonder if I'll grow up some day?"

The Captain laughed softly. "Only part of us grows up, Ronnie. Maybe two-thirds or three-quarters. The other part has a streak of perpetual adolescence that is there in us all to stay."

"What's that stuff that Celeste quotes to me about putting away childish things?"

"When I was a child, I spake as a child. When I became a man I put away childish things. First Corinthians, chapter thirteen, verse eleven," the Captain quoted soberly. "There are a lot of different interpretations as to what are childish things, Ronnie. Some men think that hunting and fishing are childish. Swimming and games, and the sheer enjoyment of fife and sunshine and nature, and the wonder of the beauties around us.

"I don't, but that's a matter of opinion. I think the childish things the Bible meant for us to put away were selfishness, gluttony, laziness, and fear of the dark. I've had to beat my fear of the dark, or it would have beaten me. Then, there certainly are a couple of childish traits we all should hang on to: tolerance, and lack of prejudice. All of us are born tolerant and unprejudiced. Children have to be taught to hate others who differ from them in race, creed, or color. Unfortunately, the world does a very good job of that teaching, which to my mind is why we're in the mess we are today."

"I've been taught plenty," Ronnie said bitterly. "Most of it the wrong way." Again he thought he might go on and couldn't.

"Growing up is always rough, and you've grown up, Ronnie. You were a child the last time I saw you. You're a man today."

The boat sped on.

Maclain pulled up the left sleeve of his zipper jacket, revealing what looked to Ronnie like two wrist watches. He placed his left arm tight against his chest, palm down, and nipped open the lid of the wrist watch nearer to his elbow.

Ronnie leaned closer and found himself staring at the quivering needle of an uncovered compass. The Captain touched the needle lightly with his finger, checking its position against some raised dots around the edge of the circle.

"North by west. Is that close enough?"

"Pretty near on the button," Ronnie said, consulting the boat compass. "But—"

"What good does it do when I can't see? Well, let's just say I like to know what direction I'm going in. This one is my Braille watch." He flipped open the lid of the other one and held it out for Ronnie to examine as he touched it with his finger. "Quarter to seven. That's fifteen minutes since you nearly amputated the flasher marking the entrance to Little Pass. Number three, I believe, from what your stepfather told me day before yesterday when we were on the *Kalua*."

"So you get a kick from just doping things out."

"No, it's more than that. Fifteen minutes at twenty miles per hour would locate us five miles from there. So you see, if you dropped dead, or fell overboard, Heaven forbid, I could turn the boat around and put her on the opposite course—south by east. Then if I ran her for fifteen minutes, I could slow her down, put her on a course toward Mandalay Beach—say east by north. If my frantic wavings failed to attract another craft, and I didn't hit anything or run aground, I could crawl into the beach and probably land in someone's front yard, hit a morning swimmer, or bump a piling on the fishing pier. Anything would please me more than putting straight out to sea."

Ronnie gave the matter some thought. "I'll bet you could do it, too. I've heard you have wonderfully sensitive fingers. What about signing on as one of my crew?"

"You think you have a job a blind man can do?"

"You've never had much luck with grouper, have you?"

"Not too good."

"I'll tell you why. They lie in rock piles on the bottom and dash out quick to get their food, then back in again. They're ferocious, fast and tricky. The trick is to find those rock piles and it is a trick. Believe me, there aren't any sign posts stuck up out in the Gulf of Mexico. Most of the bottom is sand, grass, or shell. That's no good for grouper. Did you ever sample the bottom with a sounding lead?"

The Captain shook his head.

"Well, I have a hunch. I'm going to try a new place today. It's about twelve miles up from where we came out of Little Pass, and about two miles south of Anclote Key."

"That's off Tarpon Springs, isn't it?"

"Yes. It's a long narrow key that runs north and south about three miles offshore from the mouth of the Anclote River that runs up to Tarpon Springs. A few years ago the government dredged a channel where we're going—a hundred feet wide, nine feet deep, and a mile long. On the chart it looks like it's stuck out in the middle of nowhere. But the sponge boats use it when they're headed west from shallow water into deep, and coming back in again. I think there's rocky bottom along that channel. I may be wrong, but for a long time I've wanted to give it a try. Grouper bite awfully fast, if they're there. We'll move if we don't get anything. Are you game?"

"Where do my fingers fit in? After all, I'm just the crew."

"We'll try your fingers out on this." Ronnie reached down in back of the seat and brought up an hexagonal cylinder of lead about eight inches long, narrower at one end than the other. "It's a five pound sounding-lead," he explained as he handed it to Maclain.

The Captain brailled it with interest.

"This line attached to the narrow end is knotted at three feet intervals to give you the depth when you let it down," Ronnie went on. "Now feel the larger end where it lands on the bottom."

The Captain's sentient fingers explored the length of the lead again and stopped at the feel of a putty-like substance packed tightly into a hollow in the larger end.

"It feels like it might be soap of some kind."

"Soap is right. Octagon soap. You drop the lead down until it touches the bottom, then pull it up and take a look and a feel. You can feel more than you can see. On a grassy bottom you'll bring up mud and little pieces of seaweed. No good."

"I thought that was good bottom for trout."

"We're after grouper. Bring up sand in the soap and you're over a sandy bottom. No good. Wipe it off and try again. Bring up little sharp particles and the bottom's sand and shell. No good. Then finally you bring up some tiny pebbles, mostly smooth, and that's what you're looking for. Rocks."

"What then?"

"You run a short distance against the tide, drop your anchor, and hope that the boat will drift back just enough to be right over that wonderful spot. Sometimes, if you're lucky, it does. Sometimes, the spot seems to have vanished and you just can't ever find it again."

"Maybe I can make myself quite useful," said Duncan Maclain. "Let me know when you want me to start."

"You can start as soon as I slow her down. It won't be long now. We're pretty near there."

Minutes trickled away with no sound but the rushing wind and the muted roar of the powerful motor. Then the boat turned sharply right and the motor slowed down to a purring crawl. The Captain didn't need his compass to know they were headed due east. After a moment, and for not much more than the space of a second, he was conscious of a break in the sound of the motor. It was brief, as though someone had tossed a pebble against a wall.

Ronnie said, "Try it here."

The Captain tossed the lead overside, felt three knots slip between his fingers—nine feet, and the soft contact as the lead touched bottom. He hauled it quickly up again and felt the soap.

"Shell," he told Ronnie. "Right?"

Ronnie took a look. "On the button."

Twice more the lead went down and the bottom showed up shell. Then once again came that break in the sound of the motor like a pebble tossed against a wall.

Six more times the Captain tried it as the *A-bomb* nosed slowly along. Sand. A grass bed. More shell. All revealed themselves in succession to the delicate touch of his fingers.

A brief change in the motor's sound came as he lowered the lead again. It was shallower here. Seven to eight feet, no more. He hauled up and this time found the soap in the lead was studded with rounded pebbles tiny as pin heads.

"Cut it!" he yelled at Ronnie. The excitement of finding uranium was in his tone. "We've got it! The rock bottom's here!"

The *A-bomb* reversed itself to a stop, swung its nose left and headed up north for fifty feet. The anchor splashed. Maclain felt the *A-bomb* fall back and pull against it.

Strange that sound of the idling motor now was different, continuous, as though the pebbles were bouncing back in a steady stream from against the phantom wall. Then Ronnie stopped the motor and the only sound was lapping water of the tide against the hull.

"You were speaking of show-offs—trying to prove things to the world, a little while ago. Now I want to show you that there's a lot of kid stuff left in me," the Captain said. "I'm still not above trying to prove how good I am with things I can't see."

"How's that?"

"After you turned the boat and slowed down, while I was sounding, we passed three markers. The first was a big one, a flasher. The other two were smaller. We're anchored just north of the third one now. Also, unless I'm all wet, there's another big one, a flasher, somewhere about a hundred yards to the right of where we're anchored now."

Ronnie's stomach tightened up inside of him. Sweat popped out on his forehead. He began to shake with an overwhelming ague. This man whom he'd trusted was just a phony who'd been watching his narrowed pupils all morning. Laughing to himself about this hop-head who thought he was blind.

He was hep now to Duncan Maclain. Celeste and Jack had rigged this deal, but it wouldn't work. Nobody was going to spill the truth to his mother that her precious son was a junky.

There'd be one fake blind man missing from the roll-call at the next meeting of the New York Light House at the end of this trip if Ronnie found out that Maclain could really see.

"Well, that's a hot one." Ronnie forced his voice to keep under control. "All these years I've heard you were blind when you can really see. You sure bugged me!"

"I can only see with my ears," Maclain said quickly, caught by Ronnie's distrust that was reaching out and enfolding him with tangible tendrils. "Like most people who have been blind for years I have a built-in sonar. I can tell the size of most any room by just speaking in it and listening to the sound of my voice bounce back at me. Start the boat and run it by any markers, buoys, or other boats, and I'll tell you when we're passing them. You can try it, if you don't believe me."

"Sure, I believe you, Captain." Ronnie forced a laugh that was as unconvincing as his statement. "I'm just an odd-ball and you put me in the corner pocket. For a minute it got me. I'll rig up your tackle and we'll fish some."

But the fear of Maclain's uncanny skill was still with him—an eating fear, deep and ingrained; terror of what Maclain might fathom, even though he couldn't see.

It was an addict's fear, so strong and unreasonable that it cost Ronnie Dayland, Jr., his life when the truth might have saved him.

He lied to Maclain about where he pulled up the aluminum turtle.

FOUR

Ronnie took a seat in the stern and opened his tackle box. He attached a three-way swivel to the Captain's line, and selected a heavy dipsy which he tied on in the lower eye. He cut a length of leader-wire from the coil in his box. Working silently and using his fishing pliers, he skillfully looped one end of the leader into the third eye of the swivel so that it stood out at right angles from the line. He fastened a heavy fishhook to the other end of the leader.

Half a dozen mullet were wrapped up in a newspaper. Ronnie opened them, laid one on his baitboard, and with his sharp bait knife sliced off a tempting chunk about an inch and a half wide and three inches long. He used the piece to bait the hook, giving it a twist so that the barb went through it twice and left the point concealed in the mullet's flesh.

"You're all set now! Here feel it." He passed the rig-up to the Captain and guided his fingers down the line, over the swivel, leader and sinker, warning him to watch for the hook as he touched the bait.

The Captain nodded admiringly and kept his mouth shut. He'd already given enough demonstrations of his faculties to last all day. Telling Ronnie about the markers had been a blooper. Better to take things easy until he found out why.

The boy was abnormally nervous, terrorized by something from all the indications of his jumpy reactions. Maclain decided that maybe if he relaxed and took things easy he could win Ronnie's confidence and get him to talk before the end of the day.

Meantime, if Ronnie wanted to think that Duncan Maclain was helpless, better let him think so. This was scarcely the moment to tell him that Maclain had been rigging his own tackle, cutting his own bait, baiting his own hooks on salt and fresh water from coast to coast—not to mention taking his own fish from the hooks since before Ronnie Dayland, Jr., was born.

Sure, he'd done it all in inky blackness, and been barbed and bitten, stuck and stung by a hundred mixed varieties of creatures of the sea.

Why?

Just one reason: the reason that had originally driven him into the hazardous career of a private investigator—to show a skeptical world that blindness wasn't the end of everything.

Ronnie tossed the sinker and bait overboard and watched the Captain slowly pay out line as the tide swept it toward the stern.

The boat was anchored nearly a hundred feet, north in a straight line, from the third marker from the west end of the channel. It was a single black piling. A pointed narrow board, bolted near the top, extended southward like a pointing arm to mark the channel.

There was a white five on the extended arm. Ronnie had seen it as they poked along while the Captain was sounding. He had a quick desire to ask the old boy if he knew the number on that marker.

Yes, he'd feel pretty silly if the Captain told him. He took a quick look out starboard at the group of heavy pilings with the square box on top supporting the flasher. It was about three hundred yards away, in fine with number five. The flasher was number seven, and Maclain had indicated that he'd heard the sound of the outboard bounce back from it, too.

Ronnie shut his eyes for a minute. It was a cinch that the old boy probably knew that all black flashers and markers bore odd numbers. Then he'd know that the first of the four, marking the entrance to the channel coming shoreward would be number one. One, three, five, and seven! Sure as the devil the old boy would have it pegged that they were anchored off number five now.

Ronnie opened his eyes with a snap and blinked against the rush of the sunlight. The hell with playing blindman and guessing what Captain Maclain could do. He'd already seen, or heard, enough card tricks, or ear tricks, to give him the jitters.

"Just let your sinker touch the bottom, then lift it up and down a few inches easy every now and then to be sure it's free." Now he was talking about something he knew—grouper fishing.

He was the best damn grouper fisherman in Mandalay—in Florida —in the United States—in the world. Where he'd had the shakes a few minutes before, now he was flooded with self-confidence, self-assurance, self-possession. He'd show this helpless blind man how really to catch fish. Seeing with his ears!

Crazy!

"When a grouper hits, you've got to get him free of the rocks, but quick. Otherwise before you can wink they'll have run you into one of their holes and hung you up but good. Then there's nothing left to do but break your line trying to haul up the whole bottom of the bay."

"You must have caught a lot, Ronnie."

"Probably more than anyone living," he said simply. "I've taken as high as fifty in a day. Caught my share of black grouper and jew-fish, too. One bigger than I am—over three-hundred-and-fifty pounds." The statement seemed quite natural to him, just the truth without exaggeration.

For the moment he was the mostest! The greatest! The all supreme! He had no inkling that the horse might be talking, and that the sudden change from diffident boy to bragging intrepid fisherman might have filled his voice with so much aplomb that the falseness was overflowing and leaking through.

"I'll watch my step," Maclain said puzzled, and chary of giving too much praise. "But I'm not making any guarantees what will happen if any whoppers that size come my way."

Ronnie laughed and felt better as he put in his own line overboard on the opposite side of the A-bomb. "I don't think you need to worry. Up here, five to seven pounds is the average, though you will catch an occasional whopper. The big blackies and the jewfish are farther out where the water's deeper, or farther south down off Key West, where I caught mine."

He was enjoying this role of kindly instructor. "If you start catching blow-fish—those things that swell up like a balloon and grunt—we'll move. They're a nuisance. Just like pulling up a sock. We used to toss them overboard, but now they call them Angel Fish, or something, and pop you a top price in the restaurants for a filet."

He fell silent. The sun rose burningly higher. The Captain shed his zipper jacket and dropped it in the bottom of the boat at his feet. His sleeveless shirt revealed a skin almost as dark as Ronnie's own, a barrel-like chest, sinewy wrists, and rippling biceps flat and hard as a boxer's.

He idly bobbled his sinker against the bottom, per Ronnie's

instructions, to make sure that it was free. Then suddenly it wasn't free. The line was hissing to the left through the water, raising a couple of tiny twin waves with its speed.

Maclain jerked hard, set the hook, and began to reel.

"Strike!" He yelled it loud in spite of himself, caught in that quick excitement that every normal person knows when some living creature is fast to the end of a singing line.

"Reel him up! Reel him up!" Ronnie was shouting, too.

He put the click on his reel and braced his rod firmly under the stern seat, then turned to the starboard side to help Maclain.

The line reversed its direction in high, bearing down now in an irresistible rush with the tide toward marker five.

"He's headed into the rocks!" Ronnie yelled. "Keep him out— keep him away!"

The Captain leaned back hard on his rod bending it into a bow. The star drag slipped and he tightened it. He was reeling in more steadily now and beginning to gain.

"When you hear him splash, swing your rod in to the left toward the stern until you feel me take hold of the tip. Then I can grab the leader and bring him in the rest of the way. But don't give him enough line to run under the boat."

The Captain's heart skipped a beat as the line slacked off. Then Ronnie exclaimed as though he had done it all on his own: "I've got him. He's a beauty. Over two feet long. Better than five or six pounds I'd say. Well, we've started the day."

But the day was far from being finished.

The click on Ronnie's reel started singing stridently as something seized his bait and tore for cover.

Ronnie abandoned the Captain's grouper to flop at will in the bottom of the boat and grabbed for his rod. He slipped off the click and struck back swiftly, tightening the line.

It was no use and he knew it. The few seconds it had taken him to get his rod free from under the seat was all that any self-respecting grouper needed.

"Not a chance," he said disappointedly. "I'm hung up properly in the rocks."

"You think you can get loose?"

"I doubt it. I'm giving it all it will stand right now, but it feels like he's tied me tight around a tree." He moved his rod in every direction in a vain attempt to free the line.

Discouraged with that, he put the rod in the boat and took the line in his hand to try giving it a direct strong steady pull.

"It's no use," he said finally. "There's one more chance. I'll have to slack off on the anchor line and let the tide carry us back until we're directly over the spot. If a straight-up pull won't free the line, I'll have to break it."

"Stay where you are," Maclain said shortly. "I can handle the anchor line." He stood up before Ronnie could protest and leaned forward over the low windshield. An instant later he had loosened the anchor line made fast to a cleat on the bow. "Tell me when to stop, Ronnie."

Keeping control with a single turn around the cleat, Maclain paid out line and let the *A-bomb* go slowly down with the tide until Ronnie said, "Now!"

Ronnie tried pulling straight up with a slow steady pull while he moved the line from side to side. Still it stuck. At last, not caring if he broke it or not, he wrapped the line around his hand and put all his strength into one last jerk.

The line came free. This time without breaking, for from the feel he could tell that the sinker was still on, but it only came up for a foot or more before it seemed to catch in something else—some yielding substance, maybe a mass of grass and seaweed.

Ronnie jerked on it angrily, and again it was free. This time even more than free, for as he pulled the line in hand over hand it appeared to be coming up buoyantly without the normal dragging weight of the sinker.

Then his hook popped up, still attached to the end of the leader and brought to the surface by a creature that floated—a dead thing, malignant and unmoving. A turtle—hooked through the nipper.

Ronnie pulled it aboard in shocked disbelief and set it on the floor by his tackle box, close by the Captain's gasping grouper whose flappings had subsided into an occasional twist of the tail.

He sat on the seat and stared at the thing, for a time too paralyzed to touch it.

He was silent for so long that the Captain asked, "Are you okay? Is your line all free?"

"Yes, but my line's a mess," he managed to say. "I'll have your fish off the hook in a minute. What about pulling us back up to where we were before and making us fast?"

"Sure thing." The Captain began to pull the anchor line back in.

No psychiatrist has even been quite able to analyze the working of a heroin addict's mind, nor classify the nameless horrors that might obtrude themselves into an addict's life through some unexplained break in routine.

Ronnie brushed cold sweat from his forehead and fought a retching of his stomach. Quick nervous yawns began to stifle an oncoming scream.

That thing at his feet never lived in the sea. Never lived at all. It couldn't have been there. It was a devil-made warning; the ultimate death-dealing climax of some horrendous waking dream.

He whipped his numbed senses back to the point of making calculations. It was ten inches long. Or maybe a foot, and about half that wide. Loathsome looking, mottled freakishly in brown and green.

He suppressed a quick impulse to grab it and take it up to the blind man, who called himself a detective, thrust it into his hands and scream in his ear: "Feel this since you know so much! Is it real? Or is it just some joke that squirted out of the needle this morning— something I haven't really seen?"

Then the lovely euphoria was back again, and with it a deep secretiveness. Cautiously, as though the world was peopled with spying eyes, Ronnie began to look around him.

Nothing. No one to spy, except the birds perched on the four black markers along the north edge of this channel, dredged way out at sea: Flasher One—a mile to the west; Marker Three—in line to the west, maybe a quarter-of-a-mile closer to the A-bomb; Marker Five—a hundred feet south of the stern from where they were anchored. And to his left, Flasher Seven—indicating the east end of the mile long channel. It was three hundred yards toward the mainland which was at least four miles away.

No one to spy except the birds. The nearest point of solid land was the lighthouse on Anclote Key, and that was two miles north of the bow.

Ronnie tightened up and forced himself to touch the turtle with shaking fingers. It was metal, all right. No doubt of that. The flippers, head and tail were rubber, or more likely soft leather. They were already becoming less flexible as they dried out in the sun.

"Think fast, Dad!" he told himself. "Some joker made that crazy turtle and planted it on the bottom of the Gulf for his own wild reason. This isn't any time to flip!"

There was only one answer: he'd lucked on to an underwater buoy that marked some sunken treasure. The place where he'd found it was his own secret and he intended to keep it that way.

Right now he had to get away from the channel and Marker Five as soon as he could without arousing Maclain's suspicions. Seven miles south of the channel he knew of another good grouper hole. He'd stop there and fish and fool the blind man. Trick him into thinking that the turtle was pulled up there later in the day.

He was rich if he played it cozy!

Rich—rich—rich! And that wasn't any junky's dream!

FIVE

They fished desultorily for maybe an hour with no luck. A very light breeze sprang up from the south, doing nothing to relieve the heat.

Ronnie tossed the Captain's grouper into the insulated fishbox, half filled with cracked ice. He took a couple of cans of beer from the frosty interior, and opened them.

Maclain drank his eagerly, glad when the moisture popped out on his skin and cooled him some with its quick evaporation.

Ronnie said: "Either those two grouper that struck were the only ones around here, or the fuss that one made when it tangled my line scared them all away."

"Maybe I didn't get the boat back in exactly the same place. Would that do it?"

"Could be. I don't know how you can lose a pile of rocks so easy, but you sure can. One minute you have them and the next they're gone." He hefted the sounding lead. "I'm going to toss the lead again and take a look at the bottom."

The lead splashed over. Ronnie pulled it up and gave an exclamation of disgust. "We're fishing over a bunch of hay. Pull us up a little farther and I'll try there."

Maclain put down his rod and complied, hauling in slowly on the anchor line while Ronnie tested the bottom twice more. The water began to shallow.

Ronnie said, "We're getting up close to a spoil bank where the dredges dumped the stuff they took from the channel. Let her go back again."

The Captain let the rope slip through his fingers while Ronnie sounded half-a-dozen times more. Twice he found very passable bottom, but said nothing about it.

Getting away from that spot where he'd pulled up the turtle had become an obsession. The sooner the better.

He took a look shoreward toward the long line of markers leading up to the mouth of the Anclote River. A sponger was coming out through the channel, three or four miles away. He thought he knew the boat, one that had been converted to take out twenty or more passengers fishing for the day.

If it was the boat he thought, it would be headed right for them, and the captain and mate both knew him. He was going to need help if that turtle marked a treasure and he intended to do any skin-diving for it. He'd have to confide his find in his stepfather, Jack Manning, and Skipper Otis Marble, for without them he couldn't use the *Kalua.*

Just let the word leak about that turtle, and let the *A-bomb* be spotted off Marker Five and half-a-dozen sponge divers in full deep water evening dress would be clomping all over the bottom around Marker Five the very next day.

"This looks like a washout," Ronnie said. "I'm afraid it's too shallow here, anyhow. Let's pull in our lines and move. What do you say?"

"Just what I said before—you're the skipper. I can stand a little breeze, even if it's artificial. I feel like a piece of toast."

"Can you handle the anchor?"

"Sure. I can see it just as well as you can, can't I? When it's down on the bottom."

Five minutes later they had sped down the channel westward, turned south with Flasher One at their stern, and settled down on a course of 170 degrees at twenty miles per hour.

For a time the Captain leaned overside to escape the protection of the windshield. The rushing wind was exhilarating against his hot cheeks, and he welcomed the occasional dashes of the warm salty spray.

Much refreshed, he straightened up and took cigarettes, holder and lighter from the pocket of his slacks. He leaned forward back of the windshield to light one.

Ronnie's blue eyes widened as he followed each movement of the familiar operation. Cigarette from pack—into holder—flash of lighter tested with a fingertip, and the application of the flame exactly to the end of the cigarette without hesitation or fumbling.

It was the product of years of confidence and surety, the way Maclain did everything. The disciplining of muscles and movement into flexible smooth co-ordination, as you steered a boat, or drove a car, or flew a plane.

The ease of it made Ronnie wonder; would he ever have the

stamina, the character, or the stick-to-itiveness in anything to develop that tidy fluidity of accomplishment that the world defined as skill?

"I had lunch with a very old friend of mine yesterday—the Sheriff." The Captain settled down in his seat.

"Dave Riker?"

"Yes."

"What did old Sherlock have to say?"

"Quite a lot about your father's murder." The Captain held out his cigarette and de-ashed it in the rushing wind. "There were several things that didn't make sense."

"Yes, several things. I suppose he's still hepped about that wrist watch and the diamond ring."

"And the Water Rovers."

"Call 'em the Wharf Rats, like everyone else; it doesn't bother me. Did you come up with any bright ideas?"

"Bright ideas tarnish after seven years."

"Yeah. If he told you about the Wharf Rats, he must have given you a thirty-minute show with music about me."

The Captain took a few more puffs, ejected his cigarette overside, and returned his holder to his pocket. "The sheriff said you'd been a member in good standing up until a year ago—then resigned, or quit. Or whatever the procedure is in a gang with the Wharf Rats' reputation. He wasn't sure."

"He's not too bright, or he would be."

"Sure?"

"Yeah. The next time you see him, you might tell him that he doesn't dig me or the Wharf Rats, either one. You don't just resign from the Wharf Rats. I tipped the sheriff off to a caper the Rats were going to pull and got booted out on my ear—but that isn't the end by a hell of a sight."

The Captain was silent, rubbing his temples.

"Now I'm solid-citizen Ronnie Dayland, living his li'l ole life alone—visiting the local hot-spots minus any gal friend. Of course, the only hot spot I visit is the Hi-Fi Club when I play the machine in my luxurious sitting-room in Endsville."

"I thought you were seeing a lot of Betty Hubbard."

"Mother's been giving you her current dreams about my love-life. Is that it?"

"Yes."

"Sure, I still see a lot of Betty—if I go downtown and take a look in the drugstore where she's having a Coke with Paul Fraceti. Or if I take a look through the window at the high school dance where she's doing a little rocking with Chuck Lindsay." He bit off the second boy's name on an acrid note.

Again he had a chance to put his ad in the help wanted department—tell the Captain that Betty had watched him go down the sliding board from marihuana to pills and the needle, and tried to stop him. Not until she realized he was hooked for good had she promised to keep her mouth shut and told him in words of one syllable that she wasn't dating a hop-head.

She'd made it quite clear that unless he shook the habit, cold-turkey, or by taking a cure, she was shaking him. He studied the Captain's rugged face, and chickened out again.

He had a scheme to get away from Mandalay—from Jack and Celeste, and all the people he knew. It was going to take money, but he had money: two-hundred-thousand bucks from his father's estate. It was coming to him in a couple of years, when he was twenty-one.

That is, if he could keep Celeste buttered up and thinking that her wandering boy had kept his nose clean. If she ever found out—! If she considered him incompetent—! Well, she mustn't! She had the power under the will to keep his inheritance out of his hands for four years more, until he was twenty-five.

He couldn't wait that long. He couldn't wait two years. He wanted thirty-five thousand bucks right now to carry out his scheme—to buy a charter boat that Otis Marble and he could take to Miami.

It was a sound idea and he'd talked it over with Otis a dozen times. Otis had his license and could act as captain with Ronnie as mate.

But most important of all, once he got safely away to Miami he could go to a decent doctor under another name, if necessary, and take the cure. Who cared about a mate on a charter boat?

Maclain had a lot of pull with Celeste. Ronnie determined that before the day ended he'd tell him just enough of his troubles to see if the Captain wouldn't intercede with Celeste and get him the thirty-five thousand. But it would be taking far too big a chance to tell him everything.

Of course, if that turtle was what he thought it was—some marker on a treasure, and he could get there first, before the diver who had marked the place returned—all his worries would be ended.

He brought himself back to the *A-bomb* with a start. The Captain was speaking and Ronnie had missed it.

"I'm sorry. We're nearly there to the place I want to try fishing again. I was trying to line up Red Flasher Two, and Black Marker Three, in Big Pass, between Caladesi Island and the north end of Mandalay Beach. I missed what you were saying."

"I asked you if your experience with the Wharf Rats indicated to you that a bunch of youngsters like that would have gone so far as to deliberately murder your father. You don't have to answer if it's painful to you, but the idea is almost incredible to me."

"Incredible to you?" Ronnie wet his lips. "Maybe you don't read the papers. I'm sorry, I didn't—"

"Don't apologize. I get what you're driving at. Rena Savage, Spud's wife, has been my secretary for years. Part of her work is to keep me posted on good and bad by reading the papers to me every day. I'm still not convinced, and never will be, that every kid in the country is a potential murderer just because he's young."

"Or she's young. There are some dolls in the Wharf Rats, too. Betty Hubbard was one. But she quit about the time I got booted out, or half quit. Still, she thinks I'm a fink for cooling one of their capers by going to Sheriff Riker. That's why our beautiful romance is no more."

"Want to tell me about the caper?"

"Why not? A couple of the dolls thought it up. Their names don't matter, but I'll tell you this: they have a lot of ideas in the wrong direction and like to drag their boy friends along. They were going to rob old man Baxter, who comes down here every winter and lives on his cruiser at the Yacht Club docks, alone."

"Any particular reason?"

"Big deal! He liked to play the races, and he'd made a big killing at the Sunshine track that day. Word got around about it. He was a sitting duck. Five of them were going to board the cruiser from a rowboat late that night. Excitement, see? Nice big haul of cash. Lots of brainwork needed. Case the cruiser and all that sort of thing. Everything planned down to the last detail. That's how they all start—just good clean fun."

"But you couldn't take it."

"Don't pin any medals on me, Captain. I got to thinking about what had happened to Dad and my guts flipped. I liked old man Baxter. He'd fished with me. Also he'd told me he slept with a gun under his pillow. I told them there'd be shooting and asked them to lay off. They wouldn't, so I phoned the sheriff, then told them what I'd done."

"Did you give their names?"

"No, and old Sherlock didn't like it because I refused to put the finger on anyone."

"And you really think they might have killed Mr. Baxter?" the Captain asked Ronnie after a pause.

Ronnie took his time before he answered. Finally he said, "The reason you think it's incredible, Captain, is just because you don't get the idea. You're thinking of youngsters—and there aren't any youngsters any more. I've given this a lot of thought. There's nothing but adults today.

"There's a battle on between adults over, and adults under, twenty-one. It's a nuclear war. Neither the overs nor the unders think that the others have brains enough to come in out of the rain, and maybe that's true. Dad got a bang out of passing his examinations, and getting good marks in school. That makes you an egghead, today. He said it was fun, but I wouldn't know."

"What is your idea of fun?"

Ronnie studied that a while. "Getting away with something that builds a mushroom cloud under the over twenty-ones," he said at last. "I was an adult by the time I was ten, one of the under twenty-one army. Everything the overs could do, I could do—or thought I could, and better than them. Run a boat. Drive a car. Watch TV. Talk about sex and killing. That was play. Getting money was play. The hell with right and wrong. Keep out of your parents' hair and don't get caught. If this rocket falls, push the button and send up another one."

"So you joined up with your own young army of adults-under-twenty-one?"

"Check! And until you got over twenty-one you stayed with the mob and did things their way, because all the others were against you. Get it? That makes everyone over twenty-one legitimate prey."

Thinking about his own position, he was silent a moment, then he went on: "You asked me if the Wharf Rats would kill. All rats will kill if they're cornered, and they'll kill the rats who run away."

He slowed down the boat. "I've got the range on those markers in Big Pass. We're in about sixteen feet of water. Toss over the lead and see if you can find a spot where it goes five feet more down with a rocky bottom. We ought to get a dozen more grouper if we can find it."

The motor slowed further until its purr was almost inaudible. Ronnie turned squarely to face the Captain. "There's an outboard coming out of Big Pass now with a couple of nice guys in it—Paul Fraceti, and Chuck Lindsay. Big deal, like I said. Case the joint, and all that sort of thing. They're just keeping tabs on me to make me nervous before they close in for the kill."

"For the kill?"

"You dig it! They're a couple of self-appointed trigger-men for the Wharf Rats. If I turn up with a bullet in me, or a knife in my rib while you're still here, you might ask them some questions."

The Captain ran a hand through his hair and the palm came away wet. "You can't be serious, Ronnie."

"Just stick around long enough and you'll be in on the fun. They've already made a couple of passes, but those were just fakes to scare me. The next will be for real."

"You think they will really try to kill you?"

"You dig it, Daddy-O!" Ronnie said calmly. "I'm one of the rats who squealed and tried to run away!"

SIX

There were too many facets to this boy, Maclain thought grimly. Too many contrasts and clashing sides. What in the name of all that was holy had produced such a complex creature? Was this a present day picture of the normal well-to-do American boy?

Were his parents at fault? His school and education? Or was he just a normal product of the pack that he had to be one of to survive?

Of one thing Maclain felt sure: each facet that went to make up the boy, taken by itself, might be just a simple character trait; but taken all together they could only be harbingers of disaster. Maclain, with all his prescience and training in blindness, was certain that Ronnie must have some inkling of that impending doom.

That surety made him feel futile, for he was just as certain that some badly needed strength in the boy was missing and that Ronnie Dayland, Jr., didn't care.

Heaving the lead as his thoughts ran on, the Captain found the drop-off in the deeper water on the seventh try. The feel of the tiny pebbles under his fingers could not be mistaken.

"This is it, I'm sure," he told Ronnie. "The bottom's rocky and it's suddenly dropped off from about nineteen feet to twenty-four."

"That's keen. I'll run her up north a little until you feel it shallow off to nineteen feet again, then I'll toss the anchor and we can drift back over the hole. That twenty-four-foot bottom sticks in east from the deep water of the Gulf like a finger. Do you get the idea? North, south, or east of it you have five feet less water, but it's something you have to feel, not see."

"I get the idea."

A few minutes later they were anchored and the *A-bomb* had drifted back accurately over the fish hole.

If Ronnie had been chary about giving out information concerning the place they had just left, he reversed his field now.

"Open your compass," he told the Captain while he was fixing new bait. "I'll bet I can tell you so accurately where we are that the next time you go out on the *Kalua*, you could find this same spot just by asking Jack and Otis a couple of questions."

"Maybe I'd let you down, Ronnie."

"Let's try it. Man, if you could find this place again pretty near on your own it would sure bug old Otis."

"Well, go to it, Skipper." The Captain got himself and his compass into position and touched the needle with his right forefinger. "I make it that we're pointed straight due north where we're anchored here. You give me the fill-ins."

"Getting here in the *Kalua* is a little different from making the run in the *A-bomb*," Ronnie explained. "If I could show you chart 858, it would be easy for you to see the difference."

The Captain laughed. "So you'll have to take it out in explaining."

"Well, maybe it isn't so hard at that. Coming out of Little Pass, instead of turning sharp right around Green Flasher Three, the *Kalua* would keep due west for a mile to deeper water and turn around Bell Flasher One. Then she'd hold a course straight due north from there five miles, and she'd be practically over this spot where we are right now."

"Umm." The Captain did some figuring. "That would be a fifteen-minute run in the *A-bomb*, but what about in the *Kalua*?"

"She does fourteen knots at cruising speed. Can you take it from there?"

"Yes, I think I can, even though I did graduate from high school." The Captain couldn't resist the dig at Ronnie's failure to finish his senior year. "Fourteen knots would be about sixteen land miles per hour. That means she'd do one land mile in three and three-quarter minutes. Five land miles from Bell Flasher One to here would take her eighteen and three-quarter minutes."

"Cool, man, cool!" Ronnie said. "You're practically here!" He broke off abruptly. The sound of an outboard was getting nearer— a powerful one, like the Johnson, but older and not so well muffled.

"Are those the two boys you were speaking about?"

"Yeah. The Wharf Rat killers. Chuck Lindsay and Paul Fraceti. They're coming straight at us—wide open. But don't worry. They're not risking their own hides by running us down.

I wish I'd brought my rifle."

"You mean you'd really take a shot at them?"

"Maybe not to hit them—but they've taken shots at me." There was a trace of deadliness in his tone that the Captain found upsetting. "They're chicken. I'd only have to show them a gun and they'd be back to Mandalay where the flying fishes play."

"Poetic," the Captain muttered. "Let's hope they don't think it's D-day and make a landing in our laps."

The boat came too close for comfort, at that, rocking them violently as it sped by wide open. The Captain judged it was not more than a few feet away.

There was a derisive hail that Ronnie didn't answer. Half a dozen times the boat circled around them in a widening arc. Finally the noise of the motor stopped.

Ronnie said: "Well, that's that. They've anchored about a half a mile away. The hell with them! I was telling you about our position."

"I'm not seasick. Go on."

"We're about a mile and a half west of the middle of Caladesi Island. Standing in the bow you can line up a black marker—number one—at the entrance to Hurricane Pass, with the southernmost tip of Honeymoon Island. The tip's just a half a mile beyond the marker. Say, two points off the starboard bow. Do you think you've got that?"

"Two points." Maclain touched his compass and nodded, letting his vivid imagination supply the landmarks he would never see.

"Now, facing south," Ronnie went on, "and again about two points to starboard, Red Flasher Two marks the entrance into Big Pass. That's between the south end of Caladesi Island and the north end of Mandalay Beach. Those goons just came out of there. The flasher's not more than a mile away. I've got it lined up with a black marker, number three, about a quarter of a mile behind it."

The Captain stood up, turned, and stared shoreward, once again visualizing the unseen objects as Ronnie described them. He snapped the case of his compass shut and sat down.

"I've either got it or it's got me. The only charts I have are burned into my brain. Let's see what I can tell you now—where I'd tell you to stop if you were steering the *Kalua* for me."

Ronnie waited, his eyes full of a skeptical expectancy.

"We're anchored at the western apex of a triangle. A straight line drawn due east from here for a mile and a half would bisect Caladesi Island. The northeast leg of the triangle is two miles long and runs through Marker One in Hurricane Pass to the south end of Honeymoon Island. The southeast leg, off the stern, is a mile and a half long. It runs through Red Flasher Two and Black Marker Three, going into Big Pass at the south end of Caladesi Island. Also, we're about five miles due north of Bell Flasher One, which is a mile west of the entrance to Little Pass where we came out at the south end of Mandalay Beach."

"Holy cow!" Ronnie said after a time. "Why couldn't I soak up stuff like that in school?"

"Maybe because you didn't have to, Ronnie. I do. You have to work out some sort of compensation for not being able to see."

"Do you try to work out everything in your life like that? Always knowing where you're going, and exactly where you are?"

"You try to if you want to survive, but my nose has been out of joint plenty of times. Mentally and physically from running into doors and walls. Still, you have to try."

"You make blindness sound like it could be a lot of fun."

"I've seen a couple of men die laughing in the heat of a battle," the Captain said grimly. "I don't think they thought it was fun. Blindness, of course, could be hilarious, except for one thing—"

"What's that?"

"You can't see to enjoy the fun."

This time they were really in the grouper. One of the voracious fish had grabbed the Captain's bait and taken it on a sweeping run before his sinker had touched the bottom. A few minutes later Ronnie added it to its fellow in the icebox.

Five minutes more and it was Ronnie again. Another good fish was brought in.

Twice the Captain got hung up in the rocks. The first time he freed his line, but the second time he had to break it.

The turtle was lying at Ronnie's feet. He gave it a gentle

explorative touch with his toe. When he'd pulled it in, he'd made no attempt to remove the barbed hook from the flipper. Instead, he'd merely snipped the wire leader with his pliers and twisted on another hook to resume his fishing.

While he was putting a new rig on the Captain's broken line he toyed briefly with an ephemeral plan: some means of attaching the turtle to the Captain's line.

He'd done a master job of orienting Maclain to their exact position. He was pleased with that. There'd be no question in anyone's mind as to where in the Gulf that turtle had come from, if he could just trick Maclain into believing that he was the one who had actually pulled the thing up from the bottom.

He discarded the plan almost as quickly as he'd conceived it. It would be easier to deceive somebody with eyes. They'd probably believe they'd caught the darn thing if you fastened it to the end of their line when they weren't looking and tossed it over.

Not Maclain!

The old boy would be analyzing every tug of his line, every touch of his hook and drag of his dipsy. It was a bright idea—except that it stank! It simply couldn't be done.

They had fished another hour and caught eleven grouper between them—the Captain six to Ronnie's five—when Paul Fraceti and Chuck Lindsay, apparently having no luck, pulled up anchor. This time, without even bothering to rock the *A-bomb*, the two Wharf Rats headed for shore.

Ronnie decided the time was ripe to get his show on the road.

He snipped off the hook he'd been using and replaced it with the one that was stuck through the turtle's flipper, making sure that his prize was firmly secured.

Cautiously, he dropped it overside and payed out line. The weight of his sinker pulled the buoyant turtle just below the surface. It was Ronnie's intention to fake an act about being hung up in the rocks. It had to be good. He'd have some phony reefing and pulling to do.

He let the turtle drift out with the tide until his line on the port side of the boat was almost parallel with the Captain's who was fishing to starboard.

Then fate, embodying itself impersonally in the shape of a

hungry grouper, decided to add a fillip of its own and further Ronnie's scheme of deception. The fillip was a trick that was as dramatic as it was unforeseen.

Just as Ronnie flipped the lever on the side of his free running reel to set the drag, Maclain had a strike. It must have been the biggest fish of the day, although neither of them ever saw it. It made a run for the rocks, found itself stopped, and turned abruptly taking the Captain's line in a scorching semi-circle around the stern of the *A-bomb*.

Before Maclain or Ronnie had time to reel in a single turn the grouper had gone, leaving the disgruntled Captain inextricably fouled with Ronnie's line and the floating turtle.

Soberly, as Ronnie directed, they reeled the lines up close to the boat. Ronnie lifted the tangle and the turtle in together. His purposeful silence lasted just long enough to make it seem pregnant with meaning.

Then he said: "Well, this is the damndest! We've not only got a bloody mess, but we seem to have hooked a turtle through the flipper."

"A turtle?"

"Well, it looks like a turtle," Ronnie said, "but it seems to be dead. Gosh, I'd hate to take this fish story home all by myself. I'm glad you were along. I can't tell yet whose hook it's on, yours or mine."

"You take the credit. If I told Sybella that I'd pulled up a dead turtle she'd put me on a ration of iced tea."

Ronnie was silent again a proper length of time to free the turtle from hook and lines. "I'd tell you something more, but you'd say I was crazy." A note of hysteria crept into his voice without his trying. The blasted thing was getting him again, just as when he'd first pulled it up. Or maybe the hysteria had been close to the surface all the time.

"You make it sound quite interesting. Go ahead and tell me."

"It's not only dead, it was never alive. It's metal, with a leather head and tail and leather flippers."

"Metal?" Maclain was really surprised now. He reached back, his fingers extended. "Metal? I'd like to feel that for myself."

"Go to it." Ronnie place it quickly in the Captain's outstretched hand and watched the strong brown fingers close about it, loosen quickly as though in unbelief, then tighten more slowly.

He couldn't have asked for anything better. He'd set the stage and the action had been perfect right up to the final curtain which had fallen with a bang in a tailor-made climax to his little scene. Now all he had to do was extract a promise from the Captain that the turtle wouldn't be mentioned to anyone.

He got it before they pulled up anchor and set out for home. He had definite plans of his own.

A new found confidence seemed to have flooded the boy. He'd gotten a charge from his find that was almost as strong as one from the needle. He had described the turtle in detail while the Captain traced the mottled spots that were painted all over it, a camouflage of yellow and brown.

"Aluminum," Maclain decided, testing the hardness of the metal with his thumbnail. Then he pointed out a feature that Ronnie had overlooked. "Did you notice these two small places on the underside?"

"No." Ronnie took a look.

"I think a couple of metal loops were soldered on there," the Captain said. "This thing was probably attached to something under water with a wire of some kind and we pulled it loose."

"That's my idea exactly, Captain. It's an underwater buoy shaped like a turtle to escape the notice of any diver who might see it. Don't you agree?"

"Your guess is as good as mine, Ronnie. I'll keep my mouth shut as you asked me."

With the Captain's promise of silence, Ronnie loosened up and chattered incessantly the whole trip home while Maclain fingered the turtle he was nursing on his knee.

Ronnie told him excitedly about the pirate, Don Gomez, known as the crudest pirate in the whole Caribbean, who had plied the waters and raided ships off Mandalay a hundred years before. He repeated the oft-told story of a sunken pirate ship off Honeymoon Island; a tale that had started a dozen unsuccessful salvage parties on their way. Many times sponge divers from Tarpon Springs had reported seeing the sand-covered hull at low tide in clear weather, but they never seemed able to quite locate it a second time.

"But those sponge divers saw that hull somewhere near where we pulled up that turtle," Ronnie added convincingly.

"Why didn't they go after it?" the Captain inquired mildly.

"That's just it—they intend to! One of them marked it with that turtle until they could get the necessary money for a salvage party. They'll be back any day."

"And what are your plans?"

"I'm going to beat them to it. First come first served. A treasure is anybody's prize. I'm going to get Jack and Otis Marble to take me out skin-diving on the *Kalua* tomorrow. Just the three of us. If I can get a piece of wreckage—enough to prove there is some treasure there—Mom and Jack will put up the salvage dough."

"Then what?"

"I'll have money enough to buy a charter boat and take it to Miami where Otis and I can run it. I'll be something then. If not, at least I'll be away."

"Away from what?"

"Myself, maybe," he said after a little thought.

"It can't be done, Ronnie. You always catch up with yourself some day and find you like yourself less than before you ran away."

"We're coming into the dock," Ronnie said. "Give me the turtle, I'm going to hide it. You won't mention it, will you?"

"No. I've promised." The Captain handed over the turtle, but the memory of the first time he'd touched it stayed with his fingers to worry and plague him. It had been too hot to have just been pulled from the bottom of the sea.

SEVEN

The Captain woke up to the muted hi-fi record of a combo making strenuously with the rock 'n' roll. He lay relaxed, quietly listening, allowing his senses to adjust themselves until he knew exactly where he was, and where the music was coming from.

He'd been asleep just covered with a sheet, and only his shorts on. An air-conditioner was exhaling steadily. His wrist watch read twenty past six.

But it wasn't morning—that unmistakable reluctance to get up immediately, the aftermath of eight hours sound sleep, was missing. So was the odor of cooking breakfast. In addition, he slept every night with pajamas on.

He wasn't in his penthouse apartment in New York City—there was no sound of Sarah Marsh stirring in the kitchen, no clink of silver as she set the table for a meal.

Most certain of all the record that had awakened him had never been selected from his own collection of stero that delighted him at home. Shades of Mozart, Chopin, Wagner, and Beethoven! Shades of Victor Herbert, Rogers and Hart, Gershwin, Porter, and Hammerstein!

That was Ronnie Dayland's jive coming from the adjoining apartment, way out and cool. What had Ronnie called it? "My Hi-Fi Club in Endsville."

The Captain swung his feet to the floor.

All the sensory flashes had coagulated now, revealing to him his present surroundings as minutely as a sighted man would have seen them from a waking glance around a room.

Probably revealing more: In panoramic sequence Maclain could recall with startling accuracy every event, and every snatch of conversation with Ronnie during the day.

True, some of it was garbled. "I'm afraid I'm a little too old to be a Beatnik and master all this jive talk," the Captain muttered as the bong-bong jabbed at his sensitive ears. "Their jargon is as uncomprehensible as their music. Both are just noises to me. Maybe they're just born that way!"

His pack of cigarettes was on the bedside table. He picked

it up and found that Sybella had left a poker chip lying on it—a signal that there was a recorded message for him on his Audograph dictating machine. He lit a smoke, went into the living-room and started the flexible record:

"Duncan: We've gone over to the main house. You were sleeping so peacefully. Spud has fed the dogs. I set the electric alarm for six-thirty. Switch it off if you wake before then. Cocktails at seven. Dinner at eight. Black tie stuff. Celeste has asked the Fracetis, the Hubbards, Marian Lindsay, and a lawyer, Arch Ransom. Three tables of bridge.

"You'll remember Ross and Carolyn Hubbard. He's the banker, President of the Mandalay Trust Company. Their daughter, Betty, is eighteen, but not coming tonight. This is an adult brawl. You haven't met the Fracetis—Leonardi and Donna. They have a son, Paul, about Ronnie's age. ('I came close to meeting him,' the Captain thought.) Mr. Fraceti owns the Leon's Super Market chain. Big wheel customer of Jack Manning's so be your own sweet self. He likes chess, so give him a break if you play some time, as you will.

"You'll remember Abbott and Marian Lindsay. They had us out sailing the last time we were here, and dinner at Pappas' Restaurant in Tarpon Springs. Chuck, their son, was eleven then. Year younger than Ronnie now. Quick bright boy with red hair. ('Now *that* I'd be bound to remember!' Maclain grunted back at Sybella's voice.) He asked a hundred questions about Schnucke and Dreist. This is a warning to watch your step, darling. The Lindsays were divorced three years ago. No details, but Celeste says in spite of a fat alimony Marian is bitter. Sounds like gal trouble so go easy. Also Chuck was in some kind of a hot-car scrape with the Fraceti boy last year.

"It couldn't have been too bad a mess, according to Celeste, for Arch Ransom got both boys off clear. He also handles some local affairs for Dayland Fruits, Inc. He's an eligible widower about fifty —white-haired man-of-distinction type. A 'dream boat' to quote Celeste again. Apparently, he's quite spouse shy, although Mandalay has it that our vivacious Marian Lindsay considers herself as an entry. Celeste says: 'No.' In case you want to fight with Ransom he's six-foot of muscle in a tight-packed frame. ('Bully for Ransom!' the Captain whispered to the air.)

"Your tux is on my bed. White jacket. Soft shirt. Cummerbund. Snap maroon tie. Black pumps under edge of my bed. Black sox in them. And if you don't put something on that sunburn you got today, you'll die! Now who loves you, lover boy? Over and out!"

The Captain was grinning as he clicked off the Audograph and went into the bedroom to do the same for the electric clock that had been buzzing unheeded for a minute or two.

The music coming from Ronnie's hi-fi had changed. Or had it? Unless you were hep and cool and accepted in that strange half-world more remote than being in orbit, you never knew. No wonder they called it "way out."

Yet what right had he to question anyone? Without aid from the ones who loved him, wouldn't he be way out in orbit, too?

Take Sybella's recorded message—a rundown of the people he would meet at the party. Instead of having to sort out a room full of strangers he couldn't see, with every possibility of embarrassment to himself, if not to others, now he would enter a room full of friends. He would be assured instead of awkward. So would the others, solely because of the trifling details Sybella had been thoughtful enough to gather and pass along.

He did a quick once-over with his electric razor, showered, and took Sybella's advice about rubbing some soothing cream into the high spots to avoid threatening blisters from the sunburn.

He paused for an instant outside listening to the sound of laughter and the clink of glasses from the cocktail party on the terrace, then confidently started up the flagstone walk, disdaining a cane.

Spud came to meet him halfway and offered an arm.

"Good performance!" his partner whispered sarcastically. "Slightly sophomoric, wouldn't you say? But demonstrative of your rare ability to damn near walk a straight line."

"I knew you'd be watching for me with those keen yellow eyes."

"You just haven't seen them lately, Dune. Like my yellow hair they are turning tattle-tale gray."

"Except that the whites are Martini red. You reek of gin."

"That's a lie. I've been drinking breathless vodka. You sure were flying up this path. I wish you'd tried to shortcut across the lawn—"

"I nearly did. What's to stop me?"

"Celeste has set up an obstacle course for you. While you were fishing we've been playing croquet. The wickets are still there."

"Ouch!" Maclain shuddered. "I'll stick to the broad wide path after this." He checked their walk with a squeeze of his partner's arm. "Who's that?"

A car had rolled in with a crunch of gravel. It stopped and a door slammed. Footsteps came around the house, followed by greetings from the terrace.

"Arch Ransom. Last of the party. He walks with the springy step of a lawyer who has just collected a fifty-grand fee. Come on."

The Captain held back. "How do you grade the Fracetis?"

"Class 'A'—what's eating you, Dune?"

"What do you mean?"

"You've got the nutters. Did something happen today?"

"We caught a lot of fish," Maclain said shortly. "And I nearly made contact with young Chuck Lindsay and the Fraceti boy, Paul. Or they nearly made contact with the *A-bomb* and me."

"Nearly?"

"Ronnie and I were anchored. They came within a couple of feet of cutting us down."

"Seriously?" Spud amber eyes darkened with a frown.

"Just call it close enough for a shock treatment. Maybe it was clean teen-age play. Or perhaps they just get a kick out of watching people drown. Or maybe I just need a drink. Let's leave it that way."

They walked on up to the terrace. Jack Manning's warm cordial voice greeted the Captain and immediately introduced him around.

The caviar was real Beluga served with finely minced onion and chopped hard boiled eggs on thin crisp strips of toast. The Captain elected gin instead of vodka. He sipped his Martini with real appreciation. It was perfect—cold enough and properly dry. The Mannings, as the Daylands had, did themselves well.

When Uncle Eben, the stately white-haired Negro who had served the Dayland family for more than half a century, refilled his glass, Maclain said:

"The Martinis are the best I've tasted since the last time we were here, Uncle Eben, and the canapes are superb. You must have remembered my weakness for caviar."

"Miz' Celeste don't forget you, Cap'n, sir. Neither do I. Too many years since we seen you has gone by."

"Well, I thank the host and hostess, but I still detect your inimitable touch, Uncle Eben. You can't convince me that you're not responsible for the perfection of it all."

"You' a hard man to convince, Cap'n, sir." Uncle Eben chuckled. "Better I don't try." The old man's voice lowered. "Cap'n Maclain, sir—"

The Captain took a sip of his cocktail and waited. He'd been quick to catch a troubled note that betrayed itself in the old servant's lowered tone. It was the merest hint of a guarded attempt to overstep the boundary between guest and servant that Uncle Eben had held sacred for so long.

"Eben, get the Captain some caviar from that fresh can. It's colder." Jack Manning spoke from beside Maclain, lightly touching his arm.

"Yessuh, Mist' Manning." Uncle Eben promptly moved away on his errand leaving Maclain with a sense of frustration. There was some delicate matter preying on the old man's mind. That "Cap'n Maclain, sir—" was full of implications. Implications of what? Maclain found himself full of an eager desire to know.

Given a propitious moment, Uncle Eben might make another try —that is if Maclain wasn't full of jitters as Spud had said, and building something from nothing. Or he might not. Uncle Eben was an unpredictable character.

"I'm about to plant you between two idolizing mothers," Jack Manning warned with a laugh, tugging at the Captain's arm. "Donna Fraceti and Marian Lindsay. They've been sending up smoke flares ever since you arrived on the terrace—"

"Oh, no!" The Captain belted his cocktail down and held out his glass. "Not that, Jack. Haven't I been a good boy?"

"Then you know them?" Jack asked as he poured a refill.

"Just Marian Lindsay. Chuck was about ten the last time we were here. Smart kid with red hair, isn't he?"

"Some say he's too damn smart. He's a big boy now. Also Marian is a widow. Grass. She's addicted to bracelets that tinkle like sleigh-bells. Good old Abbott took it on the lam up north with some babe where he could take a ride and hear bells on a real sleigh. Still, Marian isn't hard to take—when she doesn't effuse about her darling boy."

"She'll effuse at me," Maclain said. "What about Mrs. Fraceti?"

"Donna? She's a living doll—but she'll tell you about little Pauly's troubles, too. They're mothers, Captain. Remember? Carolyn Hubbard will tell you about Betty. Celeste will tell you about Ronnie— unless I gag her. They're mothers—all."

Behind him the Captain could hear Spud and Arch Ransom talking: "I don't know why they ask me to play bridge," Ransom was saying in a cultured courtroom voice that the Captain liked. "I'm a miserable player."

"What could be better?" Spud gave his quiet laugh. "I've heard you're so rich, Arch. It will be painless to take your money away."

The Captain said: "Look, Jack, Ronnie says that Paul Fraceti and Chuck Lindsay are after his hide. Something to do with the Wharf Rats. Has he told you?"

"Kid stuff," Jack said after a moment, but he sounded uneasy.

"But he claims they have made some actual attempts to kill him."

"His imagination has a habit of working overtime, Captain."

Uncle Eben interrupted with the caviar.

"As I got it, Chuck and Paul were shooting at jumping mullet out in the Gulf when the *A-bomb* accidentally got in the way," Jack continued when Eben had moved on. "Yes, Ronnie has plenty of imagination. Now he insists that Otis Marble and I take him out to skin-dive from the *Kalua* tomorrow. Just the three of us. Some wild idea he got today about a sunken treasure off Honeymoon Island." The Captain could sense the keen black eyes that were studying his face. The conversations around them were growing more shrill as Uncle Eben refilled glasses. The Captain braced himself for the question that he knew was coming: "Have you any idea where this latest pipe-dream came from? You were with him all day."

The Captain shrugged it off. "He did tell me something about a legendary treasure ship sunk off Honeymoon Island. Is there anything to that?"

"Enough that I've decided to take him out tomorrow." Jack paused to sip his drink before adding: "If you'll come along."

"I thought he just wanted Otis and you."

"That's why I'm asking you to come along. He's up to something, and he's full of tricks. Let's hear his objections to having you along —if he has any. Maybe tomorrow you'll recall some little thing that you overlooked today."

Maclain's promise of silence flashed disturbingly fresh through his mind. If Ronnie wanted to keep that turtle to himself that was his business. Still, he'd like to go along on the diving trip. Not only was he curious, he'd been left perturbed by some of Ronnie's actions during the day. If Ronnie made objections and they sounded valid, he could always back out quickly. He shot out a feeler to see if Ronnie had mentioned the turtle.

"You mean there might have been some little thing that Ronnie saw and I didn't see today?" Maclain raised his expressive eyebrows inquiringly. "Such as what, Jack?"

"Such as you being difficult and twisting my words. I made no mention of you seeing anything, and you know it. Now, will you come along tomorrow if I can fix it?"

"If Ronnie agrees. I'm not butting in on a private party."

"It's Ronnie's sea-hunt," Jack said. "I'll ask him and tell you his answer, pro or con. Your mothers are waving at me impatiently. No escape. Those who enjoy our lavish Manning hospitality are always presented with a bill."

"What am I supposed to tell anxious mothers, Jack?"

"You're the detective! Give them some sound advice how to keep their budding gunmen out of jail. From where I sit, all the members of the Wharf Rats, including my brilliant step-son, Ronnie, could be fitting themselves for a nice striped suit and a course in the school of hard rocks. Instructions in road building included free."

"You don't sound very hopeful, Jack, about the boys, I mean. I doubt if you think it's really kid stuff."

"Kid stuff or not it can end up bad. There's just no future in a chain gang, Captain, and you get such lousy pay. Come along."

"Captain Maclain!" There was the tinkle of Marian Lindsay's bracelets and the soft warm clasp of her hand as she pulled him down between them on the settee. "Surely you remembered

Chuck and me. Chuck is my only son—"

"And the dinner at Pappas' in Tarpon Springs, and that wonderful sail, Marian. (Thank you, Sybella, dear!) How could I ever forget it? And how is your boy?"

"I'm afraid that Chuck is no longer a boy, Captain. This is my very dear friend, Donna Fraceti. She also has an only son. His name is Paul."

"And I'm dreadfully anxious for you to meet him, Captain Maclain." A liquid voice. Another warm handclasp, firmer than Marian's, and a passing scent of heavy perfume.

These were certainly anxious mothers. Fearful mothers. Marian was afraid her Chuck had grown up, and he had. She had lost all trace of her ten-year-old redhead. Donna Fraceti was dreadfully anxious for this man who had beaten blindness to meet her only son, Paul. Maybe there was some hope here, they both must be thinking. Some solution. Was this detective clever enough to discover what had gone wrong? Could he find the thief who had robbed half a life from each of these women?

Are you omnipotent, Duncan Maclain? Then apprehend this kidnapper, Time, and restore to me my missing little boy!

The Captain sat with his lips clamped tight, speechless with futility while excuses and prayers beat against him.

"Now Sheriff Riker thinks that some of these Wharf Rats are vicious, but the sheriff just doesn't understand—"

"There's nothing vicious about Paul, Captain. He gets into scrapes like any other boy. He's so sensitive—"

Voices on each side of him, cold and warm. Warm with love and cold with fear. Not just the voices of two frightened mothers, but the strong voice of the universe speaking for us all.

And he had no answer.

The voices were suddenly blotted out. Overhead the skies were split by a thunderous roar and a deafening screech as an evening flight of jets poured out on patrol from the Tampa field.

A sharp report sounded from somewhere in the direction of the seawall to the left of the terrace. The shot, apparently lost on the others, struck the Captain's sensitive ears, penetrating with one staccato crack the jets' inhuman scream. Glass crashed in a window of Ronnie's bedroom.

Maclain yelled "Spud!" as he jumped to his feet.

Then all of them seemed to be standing in Ronnie's

bedroom, with Ronnie laughing a little too wildly as he faced them defiantly, his back against the wall.

"Another guided missile gone wrong, that's all," Ronnie said. "Now, please get out and let me finish dressing. I'm going downtown for dinner."

"Ronnie, darling—you might have been killed!" Celeste's voice was stark with terror. "Do you know what happened?"

Jack's voice answered her. "Somebody took a pot shot from the water or from back of the bushes along the seawall. I ran down to see. No boat out there. Nothing at all."

"Skip it, will you," Ronnie said angrily. "One of the fly boys probably pushed the wrong button in his jet, Mom. Now please don't go reporting this. I don't want a lot of brass tearing my room to pieces. Please now, Mom!"

"Anything you say, darling, but I shall certainly phone the General—"

"And have me laughed at all over town. No, Mom!"

"Well, anything, so long as you're not hurt, son."

The Captain thought: "Just like the other two mothers. All the mothers. 'Anything so long as you're not hurt, son.' Even if it kills you!"

And the hell of it is Celeste really believes that she loves her boy.

EIGHT

A very unenjoyable evening had dragged itself by and finally all the guests had gone.

Jack mixed drinks, passed them around, and said, "If you want to know how to drive off friends get your information from a teen-age boy. If you'll pardon me for a little, I'm going to take a look at Ronnie's room."

"Has he gone out?" Celeste asked.

"Of course. While we were still on the terrace. You never seem to hear his car." He got a flashlight from a drawer and left.

Celeste finally broke an awkward silence:

"No one would be shooting at Ronnie without some cause. He's gotten himself into some terrible mess, like he's done so many times before. You know that, Captain, and I do, too."

"Oh, come off it, Celeste," the Captain said half angrily. "You've convinced yourself so thoroughly that Ronnie is to blame for everything that you've ceased to think straight. I've been shot at a dozen times, and so has Spud, and neither of us had gotten ourselves into a terrible mess. We were always trying to straighten one out." He paused, then asked her coldly: "Do you think that Ronald was in a terrible mess when he was murdered?"

The silence that settled over the room turned out to be unnaturally long. The Captain could hear Spud twisting uncomfortably in his chair. When Celeste finally made up her mind to answer her voice matched the Captain's in coldness:

"You were my husband's closest friend, Captain. You knew him longer than I did, and probably better. You know just as much about the cause of his murder as I do. If you have no reason to believe he was in trouble at the time of his death, then neither have I." She got up abruptly. "I think if you'll all excuse me, I'll go to bed and think about that wall between me and Ronnie. Maybe I can wash some of it away by having a real good cry."

Jack came back in through the French windows, shutting the screen softly behind him.

The Captain turned sideways in his chair. "Did you find it?"

"What?" Jack crossed the room to secure the drink he had left on the bar.

"The bullet. That's what you went over to Ronnie's room to look for, wasn't it?"

"Yes, that's what I went to look for," Jack said slowly. "From the angle of the shot in the room it could have been fired from darn near anyplace. From the seawall, back of the bushes and trees on the edge of our land, from a boat on the water, or if a high-powered rifle was used it might have come from the causeway. I thought I'd turn it over to ballistics and at least find out the caliber. That would give us the possible range of the gun."

"Then you didn't find it?"

"No. I didn't find it." Jack took a liberal drink from his glass. "But I found the hole in the wall. Ronnie took a knife and dug it out before he left. I guess I'll have to get it from him."

"Unless he tells you he hasn't got it," the Captain said.

"Then who the devil would have it?" Jack asked.

"The most interested party. The man who shot it," said Duncan Maclain.

NINE

Maclain lay awake reading braille in the dark, a cover-up for his own unrest, and the fact that he was listening alertly for the return of Ronnie's car.

The MG finally rolled in, recklessly scattering gravel and sliding to a stop, ten minutes after the Captain had put his book away. Ten minutes that had seemed more like an hour.

He heard the opening and closing of the screen and the door to Ronnie's apartment, and wondered about it briefly until he remembered that the entire guest house was air conditioned and the doors and windows left closed. Each room was controlled by a thermostat on the wall. That was why the bullet had penetrated screen and glass in Ronnie's window.

Air conditioning at night gave Sybella claustrophobia. She'd turned it off at the thermostat and opened the three casement windows of their bedroom. Outside noises had free entry, including the arrival of Ronnie's car.

Now there were nothing but night sounds: the soft scrape of palm fronds, the distant lap of waves on the beach, and a goatsucker screaming "Chuck Will's widow!" so loud it could have been perched on the dresser in the corner of the room.

The Captain felt his wrist watch on the table. It was half-past two.

What amusement could a kid like Ronnie find in a decent quiet place like Mandalay that would keep him out until half-past two? Hot spots? Jive? Beatnik cafes? A girl more complaisant than Betty Hubbard who'd be thrilled to keep a late date with a wealthy boy and a bottle in an MG sports car?

Maybe Ronnie had gone to Tampa. There were plenty of joints there with jive that weren't so strict with ID cards showing you were twenty-one. Plenty of girls ready to admire and console a boy who thought he'd been rejected by his own home town—provided he was loaded with dough.

The Captain wished he hadn't thought of Tampa. It brought back that rat race with the Wharf Rats which Maclain didn't want to remember. That picture of Ronald Dayland driving back from Tampa to Mandalay alone.

It was none of his business, anyhow. Or was it?

Wasn't it more of an obligation to do his best to solve the murder of a friend who had been as close as Ronald Dayland, Sr., than to take a fee to investigate the murder of some person he had never known?

He'd come back after seven years and found himself caught in a circle that was squeezing his mind with tightening coils. There were undercurrents he couldn't fathom, and he abhorred the unfathomable.

Ronnie's relationship with his mother seemed unnatural. Did the boy have some secret knowledge of marital difficulties between his father and mother that he'd kept to himself for seven years?

Was Celeste aware that Ronnie possessed such a secret? Had her unconscious resentment alienated her from her son?

Something had.

Ronnie's one desire in life appeared to be to get his hands on enough quick money to buy himself a charter boat and get away from home with Otis Marble.

The Captain turned over and twisted the sheet around him. He was indulging himself in an orgy of wild conjectures. He was certain that Jack Manning hadn't had a chance to speak to his stepson about asking Maclain to accompany them on the treasure hunt. Because of the lateness of Ronnie's arrival home the trip on the *Kalua* might be postponed.

The Captain fell into a fitful sleep, his last thought being that no matter when the *Kalua* went out, he'd make every effort to go along.

He woke less than two hours later after a miserable interlude during which all his conjectures had turned into dreams. He'd watched a conglomeration of ghost ships sink in the Seven Seas, filled with skeletons instead of treasure.

He felt suffocated. Sybella's open windows had let in nothing but sounds, with very little of the hot night air. At least the Chuck Will's widow had signed off, maybe with the coining of dawn.

It was ten minutes to five.

He decided to get Schnucke up from her bed in the garage which she shared with Dreist, and take an early walk. Walking helped him get his thoughts straight.

He slipped out of bed and was half dressed in his fishing clothes of the day before when Sybella spoke to him:

"Heavens above, Duncan. It's only five o'clock. Are you headed out on the *Kalua* this early?" He heard the scratch of her lighter and smelled the smoke of her cigarette.

"I don't know." He went to the bed and kissed her warmly. "Sorry if I woke you. The truth is I couldn't sleep, so I decided to take a walk with Schnucke."

"Why didn't you close the windows and put the air conditioner on? You know I don't mind it once I'm asleep."

"It wasn't that," he said quickly. "I couldn't have slept anyhow. I got to thinking that I acted like a heel with Celeste last night."

"I think you helped her, if anything. You were perfectly right about her putting her social life ahead of Ronnie."

"How did I ever get a hold of the perfect wife?" he asked her fervently. "You're the only woman living who would back me up in anything, or everything. Even when I know I'm wrong. No recriminations. No questions, even about mysterious walks at dawn."

"Thanks. Shall I get up and make you some coffee?"

"Go back to sleep. Your wifely devotion is breaking me down." He zipped up the pennant decorated terry-cloth jacket that Ronnie had thought so keen, then walked to the bed and kissed her again.

"Duncan—" Her voice wasn't sleepy.

"What?"

"You could make some excuse if you wanted to, and we could pack up and leave here today."

"What frightened you, Sybella? That shot last night?" He stood towering over her, staring down with his sightless eyes that could be so disconcertingly perceptive.

"That, added to a lot of other things."

"What, for example?"

"There's an atmosphere about the Manning household that isn't quite right. It's making me very uncomfortable, darling. I don't expect Celeste to stay in mourning for seven years, but she's put aside her grief over Ronald's death with such a thoroughness that it doesn't seem quite natural."

"I've felt something of that myself, Sybella. I thought my imagination was working overtime."

"It's not. You're feeling some tension that is really here. Mention one of our former visits, or anything that happened during her eighteen years of marriage to Ronald, and she immediately grows taut and sidetracks the subject. Mention the past, where Ronald and Celeste are concerned, to Jack, and he gives it a brush-off just as quickly. Both of them have an air of: 'Why bring up unpleasant subjects? Let's all be gay!'"

"You're devilishly perceptive, darling," the Captain said. "You've brought up a lot of the questions that helped to ruin my sleep last night. Unfortunately, they are the very reasons why we'll have to stay. Someone killed Ronald, my dearest friend. I'd like to make that killer pay."

"Where are you going now, Duncan?"

"I think I'll walk down to the marina and see if Otis Marble is up."

"Do you want to ask Otis about that shot?"

"He might have heard it if he was on board the *Kalua* when it was fired. Jack said last night that a high-powered rifle could cairy here from the causeway."

"It's over a mile from here to the marina—"

"Schnucke and I have walked over five times that distance many times before."

"Are you coming back?"

"If I find that the *Kalua* is taking out Ronnie, I may stay."

"I'm nervous, Duncan. Yes, frightened, maybe. Nothing you can do and nobody you can question is going to bring back Ronald Day-land. Isn't there a chance that Otis could have fired that shot himself?"

"Sure there's a chance," the Captain told her. "There's also a chance that he was mixed up in Ronald's murder."

"How much of a chance?"

"About forty-five thousand to one," he said.

"Where do you get those odds?"

"Forty-five thousand is the present population of Mandalay."

TEN

Outside a wall of hot wet dampness pressed against the Captain's face. He paused for a moment, breathing in the dampness. There was an overtone to it that he didn't understand and didn't like, as though far overhead unseen ice clouds were churning violently, touching the mist with a most unseasonable chill.

He moistened a finger and held it up to test the wind. It was light from the west. The mist might turn to rain, but he doubted it. Later the sun might come up and disperse it. Hopeful thinking, probably. There was just as good a chance that they were in for an overcast day.

He opened the garage where the dogs were sleeping to let them out for a ten-minute run. Schnucke came to meet him, whining softly. The Captain greeted her with a good-morning pat and a friendly scratch in back of her soft ears. That over, she tore out to race about the lawn.

He made his way past the bulk of his air-conditioned Cadillac to the rear of the garage and released Dreist from his heavy chain. You didn't take chances with Dreist. With the weather, maybe, and with sunburn, but not with Dreist. The staunch German shepherd was ten pounds heavier than Schnucke, and apart they might be mistaken one for the other, for their coloring was much the same. There the resemblance ended.

Dreist was a trained protective police dog.

Yes, you had to be careful with Dreist!

The Captain kept him de-activated most of the time with muzzle and chain. Only when he thought there was every possibility that he was walking into imminent danger did he take the courageous police dog along, unleashed and unmuzzled. Then he took the same precautions that any sane, sighted man on the side of the law would take if he had armed himself with an automatic sawed-off shotgun.

Dreist was already waiting for him, twisting in pleasure and rattling his chain. His morning greeting was a muffled growl.

The Captain said, "Oh, pipe down, wolfhound!" and roughly rumpled Dreist's ears, totally unawed by the growl. He put the heavy muzzle on before he unchained him and sent him after Schnucke for his morning run.

The Captain took his supersonic whistle from the glove compartment of the Cadillac. Its wave frequency, more than 20,000 per second, was above the range of the human ear, but the dogs could hear it and were trained to answer it instantly.

He slipped the whistle in his pocket, lit a cigarette and smoked it idly, leaning against the wall of the garage by the door.

It was a nuisance not to know how light it was and the state of visibility. His watch said five-twenty. He had a sensation that he was being watched, but put it aside impatiently. He was always having the sensation of being watched, particularly after a restless night. It had nothing to do with blindness. It was a hangover from the caveman days.

Everyone living had that feeling of being watched now and again. They were usually right. Day and night your life was full of unseen watchers that man's sharpest eyes were unable to detect. A rabbit. A coon. A house cat staring motionless from the bushes. The keen eyes of a bird or a squirrel looking down from the branch of a tree.

He began a cold dissection of his own uneasiness. Sybella's offer to pack up and leave summarily had done nothing to calm him. Neither had Spud's flat-footed accusation that he was suffering from a bad case of jitters. What had caused the two people closest to him to suggest, quite openly, that he was losing his usual aplomb?

The answer was obvious: it must be true. Then he'd better consult a psychiatrist for he had nothing tangible to follow up, nothing real and concrete to go on.

From the finding of an aluminum turtle, that he'd felt but not seen; a schoolboy's account of a teen-age feud; a shot through a window that could have been accidental; and a few muttered words from an old servant, who might well be senile, he'd built himself up a feeling of doom.

It was when Sybella became frightened that he started to panic. Sybella was part of him and her misgivings rode on his back like an old man of the sea.

He blew the whistle and brought in the dogs. He took Dreist's muzzle off, chained him up, and returned the whistle to the car. He fed them both a light breakfast of chow from the sack and gave Dreist fresh water. Their big meal came in the evening. Both were trained to take food from no one but him and his partner, Spud, or Cappo Marsh, the Captain's colored chauffeur. They thrived and kept well on their two meals a day.

When they'd eaten, he took Schnucke's U-brace from a hook on the wall and put it on her. His fingers closed lightly on the brace and he ordered Schnucke "Forward."

The sensation of being watched stayed with him. He thought that maybe Ronnie had decided to take out the *A-bomb* instead of going on the *Kalua*. The boy was rash and unpredictable enough to tackle his treasure diving alone.

Maclain headed Schnucke toward the dock where the *A-bomb* was moored, and wondered some about her erratic course across the lawn until he remembered the croquet wickets that Spud had warned him about.

Schnucke halted him at the narrow slip, reluctant to take him out on it. He said, "Pfui!"—his greatest term of reproach and ordered her on.

He was certain that Ronnie would have spoken before now, had he been there. Nevertheless, he knelt down gingerly and felt the *A-bomb*. Even in the shelter of the bay the water must be choppy for she was steadily moving up and down against her fenders.

A canvas tarpaulin, fastened on with snaphooks, covered the boat snugly from windshield to stern.

That tarpaulin was to give him considerable trouble for when he and Otis examined the *A-bomb* late that night in search of the aluminum turtle, which had vanished, the tarpaulin had also gone.

Back on the lawn, he took the driveway out of the grounds, and followed the broad width of Bayside up to Hampden Drive. There he turned right, cursing the fact that sidewalks were a thing of the past.

He decided the watching eyes must belong to the servants, if there had really been any watching eyes. Uncle Eben, probably, or maybe the cook. They were the only ones who might be up so early.

Later he found his conjecture had been right. Uncle Eben had been watching him, anxious to speak, yet held back by fear of what might happen to one of his family if he revealed to the Captain a very personal matter about Ronald Dayland, Sr., that for seven years had preyed on the old man's mind.

It was six o'clock when the Captain stopped on Pier 1 of the Mandalay marina and located the wire-railed gangplank that would take him aboard the *Kalua.*

She was a beautiful yacht, a deep sea cruiser, documented at thirty tons. Built in Seattle, Washington, by a master designer to Ronald Dayland's specifications, even at 1939 prices her rakish hull of teakwood, mahogany, and gleaming chrome had cost some $2500 per ton.

She slept four up forward in Pullman berths, usually lowered into comfortable lounge seats. That forward cabin opened astern into a spacious galley, equipped with electric icebox, a four-burner bottled gas range, and a sink with hot and cold running water.

A third of the galley on the starboard side comprised a compact private stateroom for Otis Marble.

From the galley, steps led up through a companionway to the combination wheelhouse and lounge. A hatch in the deck of the lounge gave access to the engine room below.

Another companionway from the wheelhouse led aft and below to the owner's cabin. It was luxurious with two three-quarter berths, mirrors, a wealth of mahogany lockers, a well ventilated clothes closet, and a head that boasted an electric toilet, an oversize basin, and a hot and cold shower.

One step up from the owner's cabin through a screened hatch with double doors, was the fishing cockpit in the stern. It was equipped with two swivel mahogany fishing chairs, each with a gimbal set flush in the front to support the butt of a fishing rod while trolling.

A metal-lined fishbox with a lift-up lid formed a seat along the width of the transom.

Envious private skippers on less elaborate yachts that came and went around the marina claimed it wasn't any wonder that Otis Marble had stuck to his floating hotel for a dozen years. He might never get rich on his salary, but what the hell! Very few millionaires could equal the comforts of his home.

Maclain's nose quivered at the aroma of coffee coming up from the galley. He stopped on the gangway close to the outside of the screen door that led into the wheelhouse on the starboard side.

The gangways on each side of the wheelhouse gave access to the forward deck where the anchors, a large and a smaller one, lay in their chocks by a power windlass. A forward hatch gave light and ventilation to the forward cabin below. Two mahogany bosun's lockers flanked the skylight. They served the dual purpose of storage space for gear and varnish, and foam-rubber covered couches where Celeste and her guests could bask in the sun.

The gangways ended close by where Maclain was standing at the after end of the wheelhouse. There the owner's cabin flared out to occupy the entire beam of the *Kalua*. It gave more space to the owner's quarters, but the design had disadvantages. To get from the wheelhouse to the fishing cockpit it was necessary to go through the owner's cabin.

The two wide berths could be closed off with draw curtains, but Celeste protested, not without cause, that on night fishing trips when the guests were after snapper she could have found more rest on any bus station bench. The traffic was just too heavy between the fishing cockpit and the wheelhouse bar.

It had been Ronald Dayland's opinion, shared by Jack and Otis, that women in general just didn't like boats that were under the size of the Queen Mary.

The Captain smiled at a secret thought. Schnucke didn't care particularly for boats, but she was happy and contented anywhere if he was along, and miserable anywhere if he left her home.

Schnucke had found a spot that suited her on the *Kalua*. It was up on top of the owner's cabin by the dinghy. The small boat generally gave her some shade. She could lie there all day, her muzzle between her paws, staring down into the fishing cockpit to make sure that the Captain got no ideas about walking on the water without her being ready to guide him.

Maclain lifted her now, set her up there, and told her to lie down. When she was settled, he called to Otis:

"It's Duncan Maclain. Are you below there, Skipper?"

The screen door to the wheelhouse opened after a moment.

Otis Marble's flat voice said, "Glad to have you aboard. Come inside and sit down. I'm just fixing breakfast. Will you join me? Ham and eggs. Toast and coffee."

"I couldn't think of anything better." The Captain went inside and sat down. He was wondering if the stocky skipper ever altered his flat voice or allowed it to express surprise at anything. Glad to have you aboard. Unannounced. Six in the morning. It could have been the most casual call.

Eggs broke and sizzled. Then the unemotional voice drifted up from the galley. "I was sort of expecting you."

"Really? I'm rather surprised to be here, myself. Why were you expecting me?"

"You've been thinking that I know something about that pot shot taken at Ronnie last evening." The ham began to fry.

"Why should I think that?"

"Because somebody blew the whistle on me. Jack or Sheriff Riker. Both of them know it, but so did the boss. I'm an ex-con. I served my time in the Federal pen."

"You're blowing the whistle on yourself, Otis. I'm not interested in anything you've served time for. I am interested in what you know—if it will help me find the murderer of Ronald Dayland. Will you help me?"

"Seven years," Otis Marble said up the stairs. "I was beginning to think that you didn't care for the boss. He always had you pegged as a pretty smart apple. So did I. I figured you'd be back here as soon as you heard he'd been murdered, and that you'd stick until you'd fried his killer in Raiford. What kept you?"

"Circumstances," the Captain said. "And Dave Riker's competent and a friend of mine. Unless I'm asked, I leave investigations up to the local law."

"Sure, the sheriff is competent," Otis said, "and honest, too. He nailed a kid who stole three cases of groceries from Leon's Super Market just last month. Big deal, and the goons who clobbered the boss are still living it up high, wide and handsome."

"I'd need a lot of luck and a lot of help to find out any more than Sheriff Riker has," Maclain said thoughtfully.

"I might give you more help than you think," Otis said. "More help than I could give to Riker."

"Or than you would give, maybe?"

"Could give," Otis corrected. "The sheriff doesn't like ex-cons, and doesn't believe them. You may not like me, but you're not so lawbound that you wouldn't listen to me. I might let slip a couple of ideas."

"You sound like you'd given a lot of thought to the facts connected with Ronald's killing."

"You'd be surprised what you can think for seven years on a boat, Captain. Stick around and try me!"

ELEVEN

The Captain had decided through the years that some motive, either conscious or subconscious, lay behind everything that everyone did. That motive was not always readily apparent, but nevertheless it was there. Sometimes the motive had grown for years. Sometimes it sprouted full-bloom in an instant, as a man might jump from the path of a speeding car, the motive being to save his life.

For the moment he was inclined to believe that Otis Marble's revelation about his prison record belonged in the latter category, but he couldn't be sure. It was just an item, added to numerous others, that he found himself having to play by ear.

He had known the skipper for eleven years, with a seven-year interlude, but his contacts with him had been comparatively brief, limited to fishing trips on the *Kalua.*

Those trips had been just about enough to give him an inkling of the man's taciturnity, a not uncommon trait in individuals who had some phase of their background which they wished to conceal.

He had a good picture of Otis Marble's appearance from Spud's description: muscular and short, five foot four, with a small gray mustache and close-cropped gray hair. His eyes were also gray, crinkled and unwavering. At fifty his teeth were still good and all his own. His button nose was set in a round, rather flat face, which Spud had considered anti-social. His skin was like parchment, a thick battlement against wind and sun.

The Captain had added to Spud's description the facts that Otis was a moderate pipe smoker and a moderate drinker, and as captain for a luxury cruiser, tops—unobtrusive, efficient and calm; as much a part of a boat as a binnacle and a barometer, and just about as congenial. Like a compass, the extent of his conversation was usually: "We're goin' that-a-way!"

Efficient, undoubtedly. Still, as a confidant who might share his troubles, Maclain felt he would prefer Dreist. Otis Marble on the surface was as cold, hard, and smooth as his last name.

Otis had set up a folding table in the wheelhouse and

brought breakfast up the companionway. The conversation had died. As the Captain addressed himself to ham and eggs, toast and coffee, he couldn't help but think that he'd been expertly put off balance. Otis was perfectly aware that Maclain would be prying into Ronald Dayland's murder. Otis had practically said so. It was part of Maclain's life, like breathing. The skipper knew just as well what a challenge that shot through Ronnie's window must be.

So he'd tossed out a gratuitous piece of information about taking a fall and serving time, and then clammed up. But not until he had intimated that he knew much more than he was saying, and might be persuaded to tell all.

Was this canny skipper, so quick to reveal his prison record, an adversary or a colleague?

That was really one to ponder on. "I'm an ex-con!" It was a nice piece of bait to hook a detective's interest. It could also be a nice smoke screen. All Maclain could determine for the moment was that friend or foe, if he hoped to get anything of concrete value from Otis Marble the skipper had to be treated with exceeding care.

Yet the breakfast wasn't awkward. They passed a lot of nonessentials back and forth with the buttered toast. Otis didn't like the feel of the weather, but Mr. Manning owned the boat. If Mr. Manning said go, he'd take the *Kalua* out into the teeth of a hurricane. Who knew what Ronnie had stumbled on? The whole Gulf coast from Corpus Christi clear around and down to Key West might be lined with sunken treasure ships. Again, there might be none at all. Who could say?

Mr. Manning had phoned him the night before. He and Ronnie should be on board by seven. There was a hook-up with the Mandalay phone company right here in the wheelhouse. It plugged into a piling on the dock and was disconnected when the *Kalua* got under way.

Talk. Talk. Talk. Maclain ate and let Otis ramble on. Taciturn hell! He was taciturn only when it came to things he didn't want to say.

The Captain leaned back against the cushions of the lounge seat and lit a cigarette. It was a quarter to seven. A match struck and he caught the smell of Otis's pipe.

"I'll clear off the dishes." Otis pushed his chair away.

"Wait a minute." The Captain had decided there was nothing to lose by plunging right in. "It was your idea that I came down here to ask you about that shot last night."

"Didn't you?"

"It was probably uppermost in my mind." It was going to take care, caution, and a can opener to get under Marble's skin. "I think my actual reason was to find if you were really going out today, and if there was any objection to my going along."

"What's to stop you?"

"Ronnie made it pretty clear to Jack that he wanted just the three of you, but last evening at the cocktail party Jack said if he could get clearance from Ronnie, he'd like to have me come along."

"Oh. What did Ronnie say?"

"He was out all evening. Didn't get home until late. I haven't heard any more from either of them. I wasn't even sure they were going out today."

"You got here in plenty of time."

"I didn't sleep well, so I got up to take an early walk with Schnucke. I found myself near the marina and decided to check with you."

"Where's the dog?"

Maclain jerked his thumb upward. "Her usual place. Under the dinghy. I put her up there."

"She's what the Krauts call a *schiffhund.* A boat-dog. I had one once. He'd lie out on the bow all day, fair or foul, and raise the devil if I tried to put him ashore. That was a long time ago." Otis laughed shortly and began to gather up the dishes. "Bring the *schiffhund* along."

"Then you don't think Ronnie will mind if I go?"

Otis picked up the dishes and took them below. Once again his voice started coming up through the companionway. "Ronnie won't mind when he finds out how much company he's going to have. What's one more among so many?"

"You mean others are going on this trip?" he was genuinely puzzled. "I thought Ronnie—"

"Not *with* us, *behind* us, Captain. Ronnie's a smart kid. Erratic, but smart. He may go out diving today. Probably will. But it's my idea that this will be a dry run—"

"A dry run?"

"A throw-off. He's not going close to any spot where he thinks he's located a treasure. Not today."

"What do you mean?"

There was a clink of dishes and a sound of running water before Otis replied, then he came one step up in the companionway. "Break wind in Tampa and they'll hear it in Mandalay. There's a rumor out that you and Ronnie stumbled on to something big yesterday. Rumors become facts before you can turn around in Mandalay Beach and Mandalay. Faster than that when the rumor concerns a treasure."

Maclain snubbed out his cigarette, rubbing it carefully into the bottom of the ash tray. "I don't get it. Ronnie practically made me swear to keep my mouth shut about any treasure. You and Jack Manning are the only ones I've mentioned it to—and as I recall both of you spoke of it first."

"Maybe Ronnie spread it himself for reasons of his own," Otis said. "When you get to know that kid better, you'll realize that he's as slick as an eel. The rumor's around the town, anyway."

"Are you sure?"

"I went downtown last night after watching TV to get a nightcap in Schofield's Bar. It was the first thing I got tossed at me by a waiter I know. I checked it farther in a hangout of the Wharf Rats, Kaufman's Drugstore. I'm pals with a soda jerker in there. If they've heard it in Kaufman's it's been broadcast everywhere."

"I still don't get it. Ronnie warned me about how fast anything like that would spread around town. He insisted he was only telling Jack and you."

"So maybe he had a few drinks with more than ice cream in them and let something slip to some girl. Or maybe he didn't. Anyhow, there's a couple of smart young hoodlums, Paul Fraceti and Chuck Lindsay, all gassed up in their eighteen-footer, waiting just two slips down from here for me to make a move with the *Kalua*. I'll bet there's a stakeout on the *A-bomb*, too."

The Captain said: "Those two boys almost ran us down yesterday."

"Well, there you have it," Otis said with unconcern.

"But we were fishing, not looking for treasure. Ronnie wasn't doing any diving."

"They didn't read it in the papers," Otis said. "Maybe you didn't see it, but Ronnie got onto something somehow, and spread some big talk around town about it last night, too. Either that, or they spotted the same thing Ronnie spotted—some thing that he neglected to mention to you."

"Such as—?" Maclain threw out by way of a feeler.

"How would I know? I wasn't with you." Otis wasn't telling about the turtle, if he knew. "All I know is, that bunch of goons that call themselves the Wharf Rats have it in for Ronnie. Tougher ones than Fraceti and Lindsay, and a few years older. They're not going to see him get away with anything. The *Kalua* will be leading a motorboat parade if she pulls out this morning. Mark my words! Maybe no other boats will anchor near us, but there'll be plenty circling around and marking our position down."

"Ronnie must realize that, too."

"Certainly he does. Hence the dry run to throw them off the trail. It's going to take some night diving, Captain, if Ronnie doesn't want to tip his hand. He's certainly not going to do it today."

"Were you on board the *Kalua* when that shot was fired last evening?" the Captain asked unexpectedly. He felt as though the subject had been adroitly shunted out of the way. "If you heard it, I thought you might be able to judge where it was fired from."

"It was fired when those planes went over," Otis said.

"Then you heard it?"

"You jump to conclusions worse than a D.A.," Otis said.

"No more than you jump away from answers. I'm not cross-questioning you, Otis, and I'm no D.A."

"I'm question shy," Otis said. "Once I answered too many and finished up in jail. But I didn't hear the shot. Jack Manning told me about it on the phone. Also we keep a .22 high-powered rifle on board for potting at sharks. It might reach Ronnie's window, except you can't see it from here. Since I didn't fire it, and didn't hear it, there's nothing much more I can say." He left the companionway and came back after rattling some more dishes. "You didn't ask me why I took a fall."

"I didn't intend to. It's none of my business."

"I'll tell you, anyway. Rum running. I was a charter-boat fisherman out of Stuart in the twenties. I used to take Colonel

Dayland and his son out fishing.

"It wasn't long before I got to running cargoes in from Bimini, and then Nassau. We got into a hassle with the Coast Guard one night and before it finished the ocean looked like Dodge City with the cowhands in town and the sheriff not there. Two of the Coast Guard men were wounded and one of my men was killed. We had no time to jettison all the Scotch before they nailed my boat. I drew a five-to-ten spot and they tucked me away."

He knocked out his pipe against something and blew through it noisily. "I ran into the boss by accident when he got the *Kalua.* He gave me this berth or I'd be a bum today."

"You didn't need to tell me all about that, Otis."

"I thought it was better to turn up the cards before you got the story from Riker and began to wonder why I held out on you. Luckily, I had the *Kalua* down at Sanibel Island on the night the boss was killed, and could prove it. The boss and Jack Manning were driving down to join me for a week of fishing the next day. When they didn't show I called from Punta Rassa and heard about the killing."

"Why did you say 'luckily?'"

"Sheriff Riker sort of nipped when the boss was killed. He turned a spotlight on everybody in Florida from Ronnie on up to Jack Manning and Celeste. Mr. Manning was playing poker all night with five other men at a session in a house on Davis Island, and hadn't any motive anyhow. But the sheriff lost all sight of motives. I was an ex-con, and as I said, he doesn't like ex-cons. The fact that I was a hundred and fifty miles down the coast when some of those Wharf Rats got the boss, and I could prove it, was lucky for me."

"You sound very positive," the Captain said. "Do you think the youths of the country are really that vicious."

"From your tone, I take it you don't," Otis said. "Well, I've seen my share of vicious hoods in jail and out. With all your experience, I'd guess more than you. There's good and bad in all of them and all of us, but when a real hood is bad he's generally worse, and when he's young he's worse than anything. He's not old enough to have any brains. He thinks he's getting excitement, with no thought of a nice fat felony. No thought that he's murdering for nothing but dough."

"Then you think that one of the Wharf Rats might have fired that shot last night?"

The skipper gave a cynical laugh. "I think that those two boys sitting in that boat two slips from here would burn their little sister up, if they had one, then sell the melted fillings out of her teeth for a nickel and call the whole thing play."

Footsteps sounded on Pier One.

Otis said: "Here comes Mr. Manning and the treasure hunter. We'd better get under way."

The Captain had often made the complaint that blindness got you nowhere. You could take a train, a plane, a bus, or a boat and travel for hours, days, or weeks, and it never seemed to make any difference. There wasn't any scenery, nor any landmarks. You traveled in an endless tunnel where Chicago was just as black as Denver, New York as stygian as L.A. A trip held only one certainty: the formless void you had left at the start would be with you at the journey's end.

The trip on the *Kalua* ran true to form.

Ronnie and Jack had been cordial enough, and apparently not surprised to find him on board. Ronnie had even insisted that the Captain braille his diving gear, his face mask, and air tank with the harness that strapped it on to his back, explaining each detail before he took it out into the cockpit.

He struck Maclain as being depressed, lacking the exuberance of the previous day. It was far more likely that the idea stemmed from the Captain's own feelings. Low pressure areas always made him feel dejected and this promised, weatherwise, to be a particularly damp and nasty day.

The Captain followed Ronnie out to the cockpit. He reached up to where Schnucke lay on top of the cabin and took off her U-brace, then ordered her to lie down again and stay.

He heard her stretch out comfortably.

Ronnie said: "It's overcast and a little foggy, but there's a darn funny look to the sky. We may be in for a blow. That suits me fine. How about you?"

"I can take it." The Captain didn't miss the implication that there still was time enough for him to go ashore. "I've never been seasick in my life. I'd like to go."

The Diesels churned, then picked up their muffled rumble. Jack, who was on the pier casting off, tossed the stern line to Ronnie. The Captain followed the sounds as Ronnie caught it, coiled it, and stowed it out of the way.

Then Jack's voice called from the bow: "All clear!" There was a soft thud as he jumped aboard on the forward bow.

The *Kalua's* air whistle blew three times as Otis backed her out into the channel.

"Otis tells me your boy-friends are waiting to follow you," the Captain said.

"I see them," Ronnie said shortly. "Let them follow. I have a hunch they won't stay too long. If they do, their tub may sink. I'd get a kick out of watching them drown. Let's go up in the wheel-house. I want some coffee."

Forty-five minutes of up and down movement in blackness while engines throbbed and unseen markers moved silently by. Forty-five minutes of following a trackless waste with no other guide than remarks from the people around you.

"Turn of the channel."

"Flasher Two C."

More silence.

"A boat just came around the point, Ronnie. Chuck and Paul are on our tail."

"Just do what I ask you to, Jack. Leave those mugs to me."

"Bell Flasher One! We're making good time in spite of the swell. We're a mile at sea."

Terrible! Endless! One mile or twenty, what was the difference? He knew when he was completely at sea. Snap out of it! Get yourself in hand, Maclain!

"Head her half-a-point more west, Skipper."

"You said due north, Ronnie."

"Half-a-point more west. Let me take the wheel."

You're acting like an idiot, Captain Maclain, stirring up a cauldron full of fear! Your sensitivities aren't getting any stronger. You're just getting older. You can't tell the boy not to go diving. You'll sound just like a trembling girl screaming: "Don't go down in the mine, Daddy. Something will happen today!"

The longest forty-five minutes of a life that had known some very long hours. Fruitless attempts to blame unaccountable dread on the weather, to shed unreasonable nervousness that was growing steadily stronger.

"You take the wheel now, Skipper," Ronnie said. "You can stop her here."

There was a noise as the clutch went into neutral. The *Kalua* rolled slightly and immediately began to lose way. The motors took up the coughing chug that denoted they were idling.

"Come on, Jack. I want to get my tank on and slip over before those punks get any closer." The tenseness of his voice froze the Captain and left him sitting immobilized and speechless. The words of warning crowding to be uttered were less than figments. They were just plain silly, built out of nothing. That left him absolutely nothing to say.

Jack and Ronnie hurried down the stern companionway.

"Is there anything I can do to help?" the Captain asked Otis. His built-up fears had suddenly collapsed in a fine flat heap of hopelessness, reflected by his despondent tone.

"Stand here at the wheel while I go out and toss over the anchor," Otis said. "Here, feel these two throttles. If you hear an alarm bell ring, it will mean that the oil has stopped pumping. Pull the throttles back as far as they'll go and stop the engines before we burn out a bearing."

"I've got it."

"For God's sake don't touch anything else and start the screws. I don't want to cut up Ronnie." Otis went out the port door.

Clutching tight to the throttles, the Captain heard the anchor splash. Almost immediately Otis was back beside him.

Side by side they waited until Jack yelled up from the owner's cabin: "Ronnie's gone over!"

"Do you think he'll really find a treasure?" Otis asked.

"Maybe in heaven," Maclain said softly.

"Now what do you mean by that crack, mister?" Marble's flat voice was ugly.

"I have an awful feeling that he's gone forever," the Captain said. "I'd like to tell you what I mean, and where I got the feeling, but honestly, Otis, I don't really know."

TWELVE

"I don't like any part of it," Otis said after a while.

"Any part of what?" The Captain was aware of the stocky skipper stalking pantherlike around the wheelhouse, stopping for quick inconclusive looks through the port and starboard windows, then forward and astern.

"This whole damn foolishness!" Otis performed some sacred rite on his pipe that created an offensive smell, then lit it. "This weather's got me. It has the feeling of a prison mess-hall when a riot's brewing. Then this business of skin-diving alone, without any reason, ten miles from nowhere. The boy may be bat-brained in some respects, but he knows boats and weather—" He gave a few reflective puffs. "I'm going to cut the motors. Let's join Mr. Manning in the cockpit. I want to see if he's got the boarding ladder overside okay."

"Ten miles from nowhere?" Maclain repeated. "I thought this was pretty close to the spot where Ronnie and I fished yesterday."

"He didn't mark any chart, Captain Maclain. It might be here, or anyplace else. Who's to say?"

"I might—"

Otis quit his pacing. "You might tell me where you fished yesterday?"

"That's what I said. At least you can check if it's not too foggy to see the shore."

"It's not too foggy—except in my brain. Would I be talking out of turn if I asked just how the hell you can mark down a boat's position?"

"I can't, but maybe you can. When we anchored, Ronnie gave me some accurate fixes he had on the shore. I don't think he was deceiving me."

"What was the idea?"

"He thought it would be fun if I steered the *Kalua* for you and Jack north from Bell Flasher Number One and stopped her almost over the fishing rocks."

"And he told you how to check that, too?"

"He showed me how to test the bottom with soap in a sounding-lead—using my fingers."

"Yes, that would have been fun," Otis said heavily. "I don't mean any offense, but just supposing I put you on a course due north after rounding Flasher Number One. Then what? Or do you have some type of gyrocompass and chronometer wired into your brain?"The Captain pulled up his sleeve to show Otis his Braille watch and compass. "We're lying at anchor north-by-west according to this compass. We're about five miles north of the flasher according to my timing of our run. While I haven't tested the depth of the water, or the type of bottom, my guess is we're in the vicinity of the spot where we fished yesterday."

"The vicinity, hunh? What else did the kid tell you?"

He smoked in silence while Maclain explained about the black marker in line with the south end of Honeymoon Island in Hurricane Pass, and Red Flasher Number Two in line with Black Marker Number Three in Big Pass, the latter range about four points to starboard astern.

There was only the low throb of the idling motors for a while as Otis stared out of the wheelhouse toward the distant shore. He turned at last, cut the motors, and said: "I guess Ronnie stopped where he wanted to. Jack has the binoculars watching the skindiver TV show; that is, if there's anything to watch. Let's join him."

Maclain stood up. "Can't you follow the air bubbles from Ronnie's tank while he's under?"

"You might for a few minutes near the boat, but the water's choppy and trashy today. You couldn't see them very far, if at all. He'll surface soon."

The Captain followed him down the companionway. At the foot of the stairs Otis said, "That kid's sick in the head."

"What's your reason for saying that?" Maclain halted him in the owner's cabin, a hand on his arm.

"Just my opinion, that's all. He's full of pipe dreams—get-rich-quick schemes. Chasing rainbows, like this thing today."

"Aren't they all the same? Boys and girls today? Chasing unreality."

"Could be." Otis hesitated. "Only Ronnie seems just a little bit more so to me. Come on. I'm anxious to see him wake up from this particular dream."

Jack Manning was standing at the port side of the cockpit, the binoculars pressed to his eyes, moving them slowly in a semi-circle around the stern.

"What did you cut the motors for?" he asked without lowering the glasses. Maclain found his tone unnecessarily snappish, but his follow-up indicated he was more on edge than angry. "We may have to haul anchor and start looking any second, Otis. I've lost all track of the boy."

"Then what shall we start looking for?" the skipper demanded stolidly.

Maclain sat down in the starboard fishing chair. Waves were slapping smartly and steadily against the hull.

"I might think of worse things to do, if I tried, Mr. Manning. You can't see his bubbles today. It's like looking in a washing machine. Suppose we got over him and he surfaced into one of the screws. He hasn't been down very long and he's got an hour's air. If he comes up we'll see him, or he'll see us and swim here. If he signals for help, it will take less than a minute to up anchor and get under way toward him."

"You're always so damn calm," Jack said. "I'd go over myself and take a look if I could swim."

"I've got a face mask in my cabin. Say the word and I'll make a try, even though I think it's nuts. I can't see anything in that mush, and I doubt if he can. What's got you so worried?"

"Take a look through these, Skipper. Paul Fraceti's diving from that boat anchored over there. That's Chuck Lindsay in the boat as near as I can make out. The Fraceti boy went over with a spear gun—"

A moment passed while Otis took the glasses and adjusted them. "So they're spear fishing, and annoying Ronnie by watching us. Mr. Manning, that boat is nearly half a mile away from here. It's up tide from us. Ronnie may be swimming toward it, but Fraceti will be swimming the other way."

"How do you know?"

"It's easier to get back to your boat if you swim up tide from it," Otis told him. "A good skin-diver can swim a mile under water— maybe. If Paul and Ronnie get anywhere near to each other it would be some swim, and they'd both be crazy."

"Just how far is a spear gun effective?" the Captain asked.

"About twenty feet, that's all," Otis said.

"Are there different kinds of guns? Could one have a longer range than another?"

"Three kinds, Captain, CO2, rubber bands, and springs, but their range is all about the same." Otis opened the lid of the fishbox built in the stern. "Here's Ronnie's CO2—not loaded with a spear." He put a pistol grip with an overlong barrel into the Captain's hand. "It shoots a spear thirty-inches long with a retractable barb, so you can get your fish off easy. There are three spears up on top of the cabin close by your dog. Want to feel one?"

Maclain shook his head. "I was just curious. I'm a pretty good shot at sound, after years of practice, but I don't think I'll try any spear fishing for a while. I'm afraid I couldn't count on a shark to warn me he was after me by making a sound."

"Sharks!" Jack exclaimed. "That's just it, Captain. Ronnie wouldn't even take his spear gun to protect himself. Said his knife was better anyway."

"That's true," Otis said. "Wound a shark with a spear and it can be plenty mean." There was a pause, then: "Mr. Manning, did you see that other boat anchored between here and shore?"

"I saw it. There are two men in it, fishing. They're farther away."

"One of them just went over, swimming or diving," Otis said. "Diving is my guess. I wouldn't call this a swimming day. Also there's a fast cruiser showing a wake headed north between here and the shore. Was she anywhere close to us when Ronnie went over?""I was watching Ronnie," Jack said. "I honestly couldn't say. What's your idea?"

"Too many boats around today, that's all."

"Swing your glasses over here," Jack said excitedly. "Isn't that Ronnie now?"

The Captain lit a cigarette, listening to the flame of his lighter flutter against the tiny windguard. The wind had shifted and was growing stronger. He could feel the *Kalua* swinging and tugging against her anchor line.

"He's swimming toward the other boat," Otis said. There was another pause. "He's climbing in. It's the Fraceti boy, all right. Looks like they're about to take off. Chuck Lindsay's hauling their anchor in."

"Seems like they're in a hell of a hurry, Otis. What—?"

"Could be they're smart," Otis said. "The wind's hauled around into the north. We may be facing some weather. Here, you take the glasses, Mr. Manning. I'm going to get into my trunks. Not that I think it will do much good."

"You're going over?" Jack asked uneasily.

"If Ronnie doesn't show in five minutes. See, that man's back in the boat off to starboard, and they're hauling tail." He spoke next from the owner's cabin. "You'd better get your dog in here, Captain. Yell if the boy shows. It's going to be the very devil if we have to get him up that boarding ladder in a white squall."

"That seems to be one I've missed," the Captain said as he lifted Schnucke down and sent her into the cabin.

"What's that?" Jack asked absently. The Captain could picture his intent scrutiny of the choppy water, already showing spray-flung whitecaps on waves building up by the instant.

"A white squall."

"I hope you'll miss one now. It's one of our pleasant little Florida freaks that only hit about every twenty-five years, thank God! The last one had a seventy-mile wind and the temperature dropped to below freezing in an hour. That was in April, or May, as I remember. I was just a boy. Boats came in with icicles on them—those that weren't swamped, or blown out of the bay."

"Were small craft warnings up this morning when we left?"

"Frankly, I didn't notice," Jack said, "but it wouldn't make much difference. A white squall can hit with no warning at all. Where the devil is that boy?"

The screen door behind the Captain banged sharply as Otis came out. "The bottom's dropped out of the glass in the last fifteen minutes, Mr. Manning. I'm not going over in this. It would be insane. I'd be swept away with wind and tide and never get aboard again."

"And what about Ronnie?" Jack asked. "Are you just deserting him to save your own skin?"

"Boss or not, you'd get a thick lip for that if I didn't know what a sweat you're in! We're facing a squall that's first cousin to a hurricane. I'm afraid our anchor is dragging right now—"

"Are you suggesting that we run for shelter and leave the boy?"

"Shut up and listen, damn it!" The skipper's voice was even

lower than usual with menace as he fought for control. "It's too late now to run anywhere. I'm going to start the motors and keep us in neutral. It will be slack water any minute now—dead low tide. Ronnie may be waiting for that. How long has he been under?"

"Forty minutes. What—?"

"So he has twenty minutes before his air runs out. When he went over which way did he start to swim? With the tide, or against it toward the bow?"

"Straight out from the boat from what I could see of the bubbles," Jack said in a more conciliatory manner. "That wasn't too far—"

"Then the tide would have carried him astern. Now he may have surfaced without our seeing him. He'd have known instantly he couldn't get back to the boat on the surface against this wind and tide. So he'd dive again and wait for slack water."

"And then?"

"He could swim up beyond us under the surface, and when he came up the wind would blow him toward the boat. What's the time?"

Maclain, who had been almost unaware that he was keeping a finger on the hands of his watch, answered promptly: "Nine."

"So he went overside at eight-twenty. It's nine now. Low tide's at nine-three. Don't let's panic for fifteen minutes. Okay?"

"I'm panicked already," Jack said. "This is slicing it too thin. What are you going to do right now?"

"Let out lines that he can grab at along each side of the boat. You take that life-ring up there and pay it out astern in case he's blown by. I'm going forward and drop that big emergency sea anchor—"

"It takes the winch to get that in, Otis. What if he comes up astern of us or blows by? We'd never get free in time to follow him."

"I'm making up a jury-rigged mooring buoy out of three life-jackets and fastening them to the big anchor line. Maybe we can pick up the line again if we have to cut it away. Anyhow, I'm going to cut both lines if I have to. We'll just lose the smaller anchor and line. It isn't holding anyway. Whatever comes we've got to ride out this storm. I'm starting the motors now."

"What shall I do?" Jack asked.

"Keep looking and pray! You'll help, Captain, if you'll come and listen for that warning signal in case anything goes haywire with the oil pressure. You'll be drenched here soon, anyhow. There's rain and hail coming on plenty. Okay?"

"Fine." The Captain followed him inside. The steady roll and pitch of the *Kalua* was more noticeable there. Up. Roll. Pause. A strain at the anchor line. Down in a sickening slide again.

Schnucke, shivering with nervousness, pressed against his leg with a whine.

"Take her up in the wheelhouse with you," Otis advised. "I'll get a storm suit for Mr. Manning from the closet here." A door creaked and slammed. A moment later the screen door at the back followed suit. Maclain could just hear Otis say. "Here Mr. Manning, better put these on."

Up in the wheelhouse the rolling and pitching was doubled. Otis appeared and started the engines. The Captain preferred it when the engines were running. Their guttural rumble soothed him. It was probably entirely false, but the power of the idling Diesels gave him a sense of security.

"You take over, Captain." Otis was gone again outside before Maclain could reply.

As the wheelhouse door slid shut behind him, Maclain fought off a hollow feeling that was most unpleasant. The departure of the skipper had left him very much alone.

THIRTEEN

The Captain found the throttle knobs, touched them lightly, then stood swaying, clutching at the wheel to maintain his balance. Schnucke squeezed herself close to the back of his legs, her poise all gone. For once she refused his order to leave him and lie down.

A sudden blast of wind struck and heeled the *Kalua* frighteningly to starboard, then started shrieking through the metal guy lines of the radio mast with a piercing scream.

Rain smashed against the wheelhouse in a solid sheet of water. The *Kalua* heeled over still farther and hung there endlessly before protestingly righting herself from the staggering blow.

The starboard door slid open, admitted Otis along with a blast of icy air and rain, and closed again. He sidled in between Maclain and the wheelhouse wall, dripping water from his oilskins.

"I'm glad you're back."

"I know what you mean," Otis said. "I've seen the time I would have welcomed the ghost of Al Capone. I can take over now. You'd better sit down. These damn squalls. The wind blows from all four quarters at the same time. You can't—"

"It's nine fifteen, Otis. Anything?"

"Nothing. Five more minutes to go. Not a prayer!"

Thunder crashed in a double ear-splitting clap, followed instantly by a machine-gun rattle all over the boat that was louder than the screaming wind.

"That's hail!" Otis yelled above another crash of thunder. "Hail as big as pin-pong balls. They're bouncing a foot off the forward deck. Jack is sticking it out in that cockpit, but God knows what for. You can't see a foot in front of you out there."

"It's very hard to shake off hope," the Captain said, but his brave talk sounded fatuous to him when he realized he was shivering in time with Schnucke. Either the weather had really turned arctic or he was overcome with a chill of despair.

For aeons the thunder kept shattering the world until its

own ferocity seemed finally to drive it into oblivion. Then rain once more in tearing sheets replaced the bombarding hail.

Steadily, the wind in the guy lines screamed in a higher and higher key.

Each tug of the *Kalua* against her anchor lines grew longer, each drop into the trough more swift and sickening. All sailors claimed that a ship was a living thing with a soul of its own. If that were true, the Captain thought, the *Kalua* must be aware of Ronnie somewhere beneath her, and seeking to submerge and help him in some supernatural fashion.

It was ten o'clock when Jack came up the companionway and huddled down on the lounge seat in the farthest corner. The wind had increased in fury until the flattened-out waters of the Gulf gave a false sense of calm.

A new sound had been added with Jack's arrival. It took a moment for Maclain to recognize that he and Schnucke were not the only ones trembling. Jack's teeth were chattering loudly with an uncontrollable chill.

Any chance of Ronnie's life being saved had ended forty minutes before when the air in his tank was exhausted. Each of those forty minutes was a leaden weight hung about the necks of the three men in the wheelhouse. Those weights would grow heavier as seconds, minutes, and years went by. The increasing load would never be forgotten. Right now there was nothing that any of the three could say.

Otis went below into the galley.

A clink of cups mingled with the wind and the steady chatter of Jack Manning's teeth.

After a time Otis came back up carrying three steaming cups on a tray.

"Coffee laced with brandy, Captain."

Maclain stretched out his hand mechanically and received the cup and saucer. Otis moved on.

"I don't want it," Jack said, his rich voice quivery.

"Drink it, damn it!" Otis snapped. "You have things to do. Call the Coast Guard on the ship-to-shore phone. Save your chill until the time comes to break the news about this to Mrs. Manning."

"I g-guess you're right, Otis." China clinked against Jack's teeth. He gulped down some of the scalding brandy and coffee.

"B-but I'm not calling Celeste about this—n-not until we actually know." His voice was more steady.

"That may be never," Otis said. "Whole ships with every hand on board have vanished in lesser blows than this and were never heard of again, nor a body found. Do you want me to get the Coast Guard on the emergency band—twenty-one-eighty-two?"

"What the devil can they do now?" The cup and saucer rattled in Jack's shaky hand.

"Send out search boats with divers as soon as this wind drops down. That won't be long, an hour or two. Then if you're lucky the boy won't be lost at sea and leave you forever wondering."

"You call them then, Otis. There's nothing else left to do."

"Nothing." Otis crossed the wheelhouse to the ship-to-shore. Somewhere on board a generator whirred. The Captain drained the last of his cup.

"This is the yacht *Kalua* calling the United States Coast Guard," Otis's flat voice rode out on the shrieking wind. "This is the yacht, *Kalua*, calling the United States Coast Guard. How do you read me?"

"This is the Coast Guard, *Kalua*. We're reading you five-by-five. Loud and clear. How me?"

"Five-by-five," Otis said. "Loud and clear. A boy's been drowned —" He paused a second then blurted out: "Or maybe murdered. May Day, Coast Guard. Can you read me?"

"Maybe murdered," the disembodied voice of the Coast Guard repeated. "State your position and details, Yacht *Kalua*, we're reading you loud and clear! Over."

Jack said disgustedly: "Now you've played hell, Otis, mentioning murder. You must have flipped. Give me that thing!"

"So I've nipped. It was murder letting the kid go down on a day like this. Here you tell 'em."

"This is Jack Manning, owner of the yacht *Kalua*, speaking, Coast Guard. How do you read me? Over."

"Still loud and clear, *Kalua*. Please state position and give details of murder. Over."

"We're anchored at sea approximately five miles due north of Little Pass Bell Flasher Number One, and two miles west of Caladesi Island. There has been no murder on board, Coast

Guard. My captain, Otis Marble, who called you was over-wrought. No murder. Do you read me? Over."

"Five-by-five. Are you reporting a murder or an accidental drowning? Over."

"An accidental drowning. My stepson, Ronald Dayland, Jr., was skin-diving when the squall struck and he failed to surface. He's been gone ninety minutes. He had only an hour's supply of air. Request assistance to recover his body."

"Please stand by for an all-craft bulletin, *Kalua*. Do not leave this frequency. All craft on this frequency are requested not to interrupt, to stand-by, and keep this channel clear—"

The bulletin concerned the sudden squall. It was local, not reaching inland, and apparently confined to an area of twenty miles north of St. Petersburg. Winds that had reached full gale were expected to moderate before noon.

The Captain listened, swaying to the *Kalua's* unending motion: Up! Jerk! Sideways! Twist and fall!

Their bulletin repeated, and over, the Coast Guard took matters up with the *Kalua* again: "We are dispatching Patrol Boat, 25GYF, with a diver to assist in searching for a body, *Kalua*. But no search can be started before this heavy wind moderates and the seas quiet down. It is against Coast Guard regulations to pursue such a search for more than one day. However, if the body is not found we will furnish the necessary diving gear to other boats that may wish to carry on—"

It was at this point that another voice cut in: "Coast Guard and yacht *Kalua*. This is Gerry Farkas, captain of the charter boat *Stingray*, out of Tarpon Springs. I'm at sea just south of Anclote Key. I'm reading you both loud and clear. How me?"

When the *Stingray* knew it was being heard, the voice went on: "We have Nick Papalekas, a professional diver, on board. He has a two-tank gear. He has volunteered to search for the drowned boy. Do you want our help, *Kalua*?"

"By all means, *Stingray*. Do you have our position? Over."

"We have your position off Caladesi Island. You should sight us within fifteen minutes. We're less than ten miles from you. Nick says he can start immediately regardless of weather. We're on our way. Please stand by on present frequency. Over."

"This is the *Kalua* standing by. Did you read the *Stingray*, Coast Guard? Over."

"We read the *Stingray*. Our patrol boat will be dispatched as stated to join in search. Please stand by to keep us informed, *Kalua* and *Stingray*. Over and out."

"That wind is slacking off already. Take a look forward with those glasses, Mr. Manning, and see if you can spot the *Stingray*."

"They'd have to be flying a 'copter to be in sight by now."

"I thought you knew her," Otis said.

"The *Stingray*. Why should I know her?"

"Mr. Dayland knew her, and Gerasimos Farkas, Gerry, who owns her. He used to handle out of Mandalay. He and his mate, Grouch Tetter, were fond of Ronnie. Practically taught him what he knew about fishing when he was just a kid. Plenty of times, before he got the *A-bomb*, Ronnie would slip up to Tarpon Springs and go out with them for a day."

"Strange he never mentioned them to me," Jack said reflectively.

"He was close-mouthed about a lot of things, Mr. Manning. That cruiser we saw earlier was the *Stingray*. She could get here in a hurry. She's powered with two one-hundred-and-seventy-five horse-power Sterlings. She can do better than thirty-two knots. The fastest fishing boat in Florida, I'd say."

"That's interesting. Maybe you know this diver they're bringing —this Nick what's-his-name—?"

"Nick Papalekas." Otis waited long enough to make the Captain feel his reply was guarded. "He's a Greek, cousin or something to Gerry Farkas. He was a sponger. From talk I've heard around the docks they don't come any better—as divers—but I don't know him."

"You sound like you'd heard plenty about him around the docks," Jack said. "Plenty that you don't intend to say."

"Anything I've heard won't help or hinder him in finding Ronnie, will it?"

"You're a pain in the neck when you want to be noble," Jack said, "I've had about all I can take, Otis."

"Sorry. Once you told me that the captain of a private yacht was like a chauffeur," Otis said stolidly. "His job was just to drive the boat. Hear nothing, see nothing, and have nothing to say."

"I said I hated blabber-mouths, and I do. I don't know what

Ronnie came out here looking for, nor why. Do you?"

"No more than you. A treasure, he said."

"Fine. A treasure. So two young punks are on hand when he dives—and you're the one who suggested murder to the Coast Guard, not me. Now, in addition to Paul Fraceti and Chuck Lindsay we have the fastest damn boat in the state, with the best pro diver, hanging around in the vicinity during a squall like this one. We didn't notice the boat until she was leaving. That diver could have gone over anywhere at any time, and been picked up anywhere." He turned to Maclain. "What do you think, Captain. Don't you think it's queer?"

"Could be just fortuitous, Jack," Maclain scratched Schnucke's ear. "Things do happen like that. They may be wondering just what the *Kalua* is doing out here, and why you'd let a boy go diving on such a day."

"Hell, we had no warning about this squall."

"As much as the *Stingray*."

Otis said: "Let's take it easy, folks. I'm not too happy about Gerry Farkas showing up with Nick Papalekas. Nick has a rep, if you must know it. I was keeping my yap shut, because I figured we'd had enough worry for one day."

"What sort of a reputation, Otis?"

"He's a bad lad if he's crossed. There was a mess among the sponge divers down off the keys. Those Conchs resent the Greeks from Tarpon sponging down there. Figure the water belongs to them. It got rough. Three of the Conch divers out of Key West died with their air hoses cut. Papalekas got knifed in that particular brawl, but nobody could hang anything on him. He's been treasure diving for suckers since then, and not on spec. Treasure or not, Nick gets his pay. All this is hearsay—"

"You mentioned this Gerry Farkas, too," Jack broke in.

"He's no cream puff, and neither is his mate, Grouch Tetter. Some folks wonder where Gerry got the dough to buy the *Stingray*, but I happen to know. He was in the same racket I was in, running rum. He was luckier, or smarter than I was and salted his dough. But if you're thinking that Gerry and—"

"I'm thinking just that, Otis. That *Stingray* could have been in our laps and gone before we knew it in that wind and rain. That cutthroat diver could have killed Ronnie, and would from what you say."

"It won't wash," Otis said convincingly. "Ronnie knew Nick Papalekas, too. Nick really taught the kid to dive. Not one of those three would do anything to hurt that boy."

"Okay, okay," Jack said. "So they didn't come near us. They just happened to hear us over the air, and Papalekas is the first to offer some free body-searching to find his great friend Ronnie, that sweet little boy. Nuts! It's just too lucky to be true."

"Too lucky?"

"And how. For them not us. Where is the first place that hose cutter, Papalekas, will dive when he gets here?"

"He'll start searching out in circles from where we're anchored," Otis told him.

"Exactly," Jack agreed morosely. "Don't you see that that bunch of pirates is after the same thing Ronnie found? Now they'll start looking in the very place where Ronnie went down."

"You can't very well refuse their help in finding his body, can you?" the Captain asked mildly.

"Ronnie would be the first to tell me to refuse it," Jack said, "but they've got me where the hair is short. This Nick isn't diving for Ronnie, he's diving for gold. By the time another boat gets here, he'll have had first look at every inch of the bottom for a mile around. What blisters me is Ronnie's hard luck: first his father, now himself, searching for what he thought was his life's biggest And—" Jack stopped, then added almost inaudibly: "I feel somehow as though I'm letting the poor kid down!"

By one o'clock the only remnants of the squall were big oily rollers and a most unseasonable chill.

The Coast Guard patrol boat arrived and was shortly joined by four other volunteers from Mandalay.

For three endless hours the Captain sat consuming cigarettes while Jack and Otis passed the binoculars one to the other and paced the wheelhouse, watching the funereal procession of boats slowly spiraling out from the *Kalua*—crawling in a never-ending circle round and round.

Now and again the Captain started at the sound of a voice from the radiophone: "This is Patrol 25GYF reporting. Our diver and divers from four other boats report no trace of body so far. Search continues. That is all."

"Base to 25GYF. Carry on as instructed. That is all."

Nick Papalekas found Ronnie's body at ten minutes to four.

The Captain started to leave his seat on the lounge and promptly sat down again. Every muscle was cramped and sore. His face was rigid as he listened to the voice he recognized as Gerry Farkas's coming in unsteadily over the air:

"Attention, yacht *Kalua.* This is Farkas on the *Stingray.* Do you read me? Over."

"This is Manning on the *Kalua.* We're reading you, *Stingray.* Proceed with message. Over."

"Nick Papalekas has recovered your son's body, Mr. Manning. We're bringing him in overside now. With your permission we'll take the body to Mandalay Beach and await your arrival. Over."

"You have my permission, and all my thanks, Captain Farkas and Nick Papalekas, too. I'll phone a mortician to meet you at Pier One, at the Mandalay Beach Marina. It's most tragic that a boy with everything to live for should have drown. Over."

"Some one disagreed with you, Mr. Manning. You had better phone Sheriff Riker to meet us with the mortician. Your son didn't drown. He was shot through the heart with a fish spear!"

FOURTEEN

The Captain had dawdled through a supper of his favorite crab salad that Sybella had prepared in the guest house, but his usual words of appreciation for her culinary skill were missing.

He had maintained an inscrutable silence throughout the entire meal that did nothing to lighten an occasion already filled with gloom. Sybella, Spud and Rena Savage had found through the years that while he might be reticent and wary with outsiders, if he had some definite purpose in view, with them the reverse was generally true.

At last, fed up with his silence, Spud asked desperately.

"What are you working up to now?"

"I have an idea."

"That's bad news, and I doubt if we can take it, but keep talking. It's your evening."

Sybella poured Maclain more coffee. He sipped it black, his face an interesting study. "I think I'll let you tell Sheriff Riker something that I didn't tell him when I talked to him this afternoon."

Spud's amber eyes moved from Rena to Sybella in a quizzical appeal for help. "Whatever it is, I don't like it. If you've been holding out on the authorities, you're not going to make a patsy out of me."

"You're going to like it less and less." Maclain grinned maliciously. "I didn't tell Riker the real reason that Ronnie went diving today."

"Isn't that where we came in?"

"Yes, and now it's going to be your own little private clot on the brain. While Ronnie and I were fishing yesterday, our lines became tangled—"

"Shades of Isaak Walton," Spud murmured. "That is certainly something Riker must hear!"

"We pulled up a metal turtle." Maclain swallowed some coffee and waited, but no one said anything. "It was aluminum," he went on, "as near as I could guess from what I could feel. It was eight or nine inches long, and four or five inches wide, and two or three inches thick through the middle."

"You caught this thing on a line?" Sybella asked.

"We pulled it up in a tangle of lines. It was hooked through a flipper. It had a crude head and neck made of leather; four leather flippers and a leather tail. If I'm to believe Ronnie's description, it was camouflaged with splotches of paint in yellow and brown."

"You mean you actually felt this object, Dune?"

"Thoroughly, Spud." He finished the coffee and passed the cup to Sybella. "During the whole ride back home I held it on my knee."

"What was Ronnie's explanation, or did he have one?"

"He thought it was an under-water buoy that some diver had fastened to a sunken treasure ship. Turtle shaped so it wouldn't be noticed if other divers saw it—"

"And you bought that?"

"Do you have something better, Spud?"

"No, and nothing worse. I was just wondering what the hell the diver used to mark the spot until he came back the second time and—"

"Ouch!" the Captain banged a fist on his knee. "You take over the firm. I'm quitting. That blasted turtle mesmerized me."

Rena said: "What second time? It would be nice if you kids would cut the commercials and go on with the show."

"We return you now to the program," Spud said in his best announcer's voice. "A diver is strolling along the bottom of the ocean looking for what divers look for. Suddenly he stumbles over a treasure ship laden with pirate gold, he hopes. 'Ah!' he says. 'This is exactly what I've been looking for. Now to mark it in such a way that no other diver will find it!' So what does he do? He reaches into his vest pocket, or wherever divers carry such things, and produces one of those aluminum turtles that come with every complete diver's kit, leather flippers included, $4.98 at any diver's equipment store. A little item without which no self-respecting treasure-hunting diver ever goes down. He immediately attaches—"

"I'm down for the count," the Captain said. "Quit beating my head in. All I know is, I felt the thing, and Ronnie asked me to say nothing about it to anyone. So I didn't. As near as I can tell from my own calculations we were close to the spot where we pulled that turtle up when he was killed today. Take it from there."

"Gladly." Spud swore softly. "A smart-aleck kid thought he'd pull a fast one on a brilliant blind man. He had that turtle along with him when you went out in the *A-bomb*. He told you that you'd pulled it up, and you swallowed it—hook, line, and sinker, to coin a phrase. Isn't that possible?"

The Captain took a very deep breath. "It's so possible that it has me groggy," he admitted. "The blasted thing was too warm to the touch to have come up from twenty feet of water. I noticed that instantly when Ronnie handed it to me to feel. It felt as if it had been sitting out in the sun. That's why I wanted your reactions before I told Riker about it. It's tough to admit you've been played for a fool."

"Did Ronnie tell Jack and the skipper about it?" Spud asked after a moment's thought.

Maclain spread his hands in a futile gesture. "How do I know? If he did, neither of them mentioned it to me, or to Sheriff Riker this afternoon. If they know about it, and think it's important then let them have the first say. Now let me give you the whole picture without interruption."

He leaned back in his chair, closed his sightless eyes, and for twenty minutes his eidetic mind brought to life in vivid fashion every event of the previous, and present day.

When Maclain had finished, Spud stood up impatiently. "Let's take a look in Ronnie's apartment and find the damn thing."

"Let's keep out of it until we're asked," the Captain said. "This is a mess. Apparently Riker doesn't have any authority to investigate Ronnie's murder. The boy was killed three miles at sea. There's a question of jurisdiction and authority."

There was a knock at the door. When Sybella opened it, light shone out through the screen on Uncle Eben's black face.

"Mr. Fraceti phoned the house to know could he and Mrs. Fraceti, and their lawyer, Mr. Ransom, talk with Cap'n Maclain if they come here in half an hour. I tol' them I'd see. He left his numbah to call him back."

"You could have switched him to us here," Sybella said.

"'Ceptin' I wants to talk to the Cap'n before they come. Private like," Uncle Eben said. "If'n he wants to talk to me."

Maclain got up and went to the door. "Sybella will call back and tell them to come, Uncle Eben." He opened the screen door and went outside. "I'd be honored to have you talk with me."

FIFTEEN

The night air was cool and sweet. A gentle breeze rustled the palm trees and carried with it an air of tranquillity. It might have been striving to apologize for its recent bad manners, for the death that had struck in the storm.

The Captain put his hand in the crook of Uncle Eben's frail arm and found that the old man was trembling. It brought back starkly his own near chill during the endless hours he had sat in the cabin of the pitching *Kalua*.

"I've been nursin' something for seven years, Cap'n. It might have somethin' to do 'bout Mr. Dayland's killin'. Might be 'bout Master Ronnie's killin', too. It's been pesterin' at me, Cap'n, suh, cause it's somethin' the sheriff should rightly know."

"I've known you a long time, Uncle Eben. So has Sheriff Riker. You must have had some awfully strong reason for keeping anything from the sheriff that he should rightly know."

"I've got to get a promise from you, Cap'n, 'fore I go on."

"If you want me to keep anything from the sheriff, I can't give it, Uncle Eben."

"Nossuh. I 'spect you to tell the sheriff, or I wouldn't be talkin' now. That is, if you feel the sheriff should know it, after you've studied it some. The promise I wants is somethin' else."

"I'm afraid you'll have to give me the whole story before I make promises about anything." He took his hand from Uncle Eben's arm. "I'm being perfectly honest with you. I can't make promises to make promises. Either you tell me what you want to, without any strings attached, or we'll stop right here and forget the whole thing."

"I guess I trust you more'n any man livin', Cap'n Maclain. I'm goin' on, but I'm puttin' the life of someone I loves very much in your hands, suh."

"A man's life?"

"Yessuh, Cap'n. My nephew's life. My sister's boy, Job Taylor. He's the only one who could'a' knowed what I'm 'bout to tell you. 'Cause he's the only one who could'a' seen and heerd it. Now you knows why I've kept shet-up for seven years, and it's e't on me considerable to protect him. If word gets out to the sheriff where you heerd what I'm goin' to tell you, 'twon't be long 'fore others know that Job has talked." Uncle Eben's voice lowered and faltered. "Job'd die quick, Cap'n. Be kilt and ain't nobody goin' to stop it any more than Mr. Dayland's was stopped seven years ago, and Master Ronnie's was stopped today."

"Do you think Ronnie knew whatever it is you want to tell me?"

"A boy knows a heap when he's twelve years old, Cap'n, and he can get mighty skeered, like Job and me. As to what he knowed, I'd jest be guessin', I sure can't say. I do know Mr. Dayland was his daddy, and they both are daid. Only I figger you're a sight smarter than Ronnie and his daddy, an' can protect yourself better than they could, or I wouldn't tell you nothin'."

"Protect myself against what, Uncle Eben?" Overhead the palm fronds rustled and an icicle gently touched the base of the Captain's spine.

"Against bein' kilt. I'm loadin' you with a powerful lot of danger, Cap'n, 'cause the times come I got to load it on someone. Mebbe Mr. Jack, or Mis' Celeste be the next in line. But I sure knows this, Cap'n, I'm about to hand you one o' them time bombs an' unless you handle it mighty keerful, it could blow you up any minute."

Uncle Eben paused and scratched his head in perplexity. "Now I been frank with you Cap'n, like you was with me. I can stop right now, an' you an' me an' Job 'ud all be much safer, but it would weight on my mind 'till my dyin' day."

"I'll promise you this, Uncle Eben: I'll be mighty careful," the Captain said with deep sincerity, "and I'll do everything I can to protect you and Job. So say what you have to say."

"You'd have been the first to say that Mr. Ronald and Mis' Celeste was mighty happy together, wouldn't you Cap'n? Even though they spoiled the boy?"

The Captain thought back. "From our visits here, yes. I always thought they were one of the happiest couples we knew."

"You thought they was happy, Cap'n. The world thought they was happy. Up to three years before Mr. Dayland was killed, I guess that was true. Then somethin' went almighty wrong. Ronnie was about nine then. I wonder was it felt by that boy?"

Maclain stayed silent, offering no help, and after a time Uncle Eben went on: "It's not my place to judge morals of white folks or black ones, or anyone." Now Uncle Eben was talking more to the rustling palm trees and the velvet night, blanking his mind to the Captain's presence. The revelation was too monstrous to share with any listener. He might bring himself to speak the words aloud but it would have to be to an empty world. Only under that delusion could he ever reveal that his idol had feet of clay, and strip himself of his most prized possession, the integrity of an honorable servitor.

"There was another woman," he finally forced himself to say. "A very bad woman. Mighty pretty, and dangerous as she was pretty. Worse than any Jezebel. Mr. Dayland was seein' her regular like. I don't know if Mis' Celeste knew about this but I did, and Mr. Otis did. There was lots of quarrels with Mis' Celeste 'bout somethin'. If I felt it, the boy might have felt it, too. Where the house had been peaceful like, everything started goin' wrong."

"Was this woman mentioned by name in those quarrels?" Maclain felt called upon to ask it, although he knew he was taking a chance by breaking in.

"I never heard her mentioned, nossuh." Uncle had determined that nothing was going to stop him now. "They was mostly 'bout money, and the business, and what was goin' to happen to Master Ronnie. You see, Cap'n, what nobody knew 'cept mighty few, a divorce was comin' on."

His low voice trailed away and stopped. Finally Maclain risked another question: "How did you know about this woman if you never heard her mentioned?"

"My nephew, Job Taylor, was her houseman." Uncle Eben's voice was stronger. He didn't intend to falter again. "She has a big house, Cap'n, ten miles no'th of Tampa at a wide place in the road, calls hitself Chatham Springs. Mr. Dayland'd say he out on the boat with Otis. Nossuh, he right there at Chatham Springs. Oh, Lord, what trouble we got us all!"

"Man made trouble, Uncle Eben—"

"And women made. Save us all! Mr. Dayland was out at that house the night before he flew to Jacksonville—the night before he was kilt. He tol' her he was goin' to Jacksonville to see a lawyer man, a Judge Marston, to arrange a divorce and a settlement fo' Mis' Celeste and the boy.

"He tol' her he be back the followin' night, what time he get in, an' all. He say he phone her from the Tampa Airport soon as he get in. Then they goin' to marry an' they goin' away soon as the divorce come through. They fergit that Job is there. He heard it all an' tol' it to me."

"But not to Sheriff Riker."

"Nossuh, Cap'n. You can blame that on me. I tol' him not to. Mr. Dayland was daid, an' nothin' could been done fo' him. Ain't nobody said a word 'bout that divorce in seven years, is they? Others knowed about it—that lawyer man in Jacksonville, Mis' Celeste, herself. Must be plenty others 'sides Job an' me. All he do to hisself, tellin' about thet woman, is risk his skin."

"But you seem to think she had something to do with Mr. Day-land's death, Uncle Eben, or you wouldn't be telling this to me."

"Nossuh, Cap'n, I ain't said that woman's to blame, nossuh. Might be she just as skeered as Job an' me. This woman, her name is Eileen Coles—"

"You mean she's still around?"

"She still around plenty, Cap'n. She belong to a man named Lewis Barringer—"

"What do you mean she belongs to a man? Is she married to him?"

"Nossuh. She jest his'n, and was when Mr. Dayland was foolin' 'round. That's what I mean. This Eileen Coles is Barringer's woman, always was an' still is. You ever hear of Lewis Barringer?"

"No. I never heard his name until you mentioned it just now."

"Might be you're lucky, Cap'n. He's a mighty big man in Tampa, and he's got a powerful lot o' money. You can ask the Tampa Police 'bout him. Red Barringer. They know him better by that name. But ask 'em mighty easy like, so he don't get to hear 'bout you askin' for him. He own warehouses, garages, and a fleet o' shrimp boats, and plenty other things including this woman, Eileen."

"And what do you think the police would tell me?"

"Might be they tell you nothin'. That's my guess, Cap'n. But I'm goin' to tell you somethin'—ain' nobody got nothin' on Mr. Barringer, but everybody 'round these parts know one thing 'bout him. Red Barringer's mean as sin!"

"Is Job still working for this Eileen Coles in Chatham Springs?"

"Nossuh. Job come into some money fum somewhere shortly after Mr. Dayland was kilt. Job ain' say where, but he bought himself a lunchroom in Ybor City."

"Do you see him?"

"Jes' now an' again. He's still afeered of his skin."

"Do you think this Red Barringer—?"

"I done tol' you all I know, Cap'n. I don't think nothin' 'bout Mr. Barringer, 'cause my feelin' is it ain' even safe to think about him. And I don't know nothin' 'bout him 'cept what I tol' you, and that's what I know: you go askin' about him prosmiscous like, or troublin' his woman, Eileen Coles, and let word leak to him and he'll have you kilt, or anyone kilt, like he'd swat a fly."

"You seem pretty certain of that, Uncle Eben. What else do you know?"

"I know he can't be touched," Uncle Eben said with conviction. "He had a rival shrimp boat sunk five years ago off Mexico, with all its crew, an' nobody touched him for that, or so I heered. He's powerful as the very devil hisself, an' he's meaner than the seven hinges of sin!"

Uncle Eben started off up the walk just as a car rolled in. "There's Mr. and Mrs. Fraceti now with that lawyer man."

"Bring them over to the guest house," the Captain told him. When he went back into the guest house living room, he sank down into a chair and asked: "Do any of you happen to know just how mean are the seven hinges of sin?"

SIXTEEN

Arch Ransom, distinguished and efficient, came into the living room first. His shoulders were squared. There was a determined set to his jaw. Trailing after him came the Fracetis and Marian Lindsay with all the reluctance of prisoners walking the last mile.

Marian was no sooner inside than she rushed to the Captain, seizing both his hands in her own, her bracelets jangling. "Sybella said you'd help us, Captain. You have to help us. Chuck and Paul had nothing to do with Ronnie being killed." Her words poured out in an avalanche of badly dammed hysteria. "You must help us find and clear them—"

"Find and clear them?" The Captain freed his hands from her grip and placed his cigarette and holder in the tray. "I'm afraid—"

"Marian, this is no time for exploding!" Arch Ransom broke in with a touch of irritation. "Sit down and get yourself in hand, or I'm bowing out. You promised to let me handle this in my own way."

"Come on, Marian, sit over here." Sybella put a sympathetic arm around Marian's waist and led her to a chair.

"Find and clear them." Maclain repeated numbly.

"Damn it," Spud said involuntarily. "Don't say they've skipped."

"I didn't intend to throw it in your face," Ransom said. "But that's the general idea."

"They've taken a powder?" Spud asked grimly. "Did they sign confessions and leave them, or just take them along?"

"Spud! Captain! You must believe—" There was another soft jingle as Marian wiped her eyes with a wisp of handkerchief. "Chuck and Paul have done nothing wrong."

The Captain sat in stony silence.

"That's just it, Marian," Ransom protested. "They couldn't have found any surer means of admitting their guilt. They might just as well have left signed confessions, as Spud just said."

"They were frightened," Donna Fraceti said. "They panicked

and ran, like anyone would—"

"Frightened of what?" Maclain came out of his reverie.

"Facing the facts at an inquest, and questioning by the sheriff." Ransom explained. "They're a couple of boys who have been in scrapes. They think that Riker has it in for them. Good God, Maclain, look at the facts: they'd been feuding with Ronnie, not only threatened him but actually shot at him. So to top it, Ronnie is shot with a spear by another diver and Paul Fraceti is the only one diving in the vicinity. Isn't that enough to scare them away?"

"Apparently you believe so, Arch."

Ransom bristled. "Are you intimating that I'm involved in a conspiracy to—?"

The Captain flipped a hand in the air brushing the lawyer's unfinished question aside. He swung suddenly around to fix the Fracetis with his sightless eyes. "You've heard the damning facts that Mr. Ransom has presented so concisely. You, Mr. and Mrs. Fraceti, and you, Marian: You've protected these two boys all of their lives. Most of the time, more than protection, they needed a birch on their tail. Isn't that true?"

"We've always tried to do our best," Leonardi Fraceti said with a trace of resentment. "I believe I can speak for Marian, too."

"Sure, sure." The Captain nodded his head in pontifical agreement. "But the best you could do wasn't good enough to keep them out of this hellish mess they're in today. Now, you've gone to Mr. Ransom for help, and then come to me." His voice became deceptively low. "I'd like the truth. You say your boys have run away. That's deplorable, but just what help did you hope to get by coming to me?"

Marian Lindsay said in a quavering voice: "I consider you a friend of years. I at least expected courtesy."

The Captain snorted. "Courtesy won't help to find your boy, Marian. The FBI will probably be in on this. I don't know yet. I do know, if they come into it, they'll be most courteous, and can find your red-headed Chuck far quicker than I can." He turned his head. "And you, Mr. Fraceti, how did you think that I could help in finding Paul? Or did you just want some courtesy?"

"It wasn't so much in finding Paul as in what you might have heard Jack Manning and Otis Marble say on the boat. You have a reputation for keenness, Captain. Your ability to question people, and ferret things out. There are things you might have learned from Ronnie. Facts you might get from law officials that they wouldn't pass on to Ransom, or me."

He paused and tried to get some aid from the mask of Maclain's immobile face, then went on rather helplessly: "It isn't so much in finding Paul. I want the boy cleared. I'm willing to pay, and generously. But one thing I really don't get, Maclain, is the rough time you're giving Marian Lindsay, my wife, and me. Just say so if you think the boys are guilty, and you don't want to help, but quit riding me."

"We're all of us in for a ride with spurs, and the police will rake you worse with the rowels than I have, Mr. Fraceti. I'll tell you just what they'll be thinking, and what Sheriff Riker's thinking right now, assuming he knows these boys have skipped—"

"He knows all right," Fraceti said. "He's talked to me."

"Then he's bugged by the same doubts that are eating at me: Who's the worse scared? You three or your two boys? Those two boys know perfectly well if they're guilty or not. You three don't. Riker's wondering, just as I am, if you three got together and convinced yourselves that your boys were guilty of murder, and then tried to do what you thought was the best thing for them—give them money to skip to South America, or some other hideout where none of you figured they would ever be found. Wouldn't the next step be to hire a lawyer, and then retain the best private investigator in the country? I mean the best for your purpose: to look high and low but never find them because I can't see." The Captain smoothed hair back from his forehead. "I've been hired for jobs because I was blind many times before. With Spud's assistance, I've sometimes managed to earn my fee, much to the discomfiture of some clients, but always with more discomfiture to me. I'm not saying this is that sort of a deal, but in fairness to you and your boys, I had to point out the possibility. To put it bluntly: Have you come clean with me?"

Arch Ransom said: "I get your point, Captain, but this time you're wrong. This isn't that sort of a deal. Paul and Chuck have taken Mr. Fraceti's twenty-two-foot outboard cruiser and gone."

"Is that the boat they were out in today?" Spud asked.

"No. That's an open fishing boat that belongs to Chuck. The

one they took, the Donna, is much faster and they could live aboard her. She sleeps four."

"What about the Coast Guard picking them up?"

"Those boys knew what they were doing, Spud." The lawyer nervously cleared his throat. "They cashed a couple of checks at the local Leon's market, a hundred each, perfectly good, and left a note with the manager for Mr. Fraceti—"

"A note?" Maclain leaned forward. "What did it say?"

"Not much. I have it here." Paper rustled. Ransom read: "'Dad: The *Kalua* just called the sheriff's office to say that Ronnie Dayland was murdered. Chuck and I don't want another of Riker's third degrees. We're taking the Donna where no one will find us until this stink dies down. Tell Mom, and Chuck's mother, we're sorry, but we didn't even know Ronnie was lost until we heard he'd been killed. Don't worry. We'll be okay. Paul.'"

Ransom offered the note to Spud who shook his head. He folded the note and tucked it back in his pocket.

"You asked about the Coast Guard, Spud. The Donna can outrun a Coast Guard patrol in a cloud of spray. She's shallow draft and can go up creeks and rivers where any patrol boat would go aground. Those boys know the West Coast of Florida like the palm of their hand. If they really intend to drop out of sight—well, take Cape Romano, the Ten Thousand Islands. It's a hundred and fifty miles south of here but they could make it tonight. A 'copter couldn't spot them in that maze. It's still a hideout for the hunted. They could get supplies from the islanders and stay there until judgment day."

"So, we've convinced ourselves of their innocence," the Captain said decisively. "If the Coast Guard can't find them, nor the authorities, it's a cinch that Spud and I can't find them. But—" He pointed a steady forefinger at Ransom. "If by some miracle these boys are nailed and dragged into court on a murder charge, tell me, Mr. Counselor for the Defense, what are you going to say?"

"Frankly, Captain, damned if I know. That's why we came here in the first place. We hoped you might have some suggestions."

"I'll give you three, for what they're worth," Maclain said after a while. "Ask the prosecution, and Chuck, who stayed in the boat: How many fish spears did Paul have with him when he went over diving? How many did he have when he came back aboard? Ask them to prove that the spear that killed Ronnie was fired from Paul's gun.

"Secondly: I would ask the boys why they pulled up anchor so quickly and took it on the run. Was it on account of the coming storm? Or had they recognized a cruiser in the vicinity, named the *Stingray*, and been frightened off by the reputation of a diver on board, named Nick Papalekas, and by the equally bad reputation of the *Stingray's* crew?"

The Captain twirled his cigarette holder between his fingers. "Third, and most important. I'd try to find out, if he isn't too frightened to tell you, what Paul might have seen while he was diving. If he was the only living witness to Ronnie's murder—" He jabbed at his flattened out palm with his holder. "That's the answer to my question of what frightened them away."

"By God, you may have it!" Arch Ransom burst out. "If I knew a cold-blooded killer like that, and thought he knew me, I wouldn't care how innocent I was, and neither would I stick around to be skewered—"

"How right you are," Spud said softly. "I'd panic just like the two boys did—and pull those ten thousand islands up on top of me!"

"Then you'll help us, Captain?" Fraceti asked. "As I said, you name your fee, and I'll gladly pay."

"Let's just call this one on the house." The Captain studied the palm of his hand as though he might see the mark where he'd stabbed it with his holder. To prove those two boys innocent we've got to prove someone else is guilty. Also it looks like that's the only way we can get them to come back home. I said I couldn't find them and clear them, but maybe I can *clear* them and find them. That would be more than sufficient pay."

SEVENTEEN

The Captain had been sitting at a table in the living room, fiddling with a jigsaw puzzle, his fingers all thumbs, until he had lost all track of the time.

Spud came in from his and Rena's room, a dressing gown wrapped around him, and stood watching quietly.

"Can't you sleep either?" Maclain selected another piece of the puzzle and held it poised.

"Too chilly," Spud said. "Too quiet. You've been snapping those pieces of wood on the table top for over an hour. They sound like castanets. Why don't you try assembling that thing on your stomach in bed if you want to play?" He went out in the kitchen before Maclain could reply.

The Captain impatiently brushed all the pieces of the jigsaw puzzle into their box and put the lid on. It was chilly, the only aftermath of the violent squall. The stillness too was startling, as though nothing lived or moved in the house save the muted sounds of Spud's busying himself in the kitchen. Even the friendly sigh of the air conditioner was missing.

Spud came back unexpectedly and put a warm tall glass in the Captain's hand. "Drink that." He took a nearby chair.

"It's hot milk," the Captain said accusingly. "I could smell it cooking, like the diet kitchen of a lying-in hospital."

"Drink it."

"It reminds me of babies burping. Put a slug of bourbon in it." He held out the glass.

"No bourbon. Drink it straight. Otherwise I go back to bed right now instead of waiting fifteen minutes, and I don't ask any questions. Then you'll be unable to sleep for another night and day. Maybe I should go anyhow. It's after one."

"I'll drink it, you obscenity—obscenity!" The Captain gulped half the glass in two big swallows.

"All of it." Spud grinned at the Captain's grimace. "You know damn well it will help you relax, in spite of the nasty name."

Maclain drank the second half more slowly and put the

glass on the table. He could feel the hot milk coursing through him, untying knots and making him drowsy. "Your turn, Spud."

"To what?"

"Ask your questions. You've delivered your milk. Now play the rest of the game."

"What did Uncle Eben tell you? The Fracetis and team arrived while you were inquiring about the seven hinges of sin."

The Captain gave him in detail the story as he knew it from Uncle Eben: the girl, Eileen Coles, in Chatham Springs, whom Ronald Dayland was seeing; the broken marriage and imminent divorce that had been kept so quiet after Ronald's murder; the fact that Eileen Coles was Lewis (Red) Barringer's woman; Red Bar-ringer's wealth, his ownership of garages, warehouses, and shrimp boats; and Uncle Eben's positive opinion that Barringer was ruthless, a killer, and mean as the seven hinges of sin. Spud listened attentively.

"So that's the whole nasty picture," the Captain finished. "Now that you've heard it all, what do you make of it?"

"Part of it figures. Part of it doesn't."

"What part figures?"

"Big wheel gangster chief in respectable clothing," Spud said. "I've watched enough TV to buy this Red Barringer as worth looking into. If we find he's true to type, he could have had Ronald bumped off by a couple of goons. Let's make a note to inquire, while we keep out of his way."

"The Coles woman might talk, Spud, if I went to see her."

"I'm sure she would," Spud said fervently. "She must have talked to Ronald, and also to Red Barringer. A conversational piece. Shall I send flowers, or do you want to be cremated and have your ashes scattered from a shrimp boat at sea?"

"Don't get whimsical." The Captain drummed softly on the table edge with his fingers. "Eileen might have really loved Ronald, if she intended to marry him. I'm going to have a talk with Job Taylor, Uncle Eben's nephew. Eben said the woman might not be to blame, and that she was scared. If that's true, she's been nursing a slow burn against Barringer for seven years. She might be anxious to get back at him by talking to me. What do you think?"

"I think you've curdled your milk and your brains." Spud stood up. "I also think you'll commit dry suicide any time you want to, and without consulting me."

"Wait a minute. You haven't said what part of this doesn't figure."

"Ronnie's murder doesn't figure, Dune." Spud smothered a yawn. "Name me one possible connecting link that would tie in this mastermind Barringer."

"You just mentioned a dozen links." Maclain pushed back his chair and got up to face his partner.

"I mentioned nothing—or nothing that looked like a link to me."

"The missing link I've been looking for had nothing to do with your intellect. It was supplied by your facetious remark about having my ashes scattered from a shrimp boat at sea."

"That's a mighty cunning bit of deduction, old boy!" Spud gave a complimentary squeeze to the Captain's shoulder. "Glad to have been of so much help. Now go in and take another pill and knock yourself out completely. Next time you want a missing link don't hesitate to call on me." He turned and started for his room.

"There are times when you act the fool so well I could brain you, if you had any," the Captain told his partner venomously. "You mentioned a shrimp boat. Well, boats are the link, you bat brain!"

"Boats?" Spud made a half turn, his amber eyes bright with a glint of admiration.

"Oodles of boats, inboards, outboards, the *Kalua*, the *A-bomb*, Chuck Lindsay's boat and the *Donna*, that the boys pinched to make a getaway, that charter boat out of Tarpon Springs, the *Stingray*." Maclain made an excited circle with his arm that included all of Florida. "Big boats, little boats, fast boats, slow boats, spongers, Coast Guard patrols, boats full of divers and fishermen. Good godamighty, Spud, they crawl like water beetles out of every cove and slip within two hundred miles of Mandalay. And who owns the most and biggest boats of them all?" He stopped and drew a tired breath.

"Red Barringer with his fleet of shrimpers," Spud said. "But there's nothing illegal about shrimping, Dune."

"I've met a few shrimpers," the Captain told him, "and none of them seemed to have this Barringer's varied interests nor the heavy sugar necessary to acquire them. Neither did they have a chick in a private house in Chatham Springs, nor the reputation of being as mean as the seven hinges of sin."

"So—?"

"I think that Red is a smuggler, among other things," Maclain said wearily. "I think that Ronald and Ronnie both got in his way inadvertently and that he called to some of his pirate cutthroats and had them murdered." He touched his watch. "Think it over, Spud. It's nearly two. We'd better turn in."

The sleeping pill and milk took hold as soon as he stretched out in bed. Still it was a while before he fell asleep. The *Kalua* moved him up and down with gentle undulations. A ghostly wind kept whining through the *Kalua's* guy lines, blotting out the rhythm of Sybella's breathing, even though he knew that around him the night was startlingly still.

The raspy voice of Captain Gerry Farkas of the *Stingray* coming through the ship-to-shore finally put him to sleep. "You had better phone Sheriff Riker to meet us with the mortician. Your son didn't drown. He was shot through the heart with a fish spear!"

"Repeat: He was shot through the heart with a fish spear!"

Not a very pleasant pillow on which to find rest.

He woke and sat straight up in bed after an hour of dreamless unconsciousness. There was no gradual awakening. Every nerve in him was drawn as taut as the guy lines on the *Kalua.* He knew exactly where he was, and what time it was, although he had no remembrance of fingering his watch on the bedside table.

It was twenty minutes past three.

He knew precisely what sound had awakened him so abruptly, and where it came from.

Someone had set a metal tackle box on the stainless steel drain-board in the kitchen of Ronnie's apartment next door.

Someone searching for the aluminum turtle!

He got out of bed like a fleeting shadow, put soft slippers on, and went through the living room and kitchen into the garage through the house door.

Dreist stood up, clanking his chain.

The Captain working with the swift surety of habit, knelt down, unchained Dreist, and put his broad flat muzzle on. As he passed, he took his supersonic whistle from the glove compartment of his car.

A minute later he had soundlessly slid up the folding door, and with Dreist close beside him was out on the lawn.

As he rounded the guest house, his footsteps catlike against the soft buffer of the grass, he heard the click of the latch on Ronnie's closing front door.

The Captain said, "Get him, Dreist!" and stood with his back pressed hard against the guest-house wall.

EIGHTEEN

Dreist blasted off from his side like a shadowy silent missile bent on a message of destruction. He couldn't bite and tear with his muzzle on, but he could bring a fleeing person down, and his snarling presence over them packed far more menace than the pointing of an unloaded shotgun.

If a criminal was desperate enough he might take a chance that the weapon was unloaded. If he guessed wrong he died. If his guess was right, it was just too bad for the man with the empty gun. Fifty-fifty!

Somehow, once you were on the ground you didn't take chances with a trained protective police dog, muzzled or not. His compassionless efficiency robbed you of initiative. It was useless to study his demeanor, searching for fear or weakness. You already had the answer. He was loaded in both barrels, and he was there.

Feet pattered across the lawn in a run and pounded over the gravel drive. A hedge crashed in brittle protest as someone tore through it. A body thudded.

The Captain's forehead wrinkled in quick surprise as, wary of the croquet wickets, he made his way toward the sound of Otis Marble's flat voice. Unexcitedly, fluently, and steadily with a depth of feeling, the stocky skipper of the *Kalua*, lying flat with Dreist over him, had started to swear.

Maclain found the hedge and pushed through it. "Is that you, Otis?"

"Jackpot, damit! Remove this drooling grizzly bear!"

"Still steben, Dreist! Quiet! Stand still!" the Captain snapped out. The dog came close and pressed his leg. "I'm sorry, Otis. It was late and I was nervous—"

"And I was noisy as a boiler factory. I should have my head examined for not taking a course in burglary while I was in the can. You and them ears!"

"I never thought of you—"

"Cripes! Why would you? Can I get up now, or will that rabies factory start goosing me in the belly again?"

"He won't bother you again, I promise."

"Thanks." There were sounds as Otis scrambled up and slapped dirt from his clothes. "That s-o-b would eat up a baby. I'm glad you had his muzzle on. I don't think he likes me."

"He'll go after anyone who runs. Now if you'd just stayed still—"

"Hah! If you could see him, Captain, you'd run." He started to take the Captain's arm, looked at Dreist and changed his mind. "Let's go sit a few minutes on the sea wall. I've got some explaining to do."

"Not to me, unless you want to."

"I want to. Maybe if I tell you why I was prowling, you'll decide not to blow the whistle on me."

"Perhaps I know already."

"That's possible, but I doubt it, Captain. If you do, then you'll know we can save the Mannings more heartaches by not having it spread around."

"We're not on the same wave length, then. Walk up with me while I put Dreist back in the garage and chain him. Then we can go down on the *A-bomb*'s dock. We won't disturb anyone there and there's a bench to sit down on."

With Dreist kenneled they retraced their steps. Out on the dock Otis stopped and leaned over the side by the *A-bomb* before they sat down.

"Well, the Wharf Rats must have been gnawing again," he muttered.

"What's the matter now?"

"Somebody stole the canvas cover off the *A-bomb*. Ronnie never left that boat uncovered. He was too good a boatman and thought too much of her. She's damn near waterlogged from the rain in that storm."

"The tarpaulin was on there early yesterday morning, Otis. I happened to feel it before I walked down to the marina. It was not only on there, but securely fastened down."

"So some of those sea rats pinched it between the time you felt it and the storm. It's just the type of petty thieving they go in for. Anything that—"

"I'm getting fed to the teeth with everything that happens around Mandalay being blamed on the kids, Otis. Haven't you got any adult criminals in town? I thought that you—" the

Captain broke off short and sat down.

"That I what?" Otis asked succinctly as he took a seat beside him.

"Would know how tough it is to shake off a bad name, and how rough it gets to be falsely accused of things you didn't do. Or are you the exception? Maybe when you were freed from prison nobody tried to push you around."

"I'm starting to read you five-by-five," Otis said after a wait. "You may not be able to see but you can sure pick out the tender spots to stick your ice pick in. I'm the dizziest dumbbell out of captivity from being pushed around. Also I've been bounced considerable. The boss just happened to catch me on the third bounce and give me this job. If I'd hit the concrete one more time, I'd have kept going down, and finished up in the deep six underground. So you've heard the news. Now give me any reason why an adult criminal would pinch a tarpaulin off a boat and leave an engine worth half a grand, and I'll buy it."

"Maybe it wasn't stolen," the Captain said. "Suppose some one was hunting for something in the *A-bomb*, took the tarpaulin part way off and left it. Couldn't it have been ripped loose and blown away by the storm?"

"No. There's no trace of it. If it was ripped off, there'd be fragments of canvas left around with the fastened eyelets. The only loose pieces of gear on board are the anchor and lead. They're still there. Have you any idea what this adult criminal was looking for?"

"The same thing you were looking for in Ronnie's apartment. In his tackle box, maybe. An aluminum turtle with a leather head and tail and flippers."

"Would you mind repeating that very slowly, Captain? I want to be sure I'm hearing exactly what you say."

"Ronnie didn't mention such a turtle?"

"Are you kidding me, Captain?"

"Far from it. I'll tell you about it." He quickly ran through the events of the previous day. Otis listened, sitting motionless beside him. "That's it. The whole truth, Otis. I thought that finding that turtle was what took Ronnie on that fatal trip today."

The skipper remained silent and unmoving for an unaccountable length of time. Finally he asked: "Did you actually feel this turtle, Captain?" There was an overload of skepticism in his tone.

"I'll give you the same answer I gave to Spud when he asked me that: we came back in from fishing grounds to dock with that turtle resting on my knee."

"Have you ever been mistaken in objects you felt? Thought one thing could be another?"

"Quite often, many years ago," the Captain admitted. "Much less often in recent years. I can actually put a jigsaw puzzle together fairly quickly. But I wasn't mistaken about that turtle. Can you think of anything else on earth that is shaped like a turtle? Anything that might have deceived me?"

"Not offhand, Captain. You say you trust your fingers absolutely?"

"I'd have been dead long ago if I didn't," Maclain said most emphatically.

"What about the power of suggestion?" Otis asked.

"I don't understand."

"Could a strong suggestion throw you off the track? Trick you into believing that you were feeling something you weren't feeling?"

"For example?"

"This for example. Here's your turtle, Captain—minus five pieces of wide pork-rind lures that Ronnie fastened to it for flippers and a tail, and minus the soft tadpole fresh-water bass bait that he told you was the head." He laid a damp object on Maclain's pajama-clad knee.

The Captain picked it up and weighed it tentatively. He tested it with a thumbnail, top and bottom. Then, turning it slowly over and around, he let his surgeon's fingers explore every inch of it thoroughly.

The size in inches, eight-by-four-by-three, was very close to the turtle's dimensions. The rounded top was smooth and polished. The bottom was flat and metallic, with some holes around the edges. There were even rough splotches on the top that might have been paint.

The power of suggestion! "Here's your turtle, Captain—!"

He went all over the object again trying to fit those flippers on, together with the head and tail. For a few black seconds his mind went blank and he felt that his senses had failed him. He forced himself back to reality and with fierce concentration searched the metal bottom for the tiny sharp spots so clearly defined on the bottom of the turtle, the spots where the metal eyes to hold the mooring wire had been welded or soldered on.

There weren't any, and with the discovery his waning confidence flooded back.

"No dice!" He handed the object back to Otis. "I'll have to admit there are points of similarity. I don't know where you got that thing nor what it is, but it isn't the metal turtle that Ronnie pulled up and gave me to braille. That's positive."

"I'll tell you where I got it," Otis said. "I took it from Ronnie's tackle box less than half an hour ago. Now do you still say you can't be wrong?"

"What the devil is it?" Maclain demanded.

"It's a souvenir of Florida. Half a polished coconut shell with a metal bottom fastened on. I think it was filled with shot and used as a paperweight on board a boat. The bottom rusted and the shot fell out. It started to float and Ronnie hooked it, God help him. That half a coconut is what sold Jack on taking him out and—"

"What makes you think that came from a boat, Otis?"

"The name of the boat is painted on the shell—the *Casa ybel.*"

"Did you ever hear of her before?"

"Me and everyone else in the rum racket," Otis said. "She was sunk by the Coast Guard, or hit by them in a running battle in 'twenty-nine. Anyhow she vanished with her skipper and mate. The word was that she sank with fifty grand on board in a safe. Nobody knew exactly where, but news about it even filtered in to the Federal pen."

He hesitated and the Captain heard him suck on his empty pipe. "The *Casa* was one of Barringer's boats—"

"Barringer?" Maclain bit hard on his lower lip.

"Red Barringer. Ever heard of him?"

The Captain pondered. "I believe I've heard Sheriff Riker mention his name."

"Well, forget you heard it," Otis advised. "Red is a solid citizen with a house, three kids, and a charming wife on Davis Island. He's a big operator. He saves Uncle Whiskers millions in social security every year by eliminating kids like Ronnie, and anyone else that annoys him in a business way."

"Do you think he's connected with Ronnie's death?"

"Look, Captain, I'm talking off the top of my head. If that fifty grand is still aboard the *Casa ybel*, and Ronnie found that wreck —Well, the poor kid's dead, isn't he?"

The Captain nodded.

"And why do you think Ronnie didn't tell me about that *Casa ybel* coconut? I'll tell you why. He knew that I'd have died before I let him stick his neck out with anything connected with Barringer. I hate Red's guts, and I know, above all people, that he's poison and sudden death. Red's the punk who fingered me to the Coast Guard to get me out of his rum-running way."

"That may be true, Otis, but what reason would Ronnie have for describing that coconut as a turtle and deceiving me?"

"He did lots of crazy things without any reason," Otis said sadly. "Things he couldn't explain himself, if you asked him. That's what I meant by his power of suggestion, he believed things himself for the moment. To him it wasn't really lying, no matter how wild his lies might be."

"You're painting a pretty good picture of a psychopath, Otis."

"I'm not sure I dig the psychopath stuff, Captain, but if you mean the kid was a screwball, you've rung all the bells. He was hooked, Captain."

"Hooked? Oh, God, no!" The Captain locked his hands and squeezed until his fingers hurt. In a single word, so much of Ronnie's conduct on the fishing trip had become startlingly clear. "Heroin?"

"Yes. He's been a junky for God knows how long. I've known it for over a year."

"Do Jack and Celeste know this?"

"I hope not," Otis said fervently. "I didn't prowl his room tonight to get that *Casa ybel* coconut. I knew nothing about it. I went there to get his hypo kit, and any junk he might have with it. It was in his tackle box, with the coconut. I have it here.

"Look, Captain, they're holding an inquest on the kid in the morning, and Dr. Arnheit has probably performed an autopsy already. I was going to Arnheit and lay it on the line. Why break Mrs. Manning's heart any more than it's broken? What the hell good will it do to spread the word that Ronnie was a user?"

The Captain tightened his fingers more painfully. "None that I can see."

"Then if you agree, maybe you can do more with Arnheit and the coroner than I can. What about it?"

"First you'll have to answer me some questions." Maclain unlaced his fingers and flexed them. "You'll be asked them anyhow, but maybe we can keep them out of the inquest. I don't think they're material, but I'll have to talk to Arch Ransom, the lawyer, and see."

"Shoot," Otis said.

"Why haven't you mentioned it to Jack and Celeste, if you've known Ronnie was using for over a year?"

"Yeah, yeah. Why haven't I?" Otis said disgustedly. "This isn't going to be easy, Captain. I'm going to be in deeper than you know, if I ever manage to get myself in the clear. I guess I was closer to Ronnie than anyone living. The kid told me about it without my asking, and I like a damn fool promised to keep my mouth shut. You don't know how persuasive he could be."

"Or maybe I do," Maclain said dryly. "There was a matter of that turtle—Go on, Otis. I'm listening."

"This was a matter of two hundred grand that was coming to Ronnie when he was twenty-one. Money the boss had left in trust with his mother. If he got in any trouble his mother could hold up that dough until he was twenty-five. Captain, the kid was killing himself and there was nothing his mother or Jack could do. We cooked up a scheme—"

"Yes."

"He was going to get thirty-five thousand from his mother to get a charter boat. I think, if he'd lived, she'd have come through. We were going to take it to Miami, and he'd promised me he'd take a cure. That would have been out if I'd opened my mouth—"

"Couldn't Jack and Celeste have given him a cure?"

"Captain, believe me, you don't know junkies like I do. I've seen too many. Heard too many screaming in a cold turkey cure. Seen too many go right back on the stuff again. You have to give them some damn strong reason to beat the junk, and Ronnie wanted that charter boat enough to make it a reason. It was something he could really do. Away from the Wharf Rats and Mandalay. His mother couldn't have done it. There was a resentment in him against her. I don't know what. Hell, am I getting through to you?"

"Maybe more than you think, Otis. You've convinced me that Ronnie was very close to you."

"It gets worse," Otis said. "Worse as I go along. He was going into Tampa to make his buys and the scummy pushers were taking him over. Before he got it, the allowance his mother was giving him was gone. He got mixed up with a Cuban doll. She started a little blackmail. He had to borrow against the *A-bomb*. The next step, they'd have had him peddling—"

Otis's flat voice broke and he fought for a moment to get it under control. "Ronald Dayland's only son peddling junk to the Wharf Rats in his own home town. Well, I put the squitch on that one before it started, but it may land me back in the pen."

Silence pressed on the Captain's ears until he couldn't stand it, and asked at last: "What did you do?"

"I cleared off the *A-bomb*. Went to see that Cuban slut and told her I'd kill her. Then I took over the buying for Ronnie and told him he could have so much and no more. I made some contacts in Tampa by risking my neck. For the last three months I'd started Ronnie paring down."

"You say you were risking your neck?"

"You don't know the half of it, Captain. The contact I made is getting his junk from a dame named Eileen Coles. She lives north of Tampa in Chatham Springs, and she happens to be my old pal Red Barringer's girl."

Otis got up. "The name of my contact, Captain, is Nick Papalekas, the diver who recovered Ronnie's body. My hunch is that Barringer's snowing this state with heroin from Mexico. I hope to have just a little time before I'm killed or jailed again, and I'm going to burn that devil Barringer down."

NINETEEN

It was 4:15 p.m. on Wednesday, the 8th of April.

The Captain felt groggy, punch drunk from the lack of sleep. He had to force himself to pay attention to the proceedings which were going on around him in Sheriff Riker's big air-conditioned office in the Poinsettia County Court House, in Mandalay.

It was true he had caught a couple of hours rest following the morning's inquest, and a meager lunch at home, but the details of the inquest were still too fresh, and his nap had been restless. He'd been further disturbed by the newspaper accounts of the murder, read to him by Rena Savage.

All Arch Ransom's efforts at the inquest had failed to suppress the threats against Ronnie made by Paul and Chuck, and the shots fired at the *A-bomb*. That was followed by the story of the bullet fired into Ronnie's room. The Captain, called to the stand, had grudgingly had to confirm everything, and tell, in addition, of the boys' near attempt to swamp the *A-bomb*. When it came out that Paul and Chuck had deliberately followed the *Kalua*, and been diving near by, the picture looked grim.

Nick Papalekas, the swarthy, hairy diver, who had recovered Ronnie's body, had laconically told of his acquaintance with Ronnie, and what few facts he knew. He explained the presence of the *Stingray* in the vicinity without any trouble. Gerry Farkas and his boat had been hired by the Tarpon Springs Spongers Association to make a survey of marketable sponges in local waters. Nick had been diving for them for a month now. They had been close to the *Kalua* earlier and heard Jack's request for help when they tuned in on the Coast Guard channel, 2182, to get information about the storm.

But an early morning contact of the Captain's with Dr. Arnheit had accomplished one thing: Ronnie's addiction to heroin hadn't been hinted at. Also the Tampa, St. Pete, and Mandalay newspapers' stories had left the Manning and Dayland names spotlessly clean. Arch Ransom had done some spade work, too, for the missing boys weren't mentioned.

There'd been spade work by some unknown as well. Masterly spade work. The context of a paragraph in the Mandalay Monitor, read to him by Rena, was typical. His inability to deny it stuck lancets of frustration into the Captain's delicate spleen. It sounded to the furious Duncan Maclain like a release from Red Barringer's public relations department.

"According to a reliable source," The Monitor stated, "the young victim, Ronald Dayland, Jr., pulled up a piece of wreckage while out fishing last Monday with Captain Duncan Maclain, of New York City. Captain Maclain, his wife, Sybella, and Mr. and Mrs. Samuel Savage, are house guests of the Mannings.

"As Captain Maclain is blind, he is unable to confirm this fact, but our informant states the object pulled up from the deep was half a water-soaked coconut shell, painted with the name: *Casa ybel*. There have been many rumors that a forty-foot rum-runner, called the *Casa ybel*, was sunk with a sizable fortune on board in a waterproof safe during the lawless years of prohibition.

"Inquiries indicate that this money was recovered a long time ago, but evidently young Ronald doubted that fact, or more likely didn't know it. At any rate, he persuaded his stepfather, Jack Manning, to take him on the diving expedition that culminated in the tragedy yesterday."

"Unmitigated hogwash," Maclain stormed as Rena finished reading the paper. He gave her a pungent account of his encounter with Otis the night before, and their talk on the *A-bomb*'s pier. "That coconut was planted for the turtle yesterday, Rena. Were you and Sybella here?"

"No. We went to the country club with Celeste and Marian Lindsay, shortly after nine. We were going to golf but the rains came. We bridged and lunched instead and were there nearly all day."

"Pretty damn clever!" he fumed. "Anyone reading the papers will forget a turtle was ever mentioned before I mention it, and if I protest, I'll be branded as a blind blithering fool."

He stomped off to try to sleep until Riker's conference at four. Spud drove him and Jack Manning to the Court House. They stopped in the hall for a moment while Spud opened the door to the sheriff's office and took a quick look inside. "With you in a minute, Dave," he said to Riker, and closed the door.

"I get flashlight pictures for Dune," Spud explained to Jack who was staring inquiringly. "He likes to have a tag on new people's appearance. When they speak he dusts them off in his nimble brain."

He turned to the Captain, speaking swiftly. "Four men at Riker's desk. One on his left is barbered and clean-cut. Forty. Trade-mark: FBI."

"That's Burton McKelvey from the Tampa Office," Jack said. "This murder on the high seas was finally tossed in the lap of the FBI, but they're letting Dave handle details. He told me on the phone. Didn't mention any others, though."

"Thanks, Jack. The first to Dave's right is a Smithfield ham," Spud went on. "Ham fists, too. Florid. Hearty laughter when people fall. Bad man in a barroom brawl. Tough as a fifty-cent steak. Got him?" Maclain nodded. "Fourth one?"

"Withered cyanide type. A quiet prune with a leather face and teeth like a shark. Timid, like a Black Widow. Apologizes while he's swallowing you. Wears bow ties. Got him?"

"Perfect." Again the Captain nodded. "What about the audience?"

"Just Otis Marble and Arch Ransom so far. If no more come, us bad men will have the law outnumbered five to four. Shall we dance?" Spud opened the door.

They went in and sat down to the left of Otis and Arch Ransom. Dave Riker promptly introduced the three men at his desk. Special Agent Burton McKelvey of the FBI had been placed in charge as Jack had said. The other two were Treasury agents. Ben Lynch (the ham) was a U. S. Customs agent. Jim Claypoole (the spider) was an agent of the Federal Narcotics Bureau.

This was growing bigger by the minute, the Captain thought. No ordinary murder produced two U. S. Treasury men from Customs and Narcotics, along with an agent of the FBI.

He had a good picture now of all four. Dave Riker, he had known for years. Dave, squat, compact and powerful, had Indian blood in him. His grandmother was a full-blooded Creek. Dave's loudest laugh was a gentle chuckle. His honesty, tenacity, and general efficiency had made him almost a permanent fixture in the Poinsettia County's Sheriff's Office.

"Are we permitted to ask questions, Mr. McKelvey?"

"That's why we're all here," Burt McKelvey said pleasantly. "But we'll expect the same privilege. To ask some ourselves, and also to get the answers. What's yours, Captain Marble?"

"That coconut shell on the sheriff's desk. I found that last night in the dead boy's tackle box and gave it to Sheriff Riker this morning. It was mentioned in the papers. Is that the reason Mr. Lynch and Mr. Claypoole are sitting in?"

"We were interested, I'll admit," Jim Claypoole said.

"Oh, quit ducking up alleys," the Customs' man boomed. "You junkmen get so devious dealing with your pet pushers that you think the truth is a mortal sin. Certainly the mention of that coconut brought us here, or the name *Casa ybel*, rather. We hoped to get the lowdown about finding it from Captain Maclain. Does that answer your question, Skipper?"

"No," Otis said flatly. "I thought it was the fact that the *Casa ybel* once belonged to Red Barringer that brought you here. That and the fact—" He broke off abruptly.

"What fact?" Claypoole asked meekly.

"Is anything said in here going to anyone outside of this room?"

"No. You have my word on this, Otis," Dave Riker told him.

"That's good enough for me, Sheriff. Mr. Manning may know this or he may not. Maybe Dr. Arnheit told him after the autopsy. Anyhow, it never came out at the inquest, but Ronnie was hooked. I also gave Sheriff Riker his hypo and a few decks of 'H' that I took from Ronnie's tackle box along with that *Casa ybel* gadget. My guess was that the combination of Barringer and a murdered addict brought you two Treasury agents here."

"Did you know your stepson was a heroin addict, Mr. Manning?" McKelvey, the FBI man broke in.

"Let's say I suspected it," Jack said contemplatively. "Suspected it, but didn't want to know it."

"Didn't it occur to you that if he was an addict you might have found out more and tried to help him?"

"Yes. A great many things occurred to me where I might have been of help to Ronnie." There was an edge of desperation to Jack's statement. "I gave up finally. I was a stepfather and he never let me forget it, just as he never let his mother forget that he considered her a criminal for marrying me. It would have been the same with anyone. The only way I knew how to help him was keeping his worst faults from my wife—when I could."

"Do you think that helped either the boy or Celeste, Jack?" Dave Riker asked.

"Maybe not Celeste, but it helped the boy in the only way he wanted help—monetarily." He sketched out the details of Ronnie's inheritance and how Celeste could postpone it if she considered her son incompetent. Then he told about Ronnie wanting $35,000 to buy a charter boat to go away with Otis. "I was all for it. I'd discussed it with Celeste, but it takes a lot of convincing to get her to part with money. Still, I think she'd have come through if Ronnie had lived."

"For your information, she would have," Arch Ransom said. "She'd talked over the legal details with me."

"So even though you suspected that your stepson was on the horse, you kept it from his mother and you were willing to see him leave here to run a charter boat with Captain Marble. Just how did you figure that might help him, Mr. Manning?" Jim Claypoole asked in a manner that bordered on servility.

"You might ask Otis. Ronnie was a hell of a sight closer to him than he was to Celeste and me," Jack said miserably.

"What about that, Skipper?" The Narcotics agent turned his gentle attentions on Otis just as obsequiously.

"I'm going to hand it to you in a package, Mr. Claypoole," Otis announced stolidly. "All tied up with a nice strong string that will probably choke me. All of you know my record and that I've taken a fall, so don't try to kid me. I'm leveling and holding nothing back, so help me."

Otis, without attempting to excuse his own questionable part in obtaining heroin for Ronnie, had certainly spilled it all. He recounted with Spartan simplicity exactly what he had told Maclain: the blackmail of Ronnie by the Cuban girl, Julieta, no address, except an Ybor City bar—his contact with the diver-pusher, Nick Papalekas; his discovery that Papalekas was in turn getting heroin from *Eileen* Coles, the dame every mug in the Tampa underworld knew to be Red Barringer's girl friend.

Without any mitigating embellishments, Otis went on to tell of keeping the facts from Jack and Celeste solely because Ronnie had come to him instead of them and asked his help instead of theirs. He made light of saving the *A-bomb* from the loan company, and barely hinted that he had stopped Ronnie from becoming a local pusher, and the threatened degradation that one act alone had averted from the Dayland clan.

His own involvement fully exposed, he annoyed Maclain by saying that he felt positive Ronnie had hooked into the *Casa ybel* coconut shell and made a typical Ronnie attempt to deceive his blind friend by rigging up the coconut shell with flippers, a head and a tail, and suggesting that it was an aluminum turtle.

"What's your opinion, Mr. Claypoole? It's your business to understand junkies. Can't they be more convincing than a normal person, and isn't that just the sort of stunt that one of them might try to pull?" Otis asked in conclusion.

The Captain listened unmoving. The Narcotics Bureau agent lifted the coconut, fingered it, and replaced it on Riker's desk with a tiny thud before he replied.

"Junkies are people, Skipper." Claypoole's soft voice was even more wheedling now as though begging forgiveness for his inability to supply a definite answer. "I don't understand them at all, even though you say it's my business to. If they're convincing when they're high, it's only because they're just as convincing when they're low, and needing a fix. A clunk when he's low is merely a worse clunk when he's popped himself and flying the sky."

He paused to light a cigarette and sigh. "About the boy: He was convincing enough to talk you into breaking the law, deceiving his parents, and deliberately compounding a felony to get him a supply. You knew Ronnie Dayland, Jr., much better than I."

"I'd like to hear from Captain Maclain," Special Agent McKelvey said. "Did Captain Marble tell you this same story last night?"

"Exactly. With every crossed 't' and dotted 'i.'"

"And do you believe young Ronnie deceived you?"

"Certainly he deceived me, as he deceived many others. I had no idea the boy was a user. He seemed extra bright. Maybe a trifle erratic, but certainly—" Maclain told him, purposely misunderstanding.

"I was referring to this water-soaked souvenir that appears to have been salvaged from the *Casa ybel*—although it's beginning to get dry."

"Oh, that thing! I've never seen it!" the Captain snapped out so testily that Spud covered his eyes in an attitude of silent prayer. Jack, Otis and Arch Ransom couldn't suppress a grin.

"But you've felt it, haven't you, Captain?" McKelvey, trained to sense hostility quickly, modified his official tone.

"I've felt it." Maclain nodded. "Otis asked me to braille it last night, after he'd found it in Ronnie's tackle box. That was the first and only time."

McKelvey conferred briefly with Sheriff Riker while the Captain's nervous fingers fiddled with his empty cigarette holder. It was the sheriff's calm unhurried voice that asked the next question and it was directed to Manning.

"Tell me, Jack, did Ronnie show you this coconut gadget and tell you he'd pulled it up, with the Captain, when he asked you to take him out to dive for treasure?"

"No," Jack said promptly. "He didn't show me anything. He told me he and the Captain had pulled something up, and that I could confirm that fact from Maclain. He wouldn't say what or where."

"Didn't you think that was rather peculiar?"

"No, not coming from Ronnie. He said he'd asked the Captain to keep mum, and Maclain had agreed. So I agreed to take him out, if the Captain would come along. That's about all."

Sheriff Riker turned to Otis. "What about you, Skipper? Did Ronnie show you anything?"

"Nothing," Otis said flatly. "I didn't know we were going out next morning until Mr. Manning gave me a call. But there's one thing—"

"What's that?"

"The boy wasn't as close-mouthed as Captain Maclain. He must have gotten high on something. By eleven, the night before, news about his finding treasure was all over town."

Dave Riker grunted and came back to Maclain.

"What did Ronnie tell you he'd pulled up, Captain Maclain? What did he put in your hands to braille? I'm better acquainted than Mr. McKelvey with those eyes in the ends of your fingers. I know how accurately they can see."

"Thanks, Dave, but what's the use? I know what the kid pulled up, but nobody saw it, and now it's gone. I have no proof. I don't like the newspapers making a jackass out of me."

"If you say this coconut isn't what you felt in the *A-bomb*, I'll believe you against everyone in the world with eyes," the sheriff told him earnestly. "Now please describe what you did feel, to me."

"A metal turtle," the Captain said and went on to describe it thoroughly. "And now what?" he asked when he'd finished.

"I'm going to try to locate the monster," the sheriff said, "and the man who stole it and left this in its place."

McKelvey said, "You can count on the help of the FBI."

"And the Treasury, too, eh, Jim?" Ben Lynch, the Customs man, boomed out.

"Yes, Narcotics would like to have a look at that turtle," Jim Claypoole said cautiously. "Also, there's a character that the Skipper mentioned, this Red Barringer, that I'd like our pal, McKelvey, to get his outfit interested in."

"Here's where I'd like to stick my oar in," Jack Manning said. "I've been pretty close to Red Barringer for several years, and Mr. Dayland was before me. He and his wife, Marge, have been our guests, and have entertained Celeste and me. We store fruit in transit in Red's warehouses. His garage maintains our trucks. As a matter of fact—"

"Go on, please, Mr. Manning," Jim Claypoole urged in his withered voice. "The home life, social life, above all, the business life of this Tampa tycoon is of really great interest to Ben and me."

"I don't get it," Jack went on. "I was about to say that the night Mr. Dayland was killed, seven years ago, I was present at a poker party at Red's home on Davis Island. Dave has the names of those who were with me. Now, Otis suddenly blasts loose at Red, tying him up with dope peddlers and some chippie in Chatham Springs. I just don't get it at all."

"Let me tell you some facts of life about this joker," Ben Lynch broke in roughly. "They are facts we know but can't prove, like Captain Maclain is up against with that turtle. Red Barringer's a self-educated goon. That's why you don't get it, like so many others. He's learned to keep his stinking personality clean.

"He learned a hell of a lot, Mr. Manning, when he was called Larry Baraccini, or Red Bussolini, or what have you, and was a member of the Mafia and running alky for Al Capone. He's learned much more since then. How to really be one of 'The Untouchables' by hiring the proper legal and accounting talent, banking hot money in Switzerland under a numbered account, and taking twenty years to establish himself as a grand guy and a solid bulwark of the community in a decent city such as Tampa."

"The Mafia?" Jack asked unbelievingly. "Al Capone? That's fantastic, Mr. Lynch. And what 'hot money' does Barringer have? He owns four or five legitimate businesses. Maybe some folks in Florida think he's a smart trader, but everyone knows where his wealth comes from."

"Sure. Even a couple of stupid Feds, like Jim and me know where 'Red, the Respected's', wealth comes from. It's been pouring in for the past ten years by sea and air from Italy, Turkey, Syria, China, and Lebanon all routed via Mexico, where it's picked up by one of Mr. Barringer's respectable hard-working shrimpers. Put on board by Mexican boats out of Tampico, or maybe Campeche. Believe it or not, there are some clever agents in Mexico who can't be bought. Sometimes when one of Red's boats takes on a cargo, we're tipped off to the exact amount and the name of the shrimper. Two months ago it was twelve kilos. Worth let's say wholesale, a quarter of a million f.o.b. Campeche Bay. Pushed here, as it will be, a thousand new addicted kids and three, maybe four million bucks. U.S. not Mex. That guess is as good as any."

"My God, heroin!" Jack said blankly. "Red Barringer. But if you know the boat—"

"Heroin is right," Ben Lynch continued. "And Barringer is right. Undoubtedly the source that made a junky out of your stepson, and maybe the source that caused his murder. Let's see, two months ago we were tipped that this load of twelve kilos was coming in on Red's newest addition, a ninety-foot trawler of wood and steel, with double the normal Diesels in her, seven hundred horsepower. She's eight-foot draft, twenty-foot beam, ships a crew of five picked pirates and does thirty knots. The average trawler will shake her teeth out pushing fifteen. Red had her built a year ago. Has a strong streak of sentiment in him some place, or humor, maybe. He named this thirty-knot racing trawler the *Eileen*."

"Ben vetoed my suggestion," Jim Claypoole broke in accusingly. "I wanted to slip down to the shipyard the night before she was launched, string her rails with garlands of poppies and change her name on the stern to *Morphine*."

There was a moment of intense quiet broken only by a squeak as the sheriff tilted back in his chair.

"I alerted the customs in every port for miles around," Ben Lynch went on. "We sent another shrimper to Campeche Bay with agents aboard. The Eileen stayed out thirty days, finished her catch, headed straight home and docked in Tampa two weeks ago. My men took her apart, and they know how to search. We even sent a diver down to see if magnetized containers were attached to her bottom. There wasn't an ounce of junk on board. You can take my word the ship and crew were clean. Yes, we know where Barringer's dough comes from. What we'd like to know after ten years trying is how the hell he gets it in."

He paused to clip and light a cigar. Fragrant smoke struck at the Captain's nose and he snuffed it with appreciation. "I think you've met the *Eileen's* captain, Mr. Manning. His name is Carlos O'Brien, but he's Cuban. O'Brien's a common name in Havana."

"I'm afraid I can't place him," Jack said after a short reflection. "Carlos O'Brien? No. I'm sure I don't know him."

Dave Riker said, "He was one of the players in that poker game the night Mr. Dayland was killed, Jack."

"Oh, sure," Jack said. "I remember him now, but I only met him that one time. Seven years ago."

"Have you met any of the others since?" Ben Lynch inquired. 'Any of Red's so charming friends—or was it a friendly game?"

"Friendly? What's back of that crack, Mr. Lynch?"

"Just this, Mr. Manning. Red's got you hypnotized just as he has half of Tampa. He never moved in his life without a purpose. He's a hoodlum who's finally got it made. Were you ever asked to his house before the night of that poker game?"

"No, come to think of it, that was the first. I was general manager then. He called that same day and said Mr. Dayland was coming but had to be out of town. He told me Ted Norton, who was our secretary and comptroller then, would be there.

They needed a sixth player and would I fill in. Fifty-cent limit, dollar roodles game. You don't think—"

"I think it was a set-up," Lynch grumbled. "Who else was there?"

"Lars Hanssen, he's a prominent—"

"Shyster lawyer," Lynch snapped. "Barringer's mouthpiece. That's five: Red and you, Norton, Hanssen, and slippery Captain Carlos. This is good. Who was the sixth?"

"Walter Slazenger. He's very well thought of in Tampa. He's a C.P.A. You can't—"

"The hell I can't!" Lynch roared. "Slazenger has been in hot water with Internal Revenue so deep that his bottom looks like a beet. He can juggle three corporations with one hand, and three sets of books with the other, while falsifying two sets of tax returns with his nose. He's more important than Hanssen in keeping Bar-ringer washed for the public and out of jail."

Arch Ransom spoke up. "You say you think that party was a set-up, Mr. Lynch. What sort of a set-up and what for?"

"An alibi set up for Red Barringer," Lynch said convincingly. "Purpose: to have Ronald Day land murdered by a couple of his out-of-town torpedoes, while he had two of Mr. Dayland's employees present to prove that wherever the murder took place, Red wasn't there."

Arch Ransom said, "Ted Norton, comptroller of Dayland Fruits, got another job, didn't he?"

"He left us for some frozen juice outfit on the East Coast," Jack said. "I haven't heard from him in more than five years."

"I wonder if Mr. Dayland, and Norton, and Ronnie could all have found out what Ben Lynch wants to know so badly?" the sheriff inquired thoughtfully leaning back in his chair.

"You mean how Red's smuggling in that junk right under our nose?" Lynch asked. "What cooked up that wild idea? Did something happen to Norton, too?"

"He got another job five years ago," the sheriff said.

"Doing what?"

"Playing a harp," the sheriff said. "His body was washed ashore on St. Petersburg Beach. He had on a skin-diver's outfit. He'd been shot to death with a fish spear."

"All of which," Arch Ransom declared, "seems to leave my two missing clients, Chuck Lindsay and Paul Fraceti, entirely in the clear."

"Wait until you produce them," Jim Claypoole advised, as though asking Ransom's pardon. "They may be hooked like Ronnie, and Red may have wanted Ronnie killed. Cut off a junky's supply at any age from eight on up and to get it he'll do anything he's asked, anything at all."

TWENTY

Spud and the Captain dropped Jack off at the main house, with a few words for Celeste, shortly after six, and pleading weariness refused his offer to mix a cocktail.

Spud drove the Cadillac on around the big house on the gravel road and stopped it in the guest-house garage. The instant the Captain got out and failed to hear the rattle of Dreist's chain as the dog stood up in greeting, he realized that something unusual was going on. Schnucke wasn't there either, or she'd have been the first to nuzzle at his knee.

"Spud!" he said sharply. "Both dogs are gone!"

But Spud had also gone. He had ducked out of the garage as soon as he'd left the car. Listening, Maclain could hear his footsteps heading purposefully down the flagstone path toward the guesthouse entrance and the living-room bar.

The Captain's forehead wrinkled quizzically as he bent over and felt Dreist's feeding bowl, and did the same with Schnucke's, a short distance away. Both bowls were empty except for a few clinging grains of feed. There was one other person living besides Spud and himself who could feed those dogs and handle them. His name was Cappo Marsh.

Maclain got the soundless whistle out of the glove compartment and standing in the garage doorway at the back of the car gave it a long steady blow.

Instantly he heard the thud of paws as the dogs came bounding toward him over the lawn. He gave them both the pat and greeting they expected, found that Dreist had his muzzle on, and straightened up again.

Elephantine footsteps, supposed to be muffled, were creeping round the side of the garage. They were made by a pair of number twelve shoes supporting a frame of six foot four, and two hundred and forty pounds, of muscle, brains, and coordination.

Bracketed with his partner, Spud Savage, the Captain considered the owner of those feet one of the two most loyal courageous men he knew.

The footsteps stopped and Maclain heard breathing.

"You old gorilla!" the Captain said. "You're supposed to be in Georgia tending to Sarah's sick sister, not down here messing with my dogs. I suppose Sybella got scared that Spud couldn't look out for me and wired you."

"You're sure a smaht man, Cap'n, suh." Cappo gave his infectious laugh. "But a man sure got to take a lot of insulting and step mighty hard on his prejudice against white folks to work twenty years for a Simon Legree like you."

"You haven't lost any of your insolence, I see." Affection welled up in the Captain. Impulsively he wound his arms around Cappo's massive shoulders and gave a great bear hug to his giant Negro chauffeur. "Well, I'm glad you're here," Maclain said fervently as he freed Cappo and stepped back.

"And I'm glad to be here, Cap'n. Mis' Sybella wired young Mr. Dayland was killed, and come right away. I took a plane. Don't seem right to have murder hit twice in a family, Cap'n, does it now? I had a mind you might have something I could do."

"Plenty, Cappo, starting right now, and I don't mean just driving me around. Uncle Eben told me an ugly story last night about trouble between Mr. and Mrs. Dayland before he was killed. Seems there was another woman." The Captain swiftly filled in the details and asked, "You remember Job Taylor, Eben's nephew, that he mentioned?"

"Yessuh, Cap'n. I've known him long as you have, since he was so high."

"Good. Talk to Uncle Eben tonight and get the story from him again. See if he's told me everything I need to know. In the morning take the Cadillac to Tampa. You're having the wheels aligned, or something, understand?"

"Cap'n, I haven't been in Georgia so long that I've turned dumb as a pine tree. What do you want me to get from this Job Taylor boy?"

"Everything he's ever found out about a man named Red Bar-ringer, while Job worked for this woman, Eileen Coles. Everything Job knew about Mr. Dayland's relations with her. And particularly, did Job ever hear of an aluminum turtle with a leather head and tail and four leather flippers, or of half a polished coconut shell painted with the name 'Casa ybel!'"

Cappo stood silent so long that Maclain asked suspiciously, "What are you doing? Writing all that down?"

"Nossuh, Cap'n. You're just sounding off a trifle more wild than usual, that was all. I think it'd be better for us both if you started with the day you got here and told me all. Now, couldn't we just sit down quiet like for about fifteen minutes in the car while you tell me what we're up against?"

When Maclain had finished and answered half-a-dozen questions to Cappo's satisfaction, he heard Cappo's gigantic frame shift uneasily in its familiar position back of the steering wheel.

"Three people killed in seven years," Cappo muttered unhappily. "Mr. Dayland, Norton, that accountant, and now the boy. God only knows how many more—"

"What do you mean?"

"A shrimp boat this Barringer sank, you said. Do shrimpers sink each other fighting over shrimp, Cap'n?"

"I'm interested in finding the murderer of Ronnie Dayland, Cappo."

"And his father. And that man, Norton."

"And his father, my oldest friend. Also, Ted Norton's killer, if he happens to fit in. I knew Norton casually when he worked for Ronald. First Sybella, Spud and Rena start heckling me. Now it's you. What's the matter? Have I grown too old and feeble to get out of my wheel chair and uncover one lousy murderer?"

"Nossuh, Cap'n. Ain't no murderer living you can't get, but you're trying, with no one but Mr. Spud and me to help you, to uncover something the whole United States been working on for ten years now—an international narcotics ring."

"Then I've got Sheriff Riker along with the whole United States, including Spud and you," the Captain said. "What do you want me to do, chicken out?"

"You sure can be irritating, even for a white man, when you set out to be, Cap'n. You never chickened out on anything. Trouble is you're fixing right now to stick your chicken neck in."

"I'm not going near Red Barringer, Cappo. He's been proved respectable after being third-degreed by every agent and copper in the country, including Rin Tin Tin."

"Nossuh, Cap'n. We all know you ain't as foolish as all that. You're a smart man and careful. You're going to play it cool and cautious like. I'm telling you, Cap'n, anyone's going to look like a porcupine, from the fish spears sticking out of him, who tries to sweet-talk the truth out of Mr. Red Barringer's girl."

The Captain clapped him reassuringly on the shoulder. "There's one consolation anyhow, Cappo. Those fish spears have retractable barbs. If you know how to work them they're as easy to pull out as they are to shoot in."

The four tremendous dining-rooms of the Columbia Gardens, Tampa's world-famous Spanish restaurant in Ybor City, were jammed to capacity at quarter to seven when Cappo discharged Maclain and Sybella, with Spud and Rena Savage at the front entrance and drove the Cadillac around to the parking lot at the rear.

In spite of the Captain's telephoned reservations for a table at seven o'clock, he was told, as he suspected he might be, that there would be a short wait in the bar. There was often a short wait in the bar at Columbia Gardens, but the dinner was always worth waiting for.

A night of ten hours sound sleep had left Maclain in fine fettle. Up at eight, he had demolished a breakfast of ham, three eggs, toast, marmalade and coffee, then spent the entire morning on the guest house telephone.

His first call had been long distance to Judge Scott Marston, in Jacksonville, the lawyer friend who had driven Ronald Dayland to the airport after they had eaten dinner together on the night Day-land was killed.

The Captain had plunged right in, introducing himself as Ronald Dayland's lifetime friend, who was now investigating the murder, two days before, of Dayland's son.

"I feel that I know you through Ronald, Captain Maclain," Judge Marston said warmly. "Curious. I was just now reading the Times-Union account of Ronnie's murder when your call came in. Have those two boys been apprehended?"

"Not yet, Judge. Neither have they been proven guilty, although the papers seem to be trying them. I called to ask you a couple of questions about Ronald. He's been dead a long time now, so I don't think you'll be violating any client relationship."

"About Ronald Dayland, Senior? I don't—"

"Your answers may help to furnish a motive for Ronald's murder, Judge Marston, and may furnish some connection between that and the murder of the boy. Did Ronald consult you about divorcing Celeste on that last day he was there?"

"Since you already seem to have heard it, I'll confirm it, Captain. That's true."

"Thank you. Now my second question is more important: why did Ronald go all the way to Jacksonville to consult you?"

"I'm a lawyer and an old friend, Captain Maclain. He wanted his divorce handled discreetly. Mandalay is a small town. Perhaps he felt—"

"You're the top corporation and trust attorney in Florida, Judge Marston," Maclain said flatteringly. "You never handled a divorce suit in your entire career. Neither has any member of your firm."

"So he wanted the name of a good lawyer in Jacksonville who would handle his divorce. I gave him one, and Ronald went to see him. If you want the lawyer's name, I'll give it—"

"Ronald could have gotten that name from you by phone, Judge, and there are just as discreet divorce lawyers in Tampa. Nearer home. What was Ronald's idea of a settlement with Celeste, Judge? What was he going to do with Dayland Fruits? It must have been some big move for him to spend most of a day, and the evening, in consultation with you."

"He was going to liquidate it," Judge Marston said shortly.

"Liquidate a hundred-year-old company?" Maclain clutched the telephone tighter pressing it closer to his ear. "What in the name of heaven for?"

"For what he could get. A million. Maybe more, given time. The company's actually worth three or four. He had an offer of a hundred thousand on the Leesburg freezing plant from X-tra Seal. He was going to start with that, give half to me for Celeste and the boy, and even before the divorce went through, he was leaving for Tahiti, or some such place with some adventuress of a girl. Mid-age madness, Captain! I was to be left holding the bag, making appraisals, and audits, selling everything but the house, which went to Celeste, peddling each one of those wonderful groves, trucks, packing-houses, and the other four freezing and canning plants one at a time."

"Did you agree to that arrangement, Judge?"

"Most regretfully. But it was the only way I could be assured that half of everything would inure to the benefit of

Celeste and the boy. I trust that what I've told you will be of help in bringing someone to justice, Captain, and that you won't find it necessary to make it public. Also when is Ronnie's funeral? I'd like to wire flowers."

"It may very well be of help, Judge, but not if it's made any more public than it has been made so far. Thanks for your cooperation and your trust in me. I'll keep you informed. Ronnie's funeral is at two this afternoon. Hart's Funeral Parlor. Good-bye!"

Straight in his chair, the Captain sat with his hand on the phone and repeated to Spud what Judge Marston had said on the other end. "That's the first concrete thing we've had to work on in all this tangle, Spud. Don't you think so?"

"It certainly is, Dune," Spud agreed with enthusiasm. "Five bucks that we owe to Jack for a long distance phone. Plus tax. Or it may run more."

"I think you're deliberately being obtuse." Maclain released his grip on the phone and relaxed in his chair. "Nevertheless, I'm going to toss this out on the floor, as the gray-flannel suit boys have it, then I'm going to stomp on it and let you watch it suffer. Can't you see we've just been handed the motive, not only for Dayland's, but for Ted Norton's murder five years ago?"

"I've played straight-man so long that it wouldn't be clear to you if I said anything but 'No!' So toss out and stomp. You've caught my interest five bucks worth anyhow."

"As I see it, Norton's the key." The Captain rubbed his high forehead calculatingly. "Let's start with the premise that Norton, the trusted comptroller had been dipping his hot little hands into the cash box of Dayland Fruits, Inc. Ronald was a lovable cuss, but he had a self-wheeling company, and he was a pretty sloppy business man."

"I'll buy that, Dune. An embezzler, hunh? Why that could have been going on—"

"Four or five years. Maybe more, and God only knows how deep he could have been in. Let's assume it was plenty. So, something comes up. Jack or Ronald calls an unexpected audit, or some such thing, and good old Ted is caught with his breeches down. He has to raise plenty of cash in a hurry. Where does he go to get it, Spud? To a bank?"

"Hell, no! You're making a lot of sense, Dune. Loan

sharking has always been a top drawer activity of a hood like Barringer—"

"So, we're cooking on gas. Straight to Red Barringer is where Ted Norton would go. But Red doesn't want usurious interest. That's too simple and unprofitable. Red is a man who looks ahead. He has vision. His price for covering Norton's defalcations is getting a foot in the door."

"I bounced out of the side-car just then," Spud said. "What door?"

"The Dayland Fruit Company's door. Good Lord, Spud! They have boundless acres of groves all over the state with packing houses, and field storage houses, some of them abandoned and forgotten years ago. They have trucks carrying loads of loose oranges to freezing plants, and crated oranges being shipped to supermarkets all over the country. They're above suspicion. Let Barringer plant a few key men among Dayland's five hundred employees—"

"Holy jumping mackerel, Dune!" Spud clapped a hand to his forehead. "That's so simple that it's horrible! Why Barringer would have a built-in storage and distribution organization that could spread a ton of heroin throughout the United States every year. Small amounts shipped in marked crates. Abandoned old houses concealed in tangled grown-up groves—"

"And you've overlooked the most important item," Maclain said quietly. "The use of a fifty-foot private yacht, also above suspicion, with an ex-con skipper, who can slip out any time for a trial run, fish up half a dozen turtle buoys, each attached to a couple of kilos of heroin, and bring the load in, then drive it to one of the warehouses in his car."

"Otis—?"

"He's done a lot of fast talking, Spud. Just as there was a lot of fast talking done about Barringer and Norton sucking Jack into that poker game so that Red could set his torpedoes on Ronald that night. Did you spot the weakness in that alibi?"

"No. Not offhand, unless four of the players lied."

"If they lied," Maclain said, "we'd have to tie Jack Manning in. If all six players were there all night, then Otis's story of being on the *Kalua* at Sanibel isn't any alibi for him at all. He could have driven up from Ft. Myers in a hired car, or had the *Kalua* anywhere."

Maclain paused to light a cigarette. "Or if Otis was present when Ronald was killed on the parkway, the hatchet-man with him could have driven him up from Punta Rassa, and back from that Ocala jaunt where the Buick was abandoned. Riker knows Otis's prints were found in Ronald's Buick, but so were Jack's, and the prints of half a dozen others who had driven Ronald's car."

Maclain knocked off ashes, tapping his holder on the side of the tray. "This is the point, Spud. The reason why Otis Marble, for the moment at least, looks like our number one passenger for a ride in the electric chair: Riker maintains, although I'm going to have to remind him of it, and I agree, that Ronald wouldn't have stopped to help someone he didn't know on that lonely parkway. Certainly he wouldn't have voluntarily gotten out of his car."

"And the motives you mentioned after talking to Marston?" Spud asked after a little. "Would Otis kill a man who had been so decent to him for stealing Barringer's girl?"

"If he was forced to. The girl was only a minor factor." Maclain ejected his cigarette, blew out his holder and tucked it away. "Ronald was about to liquidate. Audits. Examinations of assets, and income and disbursements. Not only show up Norton's embezzlements, but sell off Barringer's carefully erected dope distribution center, and probably the *Kalua*, their method of getting it in. Pouf! Out the window with a million bucks a year! They had to hit Ronald and hit him fast. They did."

"And Ted Norton?"

"He hung around long enough to file reports on the inheritance tax and leave everything in the clear. Maybe Red supplied the money to stop any holes. It was only money, and Jack, if he wasn't to smell a rat, must be left with a nice clean company. Then Norton quit to seek a new atmosphere, and along with leaving, he might have conceived some blackmail scheme. That didn't sit well with 'Honest Red' and Norton got paid off with a fish spear."

"Well, we know damn well that Otis didn't kill Ronnie," Spud remarked thoughtfully. "Why would Barringer hit the boy?"

"Same answer," the Captain said. "Plus the aluminum turtle. Ronnie must have shown it to Otis. Otis must have used the phone, and Barringer likewise. Orders went out to get the kid before he led Customs men to that cache in the Gulf and blew up that million dollars income a year."

"And what about you?"

"Haven't you heard?" the Captain said. "I'm blind. I never saw a turtle and don't know where it came from. That's why my health is still good."

"Nuts to your health," Spud said. "You're doing your best to ruin it right now, and mine, too. What's your next step in breaking the Barringer bank?"

"The weakest point in his set-up," the Captain said. "I'm going to get the low-down out of that girl, Eileen Coles."

Persuading her to talk with him in person proved surprisingly easy, once the Captain had reached her on the telephone. Perhaps she'd agreed too readily, he thought afterward, in view of what happened. She could well have been under pressure to get in touch with this inquisitive blind investigator, herself, play along with him, and find out just how much he knew.

His belief that she intended to marry Ronald, and must therefore hate Red who had had him killed, might well have been the weakest point in Maclain's own set-up, too. Or was it? Wasn't his weakest point his concentration on a fixed idea to the absolute exclusion of everything else, even the red lights of warning flashed so brightly by the two men whose judgment he trusted the most, Spud and Cappo?

Yet, he had nothing but a sensation of callow elation when he heard her husky warm voice answer the phone: "Eileen Coles here. Hello."

"This is Captain Duncan Maclain, Miss Coles. We've never met, so I'll introduce myself by telling you that Ronald Dayland was my oldest and closest friend."

"Captain Maclain?" she asked, accenting the title with less warmth in her tone. "If you're the police, why not say so?"

"Neither police, army, or navy," Maclain told her with a placating laugh. "The rank has hung on, in spite of me, probably because I was blinded during the war and people don't like to say 'Hey you!' I thought that Ronald might have mentioned me to you."

"I knew a Ronald Dayland quite casually," she admitted at

last. "That was many years ago. I scarcely knew him well enough—"

"I knew him well enough to have him tell me he was divorcing his wife, Celeste, and leaving her and his twelve-year-old son to marry you, Miss Coles," Maclain stated with an edge to his words. "Your romance ended with his murder, Miss Coles. And if you've read the papers, you'll know that his son was murdered day before yesterday. It's essential that I talk to you."

"Why essential? I don't know anything that I can't tell you over the phone."

"I might refresh your memory if we met face to face. I'm totally blind, so there's nothing you can't hide from me if you care to. I can take a taxi out to your house from Tampa any time you say. I'll come alone and leave that way."

She waited so long the Captain asked: "Are you there, Miss Coles?"

"Tell the cab you want the Green Lake House, to the left on U.S. 41 in Chatham Springs. Be there at ten tonight."

"Ten tonight. Thanks."

There was another pause, then she said, "I hope you know what you're doing, mister. I don't," and disconnected the phone.

"Ten tonight," the Captain said. "She has a nice voice."

"So did Lorelei!" Spud said. "And how many boobs did she lure on the rocks with her siren song? Glad to have you aboard, Captain! Anyone for tennis?" He went out slamming the door behind him and left the Captain alone.

The Captain, his high spirits dampened, called Riker and gave him a rundown on the information from Judge Marston. The sheriff was interested, but insisted that he had checked out Otis's alibi and found it solid. That had brought him right back again to Bar-ringer's hired torpedoes, or more credible to him, though more distasteful, some members of a teen-age gang that Dayland had known.

He did have one new piece of information: the FBI had determined from the hole in the screen of Ronnie's room that the shot had been fired from a .45 caliber pistol shot at fairly close range. Probably from behind the bushes along the Dayland's seawall. There was another place Otis could be fitted in again. There was still no trace of the boys or the Donna, although an intensive search for both boys and boat was on.

Maclain hung up without mentioning his idea that the Dayland company had been taken over. It wasn't the time, without any proof to clutter up the Treasury Department and the FBI with a lot of unproved theories that were entirely his own.

Next he talked at some length to Arch Ransom and ended convinced that neither the Fracetis nor Marian Lindsay had heard a word. Decidedly those boys were hiding out in terror and not in touch with or being protected by parents at home.

His elation returned when the ordeal of the funeral was over, and they were dropped back at the guest house by one of Hart's funeral limousines. Jack and Celeste had driven to the services alone. Celeste had been put to bed with a nurse on Dr. Arnheit's orders immediately she was home.

Cappo was back from Tampa and he had certainly collected some astonishing facts from Uncle Eben's nephew, Job Taylor, and one highly important item from Uncle Eben. The Captain was quick to realize he could never have obtained the information that his chauffeur had, if he'd tried it on his own.

First, according to Uncle Eben, a man who said he was a deputy sheriff had made a thorough search of Ronnie's apartment about eleven o'clock on the morning Ronnie was killed. That was while the women were at the country club. He had been tough with Uncle Eben, and insisted on searching the place alone.

"So that ornament was substituted for Dune's turtle," Spud said. "Thank God the rep of those fingers is saved."

The rest was so astonishing that it kept plaguing all of them through their cocktails in the Columbia Gardens bar, and lingered with them all through the wonderful dinner of pompano, stuffed and baked in tin-foil Spanish style.

Job Taylor had instantly recognized Cappo's description of the coconut shell with *Casa ybel* painted on it. It had sat for years in the bottom of an aquarium of tropical fish in the Florida room of Eileen Coles' home. Job had cleaned it many times when cleaning the aquarium while he worked as houseman there.

Had Job ever heard of an aluminum turtle, with leather flippers, head and tail?

Better than that. He had heard of six! They were ornaments set in the lily pads around the edge of the goldfish pool in the center of the terrace at Green Lake House. They were painted and when the pool was lit at night, they'd glow.

Strange about those turtles. He'd been forbidden to clean or touch them, and then sometimes for several days they wouldn't be there. Yes, he'd mentioned them once to Miss Eileen right after Mr. Day-land was killed. Told her they were missing.

Result: Job had been told he was too damn nosey, and kicked out to own a lunchroom. Since that time Miss Eileen had had no regular servants there.

Job's information was still very much occupying the Captain's mind when he stood up abruptly to leave the others at the table at quarter past nine. The more thought he gave to those six turtles and that aquarium ornament, the more perplexing he found them. The more distracting, too. Eagerness to get to Chatham Springs and worm an answer from Eileen Coles was blunting his normal sense of caution, lulling him with the fanning wings of a false security.

"You three will go to the Hillsborough Theatre downtown on Florida Avenue as arranged," Maclain said. "Leave your name at the box office, Spud. I'll take a cab back and join you there. Is that understood?"

"Let me see," Spud said. "We've been over it ten times now, but I believe the campaign is finally clear."

"Do you have your gun?" Sybella asked.

"Certainly not," Maclain said impatiently. "I'm not going there to shoot anyone and no one is going to shoot at me. Do you think they want attention drawn to that place by a murder there?"

"No, I suppose not. I'm nervous, that's all. Just be careful, darling." She touched the back of his hand.

"Isn't this fun!" Spud exclaimed brightly. "Turtles that glow. Tropical fish. A mysterious woman. A sightless, fearless detective. Dope, and a ruthless murderer who kills with a fish spear. Yeeks! I feel just like a schoolboy." But there was nothing bright about his strange amber eyes as he watched his partner stride accurately through the maze of tables and go out the door of the bar. They were hooded with apprehension.

A cab pulled up from the waiting rank and Maclain got in.

"How much to Chatham Springs? I want a place called Green Lake House there. Do you know it?"

"Five bucks," the driver said. "And you can't very well miss Green Lake House. The grounds are bigger than Chatham Springs."

"Can you make it by ten?"

"Running backwards."

"Well, let's try it the usual way. I get carsick riding backwards." The Captain settled back in his seat. He couldn't see the lights that came on in another car that was watching half a block away, and his driver didn't. When some time later the cab swung north on Route 41, the other car was on their tail.

TWENTY-ONE

There were landmarks along every highway available to Maclain through the open windows of a car. Hills, and valleys, and rivers had distinctive odors once you learned to sort them out. That would be a roadhouse from the faint mingled smells of bar and cooking. There another filling-station, unmistakable with that lingering smell of oil and gasoline. Now the smell of wool from a hundred sheep, or the clean pungent smell and the lowing of cows as you passed a dairy farm. A million different noises and smells, challenges all with the windows down!

And tonight, riding in the taxi up to Chatham Springs, he remained unconscious of them all. Not that he would have had a chance of detecting the trailing car, although he had done just that half a dozen times in his long career. Done it in heavy traffic, too, by the distinctive sound of a motor, the squeal of brakes or tires, or as on one occasion in winter the slap of a loose tire chain.

But the driver who had picked up his trail at the restaurant had dropped far behind. There was no need to keep the taxi in sight for the pursuer knew where Maclain was going. What he didn't know, or the Captain, either, was that Spud and the women had left Columbia Gardens immediately after Maclain's departure. Instead of going in town to the Hillsborough Theatre, as Maclain had planned, Sybella and Rena had dropped off at a nearby movie in Ybor City. Less than twenty minutes behind the tailing car, and headed for the same destination, was the Cadillac bearing Spud and Cappo.

Oddly enough it was no premonition of real danger to the Captain that had caused Spud to change their plans and follow him. Job Taylor had given a very accurate layout of Green Lake House and the surrounding grounds to Cappo.

The big house was old, white stucco and red tile, dating back to the twenties, but had been kept in good repair. It was shielded from passing traffic on U.S. 41 by an eight-foot-high wall. The entrance, flanked by two pillars, was through an ornamental iron gate, never closed, that gave access to a circular driveway. The wall was really only a front, according to Job. It ended at a very passable sand road at the north end of the square estate of some twenty acres.

Delivery wagons used that road, which also led to a double garage in the rear. Back of the garage was a small round lake and between the garage and the terrace, which opened off a Florida room at the back of the house, was a kidney-shaped swimming pool. In the center of the flagstoned terrace was a small fountain that spouted water into a circular goldfish basin.

It was the six aluminum turtles casually placed around as ornaments in that basin that Spud had determined to see. Then he'd have concrete evidence to back up his partner. The word of a man with two perfectly good eyes to take to the FBI and the Treasury men.

He hadn't forgotten that Job had said that at times the turtles were missing, but Spud didn't think they'd be missing tonight. If Maclain's theory about Otis and the *Kalua* being the key to the heroin smuggling was valid, Ronnie had pulled up one of six other turtles attached to canisters of heroin, each holding two kilos, that were waiting for recovery on the bottom of the Gulf right now. One of them with a marker missing.

The normal routine, Spud believed, was for one of Barringer's henchmen, maybe Carlos O'Brien, or another shrimp-boat captain, to collect the turtles from the fountain and sail for Mexican waters with the buoys on board, *but only after one shipment was safely pulled up and stored in the Dayland groves, and arrangements had been concluded in Mexico for another 12 kilos to be smuggled in.*

Sure. That made sense. Two sets of turtles instead of one. Six of them readily available at Eileen Coles to be picked up and taken to Mexico while the other six were cached in the Dayland groves. Or maybe still sunk in a prearranged spot on the bottom of the Gulf, waiting to be run in on the *Kalua* when the coast was clear. When one set moved out from the fountain, the second would replace it as soon as possible, brought in from Mandalay. Who the devil would become suspicious of ornamental turtles decorating a fountain?

Now Ronnie's freak discovery, and his subsequent murder had really put the heat on! Barringer wouldn't be having turtles carted from Mandalay to Tampa right now, nor putting them aboard his shrimpers. They'd be right in that fountain at Green Lake House. While Eileen was busy with Maclain, Spud had determined to see them.

Cappo knew the plan. All they had to do was take the sand road at the end of the wall, run down it a tenth of a mile and stop there. A path to the left led through orange, guava, and mango trees straight to the swimming pool. It was just a few steps from the edge of the trees to the terrace.

Huddled in the corner of his seat the Captain rode morosely oblivious to sounds of the trip, Spud's change of plans, or the trailing car. His mind was entirely occupied with conjectures about Ronald Dayland, Celeste, and Eileen Coles.

Celeste, he and Sybella would say, was beautiful, hospitable, gracious, and generous with her friends. Had she been as generous with the love she bestowed on her husband and her boy? Somehow she had lost them both. Was she fundamentally cold? Frigid, maybe? Was the warmth she displayed to her friends just a pose, and actually insincere? Or had her love for Ronald died years before and been replaced with a passion for the younger Jack Manning? Only two people outside of Celeste, herself, were qualified to answer those personal questions and both of them had been murdered, the man and the boy.

Or was Ronald Dayland entirely to blame? No man Maclain had ever known had been endowed with more personality and charm. But Ronald had never been without ample money, nor known a moment's hardship. Had Celeste discovered that her husband lacked integrity and faithfulness? Had she waked one morning to find that she was just another incident in the love life of a philandering Don Juan?

And what of this woman, Eileen Coles, the one Maclain was on his way to talk to? Mighty pretty, Uncle Eben had called her, and dangerous as she was pretty. A very bad woman. Worse than any Jezebel. The Captain hadn't swallowed that entirely. There could be no lower depths of depravity to Uncle Eben than a woman who disrupted a Dayland home.

Job Taylor had agreed on her beauty, but not on her depravity. According to Job, she was a small, slender, exquisitely formed brunette, with jet black hair worn in a boyish cut. She seldom smiled. Her black eyes were deep, sympathetic, and sorrowful to a point of being haunted. She seldom, if ever, left the house, occupying most of her time with two parakeets, a white Persian cat she called Emperor, and her aquarium of tropical fish, when she wasn't at the big white grand piano playing music that Job didn't dig.

Men? The only men he had ever seen admitted to the house, outside of workmen, in the time he'd worked there were Mr. Barringer, who sometimes came with another man, and Mr. Dayland, who always came alone. Job didn't think Miss Eileen had any women friends at all. Job summed her up to Cappo as the kindliest, most tolerant, the loneliest, and most unhappy woman alive. "The good Lawd done give her all the looks 'n' money in creation, Cappo, 'n' she ain't got nuthin' 'ceptin' them birds, cat, 'n' li'l ole fish. Thet Barringer jes' white trash in good clothes. He'd leave her quick as wink an eye. Time come he cain't use her no mo'h."

And that was the picture Maclain carried with him when he paid off the cab and she opened the door to let him in. But he had shrewdly guessed before he felt the cold clasp of her hand, and heard the soft huskiness of her voice, that it was the medical definition of the word "tolerant," and not the one Job had used, that kept Eileen Coles a hermit and Red Barringer's helpless vassal.

She had learned her tolerance the hard way, but it wasn't tolerance for the man who held her captive, it was tolerance, increasing every horrible day, for the drug she must have to stay alive, the drug that Red supplied so freely, that terrible unrelenting master, morphine.

"Are you truly blind?" she asked immediately as though it was a matter of great importance. "I don't mean to be rude but— Well, I expected a dog or a cane."

"The cab picked me up at Columbia Gardens where I had dinner and let me out right at your door." The Captain smiled. "Now, if you'll let me take your arm, you can plant me in a chair. Have you ever eaten at Columbia Gardens?"

"Once," she said as he placed his hand in the crook of her arm. Under the long sleeve of her dress she felt very frail. "It was a long time ago, way back in a dream world. This is the sitting room. I have some very lovely things. I wish you could see them. Two steps down here. This is the Florida room that opens onto the terrace. Here! You can sit beside me on this divan. Would you care for a highball? I have scotch, or if you'd rather have it, bourbon."

"I'll fall for the scotch. With soda, please." He felt it would make her happier. Help put her at ease. He could sense the surrounding luxury. Unlimited funds in the texture of her sleeve, the thickness of the carpeting, and the eiderdown cushions of the club divan he was sitting on. There was money even in the highball glass she brought him, initialed crystal with a heavy bottom.

Yes, Eileen Coles possessed a warmth that was lacking in Celeste. But with a sudden flash of insight the Captain knew that her warmth alone had not been enough to separate Ronald Dayland from his wife and son. Ronald's greatest asset was his kindness of heart. He couldn't bear to see suffering and would go to almost any lengths to alleviate a fellow creature's pain.

Everything about this sensitive, delicate woman, Eileen Coles, from the mortuary luxury that surrounded her, to the knowledge that she was a helpless prisoner in the toils of her own weakness, and could never escape without loving help, had been designed to arouse the sympathy of a man such as Ronald Dayland. He might have loved her more than Celeste. Maclain didn't know. He did know that Ronald had wrecked his own marriage, and lost his life in an effort to smash through the solid gold bars and free Eileen.

"Strange, your calling me this morning—" A bundle of silky fur jumped on the divan with startling quietness and settled itself between Eileen and Maclain. "That's Emperor, my cat. I hope he didn't startle you. We're much alike, Emperor and I. We both love comfort more than freedom. We're both amoral, and caged, like those two parakeets you hear twittering. That's the price we pay."

"Why was it strange I called you today?"

She sipped her drink slowly, stroking the purring creature beside her. "I'd read that Ronald, Junior, was to be buried this afternoon. I'd reached a decision. I'd have refused to let you come here, if you'd called me yesterday—"

"Then why today?"

"I'd decided to do what Ronald wanted me to do. Leave Green Lake House and run away. You see, I'd looked at my hands this morning—"

"Your hands?"

"They were red with blood. Ronald's blood. The blood of his son, and others. I scrubbed them for two hours and it wouldn't wash off. Then you phoned, and I knew that Ronald had sent you out of that dream world to give me a second chance to escape. So I told you to come here and talk to me."

"I'll do everything I can, Miss Coles," the Captain said kindly. "But you'll have to tell me more about this second chance. How can—?"

"You've done everything you can already, in spite of yourself. You've made my decision a final one, that even a weakling like me can never go back on. Your visit tonight was all that I needed. I'm afraid you don't understand me, do you?"

"I'm afraid I don't." The Captain was chilled by the hopelessness in her words.

"Ronnie Dayland was an 'H' user," she explained with deadly calmness. "I had a part in making him one. I'm a small distributor for this district. A jobber for southern Florida, you might say. Not a very important cog in a big machine. Why do I do this? Why have I kept quiet about the murder of the one man who was ever decent to me? I'll tell you why, Captain Maclain. I'm a hopeless, incurable morphine addict. My only road to freedom is the road that was opened to Ronnie: violent death."

"Violent death? You mean—?"

"I'll get what I asked for by telling you to come here. You see, I'm not even remorseful. I'm just an addict who has grown tired and decided to jump off at the end of the trail. Now ask what you want."

"I'm trying to save a couple of teen-agers who are going to be charged with killing Ronnie. They were much too young to have murdered Ronald, but one of them could have shot Ronnie under water with that fish spear. Then there's a Greek diver named Pa-palekas—"

"Good old Nick, the Greek. He taught me skin-diving. The only sport I enjoy." She gave a throaty laugh. "He could have shot Ronnie, too, I suppose. He's an occasional customer of mine. Nobody knows who Nick would double-cross, but he's been useful as an undercover Federal Narcotics man. He's a killer, too, if he's paid enough." She sat up straight. "There's a book you simply must read, Captain. Its title is 'Tiger Man'—"

Spud's voice yelled from the doors to the terrace. "Duck, Dune. There's a spear sticking out from the curtains behind you!"

The events of the next few seconds were never clear.

The Captain ducked forward automatically, dimly aware of a click and a pouf and a shaft whistling close to his ear. Then the side of his face, and the arm of his coat, next to Eileen were showered with blood as the barbed spear, shot from a foot away, went into the back of her neck, severing a carotid artery and her spinal cord at the same time, and killing her instantly.

A second later, as he touched the barb sticking from the front of Eileen's throat, two shots crashed out from behind him, unmistakably from a .45. He jumped to his feet, smashing into a chair and falling prone in his blind rush forward to the spot where he had heard Spud fall.

"Spud! Spud!" Maclain pushed himself to his hands and knees and began to crawl. A gun butt thwacked down from above him, striking at the base of his skull and that was all.

A moment later when Cappo charged in, his mammoth Mauser clutched in his fist, the only sound in the Florida room was the senseless chattering of the parakeets in their cage beside the grand piano.

Cappo took one quick glance at the body on the couch, Spud's blood-soaked white shirt, and the Captain's gore-spattered face and gray suit and fought off a frightful wave of nausea.

He staggered into the living room, found a phone, and dialed "O."

"Get an ambulance out to Green Lake House at Chatham Springs, Miss! And call the police. Who am I? God in heaven, lady! One woman's been murdered, and two men shot. Ask me just a couple more questions and you can send out hearses for them all!"

He dashed back to the Florida room, soaked a couple of napkins in melted ice-water in the silver ice bucket, and tenderly bathed Spud's and the Captain's foreheads. Spud had been hit bad. Chest and belly. He couldn't find anything on the Captain but a lump and cut in back of his head.

Cappo kept softly intoning their names with the cadence of

a prayer.

His only answer came from under the piano. Mingling with the chatter of the parakeets, a blood-spattered Persian, instinctively aware that his life had been disrupted, suddenly started to caterwaul.

TWENTY-TWO

He woke with Sybella holding his hand. He had a headache, but his mind was abnormally clear. He seemed to be sitting in the dark outside, and peering into a lighted room where he was watching himself fit his brain together. He knew precisely where each piece belonged and could even see the picture on the assembled jigsaw puzzle. It was slightly frightening, like playing God, but the details were bright, unclouded, and very clean.

He had some unimportant questions to ask before he could summon courage enough to risk the one that was filling his heart with fear.

"Where am I?" He tightened his grip on Sybella's hand.

"Memorial Hospital. Tampa."

"What time is it?"

"Ten past eight in the morning."

"I remember everything quite clearly now. Somebody sapped me."

"Yes. An ambulance brought you and Spud in here." She told him about the change of plans, and the Ybor City picture show. Then about the dead girl and how Cappo had called the police. "She was shot from a foyer behind you with her own speargun and spear." The news about Spud must be very black. Sybella appeared to be holding it back deliberately.

"Is Spud dead?" He'd reached the point where he had to hear.

"No," she said, "but he's on the critical list. Two bullet wounds from a forty-five. Chest and abdomen. He just got out of the operating room two hours ago. He may be unconscious for days. The surgeon, Dr. Maxwell, says if Spud can withstand the extended shock—"

"Have you and Rena been here all night without any rest?"

"We dozed some in the waiting room."

"Phone and get us a suite of rooms at the Tampa Terrace," he told her decisively. "You both need rest, and you're doing no good waiting around here. They'll phone if there's any change."

"But what about you, Duncan?" Sybella asked

apprehensively. "The doctor said you were to stay in bed and sleep all you can."

"I've already been asleep since Monday," he told her, closing his grip still tighter on her hand. "If I'd been awake I'd have known that the place where Ronnie pulled up that turtle was off Marker Five. Seven miles north of where he was murdered. Ronnie and Eileen Coles would still be alive, and Spud wouldn't be fighting to save his own life." He swung his long legs off the edge of the bed. "Get me my clothes, please, darling."

"Duncan, you can't—!"

"I *can't?*" His voice was heavy with sadness. "You're the one who's directed my life by always saying there wasn't anything beneath the sun I couldn't do. Have I made such a mess of things since Monday that you've lost belief in me, too?"

"It isn't that, Duncan. You know it."

"Then what is it?"

"Nothing." She went to the locker, brought his clothes, and started to help him dress. "Your coat's all bloodstained."

"I want Cappo to drive me to Mandalay after we drop you and Rena at the hotel. I'll leave the coat at a cleaners and change out there. Phone Celeste about Spud, and tell her what things you and Rena need and I'm sure she'll bring them in. It will give her something to get her mind off Ronnie."

"Duncan." She made one last feeble protest. "Your head's all bandaged."

"I'll get Dr. Arnheit to put on a smaller dressing."

"Duncan, what are you going to do?"

"Don't you know, Sybella? I'm going to get positive proof on Red Barringer's hired bloodthirsty killer, and either send him to the chair or kill him myself, Greek or American, man or teen-age boy. With him, I'm going to wipe out Mr. Barringer, and his heroin empire, too. It's as simple as that."

She started to speak, looked at his face, and was stopped by a sudden chill. His features were contorted into a stony mask.

She realized then that those bullets in Spud had also left metal in the Captain's soul, and that Eileen Coles' bloodstains on his coat would always be partly his own. For the moment she'd lost the man she loved, and she couldn't regain him until justice was done, and murders paid for. Right now her husband was scarcely human. Duncan Maclain, with his partner close to dying, had become a human juggernaut, an inflexible, inexorable, blind machine.

Maclain and Cappo spent an hour closeted with Sheriff Riker pouring out everything they knew, while Riker let a tape recorder take it down to pass on to the FBI.

When the Captain told him about Marker Five, a couple of miles south of Anclote Key, and his belief that Ronnie had pulled up the turtle there, Riker emitted a soft whistle.

"That would mean there's twelve kilos of uncut heroin sunk in that channel." He got a copy of Chart 858 and bent over it with Cappo. "That would fit with Red's shrimper, the *Eileen*," he said after a little study.

"Fit how, Dave?"

"The *Eileen* draws eight feet. There's nine foot of water in that channel at dead low tide. Also, at night, she'd have a perfect range to guide her from the Gulf by holding Flasher One at the west entrance to the channel in line with the lighthouse on Anclote Key. Running with no lights, she could slip in there, lay her six $30,000 eggs and be out again and on her way to Tampa without being seen."

"You mean that junk's worth fifteen thousand dollars a kilo, Mr. Riker?" Cappo asked.

"That's the pitch, Cappo. A hundred and eighty thousand dollars a trip, wholesale. But if Red's been pushing retail heroin, it's been cut twenty times. Let's see, that's three million six hundred thousand dollars for each batch smuggled in. Buy a lot of dead men, won't it?"

"It's the live ones its bought that I'm interested in," the Captain told him. "You'll pass this on to Claypoole and Lynch, won't you?"

"Right away."

"What'll they do, Dave?"

"Nothing. They'll put a twenty-four hour stake-out on that channel and wait. They don't want the stuff, Captain, they want the boat and its crew that will pull it up."

"Will that get Barringer?"

"Certainly, if they can prove the boat and crew—"

"If—if—if!" Maclain sputtered disdainfully. "They haven't been able to charge Barringer with illegal parking in ten years, any more than you've been able to burn him for Dayland's murder in seven."

"That's pretty nasty fighting from an old friend, Captain," the sheriff said in a voice that was trying hard to cover his injury. "Have you ever resorted to pulling hair? Spud's shooting can't be blamed on me."

"I'm sorry as hell, Dave. That wasn't meant as a crack about Ronald, and certainly I wasn't accusing you of inefficiency. If it sounded that way, please forgive me!"

"Maybe I had that jolt coming to me," Riker said, quickly mollified. "I'd welcome a few suggestions that could blow the whistle on Barringer. Particularly any bright ideas that might send him to the chair. Are you nursing any?"

"Four."

"Four? Want to tell me? My seven-year failure might be offset since I'm getting help from Uncle Sam."

"That counter-punch was well delivered, Dave." The Captain rubbed his chin. "I'll tell you everything under one condition, and you can go the limit."

"Name it."

"Get some help from Uncle Sam for me, and from the Tampa police as well. I think they're probably after me for questioning."

"I can handle the Tampa police," Riker told him. "As to the T and G-men—"

"You're not so sure. Well, neither am I. Here's what I want you to do, Dave. Call Arnold Cameron, special agent in charge of the New York City FBI. Tell him the works: that this is sort of an open field case on jurisdiction, that Spud's been shot and I've flipped my lid. Ask him to get some Washington brass to contact McKelvey, their agent here."

"And tell him what?"

"To put up with my strange blind whims for a couple of days. That sometimes they work. And that I'm really not a drooling idiot, but a licensed New York private eye. Promise?"

"I'll call him right now if you want."

"No, wait. I'm pressed for time."

"Okay, Captain. Now the four bright ideas?"

"Not ideas, Dave. Three men and a boy, or two boys that we can class as one."

"I know the boys," Riker said. "They've dropped off the earth. Who are the men, and why?"

"Otis Marble first," Maclain said, "and I'm playing no favorites by the rotation. One or all may be hooked in together in the Barringer network. Otis is an ex-con and proud of it. He talks too much. He was too damn anxious to have me think Ronnie had pulled up that coconut shell. He could have been in on Dayland's murder and Ronald would have stopped his car. He could have shot that .45 slug through Ronnie's window. He could—"

"One thing he couldn't have done is kill Ronnie," Dave Riker broke in.

"Neither could Jack—"

"Jack Manning? Good God, Captain, aren't your pitches—?"

"Sit tight, Dave. For the moment we'll have to confine Ronnie's murder to Nick Papalekas, or the Fraceti boy. I'll take up Manning in a minute. After all, he had the best motives of any of them."

"Jack Manning? Why he married—"

"You just said it, Dave. If Jack and Norton, that comptroller, had been dipping into the funds of Dayland Fruits, and had been forced to get a cover-up loan from Barringer—" He went on to tell about his talk with Judge Marston, his own thoughts about the groves as a distribution front, and concluded: "Jack couldn't have played it cooler than by getting Dayland and Norton both killed and then marrying the Dayland groves, dope distribution center, *Kalua* and all."

"You make him look worse than Otis," Riker said.

"No, not at all," the Captain protested. "They both fit in in a dozen places, but Jack's record is clean, as far as you and I know, and Otis Marble's record smells like a dead fish. Then there's the matter of that poker alibi. Five witnesses to where Jack was, and Otis has only his own say-so which is nothing at all. And, putting it baldly, outside of that knock on the head I got last night, that's what we have, Dave—nothing at all."

"What's so remarkable about a conk on the head?"

"Crooks don't conk me, Dave. In all the years I've been in this racket, I've never been sapped before. Plenty have tried to kill me, by most ingenious methods, but that was always because of what I knew, not because of what I might see."

"I get it now, Captain. What's your explanation?"

"Our lad just intended to kill that girl before she said too much. Then he was going to lay me cold. Spud, who'd gone there with Cappo to check on those six turtles—by the way, where are those things, Cappo?"

"They were taken by Mr. McKelvey, Cap'n."

"Good. Now he may believe me. Anyhow, Spud charged in unexpectedly. Maybe he saw our lad between the curtains, or maybe he didn't. Our killer was taking no chances. He shot Spud. Now why did he conk me?"

"You're doing the talking," Riker said. "Tell me."

"On account of you," the Captain said. "If it happened to be Jack or Otis, either of them had to get back here to Mandalay. Thirty-five miles. Cappo didn't think of it, but I'd have phoned you instantly to check on Otis and Jack, find out if either was out and when he got in. Now, one of those boys might have spear-gunned Eileen—"

"Why?"

"Barringer's orders, or no more horse. Barringer may be hiding them out. Or it might have been Nick Papalekas. The girl told me he would kill for a proper fee. The question is, since I have no idea where the two boys are, nor where Papalekas hangs out, and they know it, would one of them have taken the time to sap me?"

"An interesting question, Captain. I'll add it to the file of other interesting theories that you've given me and McKelvey to work on. Am I out of line in asking what you intend to do right now?"

"I haven't the faintest notion, Dave. The rest is up to you and the FBI." He reached across the desk and flipped off the tape recorder. "Now, I'll tell you, off the record, what I'm going to do. But no squealing to McKelvey, hunh?"

"No squealing, Captain. Honor bright!"

"I'm going to find those two boys and get them to turn themselves in."

"Do you mind saying how, when they've ducked the Coast Guard and the FBI?"

"I'm going to get a girl to talk, even if I have to spank it out of her. You could kill her, I believe, and she wouldn't give you the time of day. You're the law and that's the code of a teen-age gang."

"It wouldn't surprise me a bit if you did it, Captain. Now I'm going to give you something to think about, since you've choked my recording machine. You're acting for the Fracetis and Marian Lindsay, aren't you?"

"That's right, Dave. I'm also acting for Spud and myself, win, lose, or draw."

"Well, the FBI has a hell of a lot more on Paul Fraceti than all the theories about those other characters, as damning as they may prove to be."

The Captain sat poker-faced, waiting.

"They have Chuck Lindsay's boat that the boys were in," Dave Riker continued smoothly. "In it were a couple of fish spears and Paul Fraceti's CO2 spear gun. FBI ballistics can prove that the spear removed from Ronnie's body was shot from Paul Fraceti's gun. What will a jury think of that, Captain?"

Maclain stood up. "If they have the brains of twelve dirt daubers, they'll think the same as I do. It's the pin-up of Mandalay, Dave: the perfect frame!"

TWENTY-THREE

Celeste and the Captain ate lunch together with Miss Fitch, the trained nurse, in the main house. Sybella had phoned, and Celeste was driving in that afternoon with clothes for her and Rena. Dr. Arnheit had agreed when he dressed the Captain's head, replacing the turban with a strip of plaster, that the trip and new interests in someone else's troubles were excellent therapy. He had called and said that after lunch Miss Fitch could go home. Try as he might, Maclain found it almost impossible to skirt the subject of Ronnie's death, and the murder of Eileen Coles the night before. It was obvious that Celeste had much more than a passing interest in Eileen, although she never actually said so.

The Captain kept questioning her about Red Barringer, but the facts she gave him were slim, and only served to confirm what Maclain already knew: That Barringer was an artist at tucking in his own rough edges. Celeste in turn kept prodding him with questions about Eileen.

Finally, Maclain gave in and painted a flattering and sympathetic picture, deliberately keeping it far enough away from the truth to give Ronald some justification. It might arouse Celeste's jealousy he thought, but at the same time it would bolster her self-esteem to feel that Ronald hadn't been about to leave her for some old hag of a dope-fiend.

Lunch was nearly over when they heard the starting of the motor on the *A-bomb.*

"Jack's in Sarasota!" There was a clatter of silver against a saucer as Celeste dropped a teaspoon. "That's Ronnie's boat—! Who—?"

"It's my fault, Celeste," Maclain explained quickly. "It's my chauffeur, Cappo, warming up the motor. We're going out for a couple of hours—"

"In the *A-bomb*? This afternoon? Fishing?" The reproach in Celeste's voice couldn't be missed. It took in Spud in the hospital, and Rena and Sybella left alone in Tampa to bear the brunt, while Maclain went fishing with his chauffeur.

"It's not exactly protocol, is it?" Maclain remarked, stirring his coffee. "Next to Spud Savage, Ronald Dayland was my dearest friend. The fishing trip I'm going on with Cappo isn't for pleasure, believe me. I'm going fishing for facts that can't wait. Facts to uncover who shot Spud, and killed that woman last night, and who murdered your husband and your son."

"If you'll excuse me, I'll go over and collect Rena's and Sybella's clothes." She left the table and turned at the terrace door. "I mean really excuse me, Captain, and God make your fishing successful. Miss Fitch, I won't be needing you any more."

"I think she's snapped out of it, Miss Fitch," Maclain said when she'd gone. "I suppose Jack took the Imperial when he left last night, but then—"

"Mr. Manning left this morning, but Mrs. Manning has her own car, if that was bothering you."

"Of course. Then you and Celeste didn't have to spend the night here alone. She was so nervous, I felt a little guilty about all of us going in to Tampa for dinner."

"You needn't have, Captain. Dr. Arnheit had given her a sedative, and I read until late. Mr. Manning was here all evening watching TV in his own room."

"Oh." The Captain touched the strip of plaster on his head. "I guess he didn't get a chance to go down to the *Kalua*, then. I was in hopes—"

"I don't believe he left the house," Miss Fitch said. "From Mrs. Manning's room you can hear every car on the drive, and none went out or came in. He looked in on us to say goodnight just before twelve, but Mrs. Manning was asleep. He'd made some coffee, so I had a cup with him here in the dining room. He seemed nervous, so I got him to take a Seconal, what with the funeral and all."

"Well, it isn't important," the Captain told her. "It's been very nice meeting you, Miss Fitch. I'd better be going before Cappo burns up all the gas and oil."

As the *A-bomb* sped out of Little Pass, the Captain repeated his conversation with Miss Fitch to Cappo. "Looks like the needle is pointing away from Jack. Don't you think so?"

"Nossuh, Cap'n. It's still swinging round just as crazy as ever. If I was planning to drive to Tampa for a nice cool murder and I had a man like this Red, with his goons and garages, nobody would hear me driving in and out, for I'd walk down to the road over the grass, where one of Mr. Red's chauffeurs would take me in to Chatham Springs and bring me back. Let some nosy parker spot a license, it sure wouldn't be on *my* car."

"You have all the instincts of a murderer, yourself." Maclain gave a sigh that was whipped away by the wind.

"Yessuh, Cap'n. A man sure learns to cut around corners or he ain't much use to you. Once I used to dive for pennies around the docks at Nassau. Now you got me diving for heroin. You're not foolin' me, Cap'n, with that mooring buoy and all that heavy fishing line. I know just as well as can be what you're fixing to do."

"I've already told you, big dome! I want that surface buoy attached to the canister where that turtle's missing, and all the canisters connected together on the bottom with that fishing line. Did you get that air tank, like I told you?"

"I keep my own air in my lungs, Cap'n. When I need more I come up to get it. I brought flippers and a face mask. Nobody's getting me under water with a lot of bubble-blowing machinery weighing me down. Don't worry. I'll attach your containers together so when you find one you can find the others just by following the string along. I know what you're fixing to do."

"You've said that before. I want to be sure I'm right about those turtles and that dope and make the others easy to locate after they've found one. That's all."

"After you've found one," Cappo said disgustedly. "You're not satisfied with your head bashed in and Mr. Spud shot. If this killer don't show quick enough to suit you, you're fixing to set one of your booby traps. You think if you go diving here at night in pitch black water that this killer will follow you down. You better train a porpoise like Dreist, Cap'n, or this time you'll be the one to drown."

They were back at five with the job all done. At least he hadn't made a blooper this far. He called the hospital, got Sybella, and found there had been no change in Spud. He told her he didn't know when he'd get to Tampa, but if there was any news to phone him. Then he slumped dejectedly in a chair.

Cappo came in and mixed him a couple of dry Martinis. At six o'clock he bathed and shaved, then called the Hubbards and got Betty on the phone.

At first she sounded frightened. Then, after some hesitation, she agreed to meet him and have dinner at Luigi's, an Italian restaurant across the causeway in Mandalay.

Betty's Renault Dauphine felt cramped to the Captain after the space of the Cadillac, but he hunched his long frame down more compactly and thanked his stars that the girl drove so well.

He'd talked long and earnestly through dinner, and he'd hoped persuasively. Still he didn't know what had finally decided her to take him to talk with Chuck and Paul. Even now, after thirty minutes driving, up U.S. 19, then twisting eastward through a maze of bad roads that had him baffled completely, he wasn't sure that the boys, and their hideout, were her destination.

She had toyed her way through dinner, speaking only when he asked a direct question, and then answering most evasively. About all he'd learned was that she'd known Ronnie and been fond of him, and that he already knew. As to Chuck Lindsay, and Paul Fraceti, beyond saying that she'd met them, she'd admitted nothing.

He was discouraged and ready to admit defeat when he paid the check. Then just outside of the restaurant door she'd taken his arm.

"Can you stand a rough ride and a worse walk?"

"As well as you, Betty. If while we're walking you don't try to drag me and just let me touch your arm."

"Then tell your chauffeur to go on home and not try to follow me. Not that he could, without ruining that big car. We'll go in my Dauphine and I'll drive you home."

Finally after half an hour, and four cigarettes snuffed in the ashtray he asked her directly: "Are you taking me to Chuck and Paul?"

"I don't know yet. I've been thinking it out. They may not want me to. I'm taking you to where I can talk to them while you wait in the car. The ride hasn't been much better than the dinner, has it?"

"Well, it's been longer." He lit another cigarette.

The road got worse. Hard-top, unrepaired for years, that

bounced them unmercifully. He welcomed it when Betty turned sharp left into a sand trail where branches swept each side of the little car. At a guess they were somewhere to the east in the country back of Tarpon Springs. She hadn't exaggerated when she told him that Cappo couldn't have followed without ruining the big car.

He had just put out his cigarette when she pulled off the trail to the right and stopped. Foliage was close to the window and he'd heard the scrape of branches on the top. He felt certain that even in daylight the Renault in this spot would be shielded from any searching 'copter.

"I may be fifteen or twenty minutes," Betty said. "The mosquitoes are murder here, but I can't help it. I'll hurry. Here, put some of this repellent dope on your hands, face, and ankles." She handed him a tube and got out, shutting him in the car.

He used the evil smelling stuff and still the mosquitoes attacked him viciously. The ancient smell of old trees and fertilizer was heavy. An orange grove, without doubt, but grown into jungle now. She was back in what seemed like hours but couldn't have been more than fifteen or twenty minutes.

"They're glad I brought you," she said in a relieved tone. "Chuck remembers you well. He's the redhead. Paul's dark and likes to think he's sour. It's rough from here on in. You'll probably ruin that keen suit. Still want to go?"

"I can buy a new suit, Betty. New boys aren't on the market at any price. Let's go."

She led him onto a winding path that seemed to grow more impassable as they pushed along. Briars scratched him. Twigs tore at his face. Trailing Spanish moss caressed him eerily. Once his head struck a branch. A bull's eye on Dr. Arnheit's dressing. Pain shot through him and he had to stop, clutching dizzily at a tree.

"It's not much farther. Can you make it?"

"I couldn't make it back without a rest. That's for sure." He set his teeth. "Finish your good deed, Girl Scout! Ever on!"

Five minutes later, after going through two doors in a rough pine building, he was shaking hands with a powerful Chuck Lindsay, and being introduced to Paul Fraceti, a boy with the whipcord strength of an expert swimmer, evident in the tensile fingers that wound around the Captain's palm.

"You look like Betty had worked you over," Paul said. "Sit down here. You're the first non-member ever to visit the Wharf Rats' club house."

"It's an honor I hadn't expected." Maclain sat down gratefully in a comfortable chair. "I won't waste time. You fellows are really in a bind, a terrible jam. I've been retained by your families to find who really killed Ronnie. Arch Ransom will defend you, if you decide to play it smart and come on back."

"Great snakes, man!" Chuck Lindsay said. "They don't think Paul and I had a hand in that caper, do they? Why Paul didn't even have his spear-gun with him when he went down."

"So, I said you were in a bind, boys! FBI ballistics have matched up the spear that killed Ronnie with the markings in Paul's CO2 gun. It's going to be hard to fast talk your way out of that one, since you've taken it on the run."

"Somebody's lying, mister," Paul said. "Does my old man and Chuck's old lady go along with this gag?"

"I can't read their minds, boys. They've retained Arch and me, but the town thinks your parents wouldn't believe you were up to anything if you were caught in a bank vault at two in the morning."

"And what do you think?"

"I'm here, wherever that is, but your press releases during the past few years haven't been any better than they should be. You became a couple of sitting ducks when you pinched the *Donna* and took a powder. It might help if you could give me some reason for making yourselves look like fugitives from a chain gang."

"We were sitting ducks if we stayed home," Chuck said.

"I'm listening, boys. Keep recording."

"Nick Papalekas," Paul said. "Ever hear of him?"

Maclain nodded. "Adversely. I've opened a file."

"Put this in it," Paul said. "Ronnie was a junky. Did you know that?"

Again Maclain nodded. "Go on."

"Papalekas was the pusher who supplied him. The Feds knew it, but he was stooling for them and they kept him running loose, hoping he'd turn in bigger game."

"How did you find all this out, Paul?"

"Maybe I sould take the fifth, but I won't. I'm too bugged. Papalekas used to push us some tea for our parties. We had—"

"Tea?"

"Weed. Marijuana. Now and then some Red Devils, or Yellow Perils, Seconal or nembutal. We've tried everything, I guess, but most of our gang grew up and laid off. Ronnie never did. He had to move on to the snow. Big-time Dayland! So, we figure Ronnie got too much on Nick, and Nick, and Otis Marble, who was buying junk from Nick for Ronnie, decided Ronnie must go. Then I had to stick my nose in—"

"Did you actually see Papalekas shoot Ronnie under water, Paul?"

"I saw Papalekas and he saw me, Captain Maclain. That was plenty. Look, the Feds may not know it but that Greek's worse under water than a depth bomb. He's been a tigershark for the spongers for years in their battles down off the Keys. Does it mean anything that he found Ronnie? It did to Chuck and me. When we heard he'd found Ronnie's body, seemed like he knew where it'd be—well, from the radio news and the looks of your head, my guess is you had a taste of Nick yourself last night. Chuck and I went lame, if you like, panicked and spooked. It looked like a question of blow town or die to Chuck and me. So we blew!"

A descriptive phrase had caught the Captain's attention. "Did you boys ever hear Papalekas called 'Tiger Man?'" he asked curiously.

"It would fit," Chuck said, "but it's a new one on me. Paul?"

"No, not me. You've had it, Captain. What's the verdict now? Turn ourselves in?"

"First, level with me. What was the big idea back of shooting at Ronnie out on the Gulf and damn near running us down?"

"We were trying to spook him," Chuck said. "He'd gone hog wild. Tarts in Tampa. Popping himself. Mixing with pushers and pimps. Drunken driving. The Wharf Rats had built up a bad enough name without his help. Next thing would be a teen-age curfew if Ronnie kept on. He'd talked of going to Miami. Big deal. He was a one-man crime wave, and we kept him reminded that we wanted him out of town."

"Why did you follow the *Kalua* and go diving there?"

"He'd showed some sort of a turtle to Betty the night before and said it came from a treasure ship. She blabbed to us—"

Betty put in: "Ronnie had kept promising me to get wise to himself. Instead he was getting worse. I was really fond of him, and I was sore."

"Anyhow you blabbed," Paul said. "So I went diving to bug him. Put the heat on more. I got burned myself and fixed Chuck up good, hunh?"

"Did either of you boys fire a slug into Ronnie's room the night before?"

"No," Paul said. "We didn't think of it. Anything more?"

"Could Papalekas have gotten hold of a spear that was fired from your CO2 gun, Paul?"

"Like a breeze," Paul said. "I had three, all used, that I kept in the locker of Chuck's boat. Nick could easily have taken one of mine, day or night, and left another one in its place."

"Then why wouldn't it show different markings if he'd shot Ronnie with his own gun?" The Captain wrinkled his brow.

"Easy," Paul said. "He used a spring or rubber-band job. They shoot from a trough, like a cross bow. No markings. But there's a tight fitting barrel on a CO2 gun. Can you nail him, Captain? We'd like to come home."

"One more thing," Maclain stood up. "I suppose the Donna is hidden too far away for you to reach her."

"Why?" Chuck asked suspiciously.

"I had an idea. It won't work unless you can get to a ship-to-shore phone."

"We'll listen," Paul said. "The *Donna's* hidden in an old abandoned boathouse way up the Anclote River. She's less than five minutes walk from here."

"I'll send you details by Betty tomorrow. Stick around, boys. I'm afraid the atmosphere is healthier here than at home."

He hadn't asked them outright if they were hooked like Ronnie. He felt sure that he already knew.

TWENTY-FOUR

He'd spent the whole morning selling his scheme to Riker, the Treasury men, and FBI Agent McKelvey. It hadn't been easy. He knew he couldn't have put it across without a phone call to McKelvey from Special Agent Arnold Cameron in New York. Now the rest of the day was gone and still nothing done.

The sun dove down with its usual trick in Florida of eliminating any twilight and suddenly turning day into night. Sitting alone in the guest house, close by the phone, the Captain didn't know the difference. He'd been there most of the afternoon, vainly trying to keep his mind from working crazily by trying to concentrate on a book, his jigsaw puzzle, or the radio, in turn. None of them served to relax him. The kaleidoscopic patterns of mistakes he had made, past and present, kept forming in colorful mockeries.

If he could just get through to Spud long enough to tell him: "Those weren't any magic bullets, Spud! Just .45 slugs from some creep's automatic. Some moron who murders women and kids with fish spears. Even old Arnold Cameron, with the great stone face, is pulling for you. I've never let you down, have I? I swear it, Spud, if you'll stay alive you can watch this killer fry!"

Big talk. Brave talk. Bombast. He'd better get a new script writer.

He mixed up some mess of a salad from stuff in the icebox, tried to eat it without his usual cocktails, and consigned most of it to the garbage can. He had never felt so much alone and so utterly helpless.

At nine-thirty he could stand it no longer. He called the main house and got Jack Manning on the phone.

"Can you come over to the guest house for a while? I'm sitting here consuming myself like a snake swallowing it's tail."

"Godamighty, Captain. We thought you'd gone in town. Eben said Cappo left with your dogs this afternoon. Why didn't you come over here? Anyhow, come on over now. Arch Ransom's here, and the Hubbards."

"I don't want to see them, Jack. Particularly not the

Hubbards. Make some excuse for me, if you will. Come on over and I'll explain. I'm stuck here by the phone."

Jack came over a few minutes later and exclaimed in surprise when he switched on the lights in the living room. "You look slightly the worse for wear."

"So they've been telling me." His fingered his Braille watch nervously.

Jack sat down. His penetrating black eyes flickered over Maclain's zipper jacket, khaki pants, and Topsider boat shoes. Not attempting to hide his amazement, he asked: "Are you figuring on a trip with those fishing clothes on?"

"I ruined a perfectly good suit last night prowling through jungles. I may have to repeat it when I get a call. I've found the boys, Jack." He told him about his trip with Betty. "The only reason she took me is because I still don't know where they are. I thought if she called tonight, I'd tell her I was grounded without Cappo. Then she'd have to come here and you might follow in Ronnie's MG. You can't get through a lot of those trails in a man's size auto. Even if you stayed way behind, you know the groves around here well enough to guess where they are."

"I have a hunch where that club house is right now," Jack said deliberatively. "We own a lot of freeze-outs back of Tarpon Springs. Abandoned. Could be Ronnie—"

The telephone interrupted.

Maclain answered and listened to the excited voice without speaking until it was finished.

"Thanks, Betty," he said, then after more talk from the other end. "Look, Honey, you've done the right thing. Believe me, it's the best for everybody, including the boys and you. Hang up now, and I'll see what I can do."

"Those boys are about to haul it again on the *Donna*. Either they got alarmed at my visit, or they've played me for a fool." He touched his watch. "It's nine forty-five. Is Otis on board the *Kalua*?"

"Otis Marble has packed up his duds and is gone," Jack said woodenly. "Do you suppose he's mixed up with those kids?"

"Up to his ears," the Captain said. "I haven't time to explain. Get your car and drive me down to the marina. Can we make it by ten?"

"If we hurry. What's cooking?"

"We've got to get to the ship-to-shore phone on the *Kalua*. Those boys will be standing-by on the *Donna* for a message at ten. We've got to listen in to that call."

"The damn light's out on the end of Pier One," Jack said when they got there. "It's black as pitch."

"Not to me," the Captain said. "Hurry! I'm not going to fall."

Two boats were talking back and forth on 2182 when the ship-to-shore began to buzz, filling the *Kalua's* wheelhouse with its droning sound.

Almost instantly the rasping voice of Gerry Farkas broke in. "This is the charter-boat *Stingray* calling the yacht *Donna*. Repeat—"

"This is the *Donna*, *Stingray*. No need to repeat. We're reading you loud and clear. How me? Over."

"Chuck Lindsay's voice," the Captain whispered.

"Loud and clear. We're meeting at the Turtle Bar, table five, and bringing Nick. At one. Otis knows where it is. He's with you, isn't he? Over."

"Yes. He's here. We can get there earlier if you'd like us to. Over."

"No earlier. We can't make if before one. We'll lift a few for you. Maybe you and the Skipper will pick up something you'd like to take home. We'll see you then. Over."

"At one," Chuck's voice assured Farkas. "Roger. Over and out."

"Now, what was that Turtle Bar stuff about?" Jack asked as he switched off the S-to-S phone.

The Captain rapidly explained and added, "Cappo saw those six sunken containers and hitched them together with a guide line yesterday."

"Why?"

"We're wasting time, Jack. We thought he might have to dive for them again. Cappo says the containers must weigh a hundred pounds each. Now call the Coast Guard on the ship-to-shore phone and I'll explain things. The *Stingray* and the *Donna* are going out there to get that million bucks worth of heroin. The *Stingray* has a winch to pull it up. The *Donna* hasn't. They'll load it on board the *Donna*, and Otis, who knows every cove on the coast, will run it in."

"But what about those boys, Captain?"

"They're both hooked, like Ronnie was. This looks to them like a hophead's dream. Sooner or later, just like Ronnie, Papalekas may find their bodies, near where that bunch of pirates have murdered them, and bring them ashore. You don't believe they're going to be allowed to live and talk, do you? Now, turn on that ship-to-shore."

"Like hell!" Jack said. "Not and let the whole world listen in. This blasted shore phone in here is out of order. I reported it when I tried to call Otis today. He probably silenced it before he left."

"What about the marina?" Maclain asked.

"Good. I'll run up and phone St. Petersburg Coast Guard from the pay booth there."

"You know what to say?"

"God above!" Jack was halfway out the door. "Yes, I know what to say."

It took him ten minutes, and then he came back storming in: "Damn bureaucracy! That place off Anclote Key is five miles out. They have no jurisdiction. They're dispatching a patrol boat, but it's way down the coast. It couldn't possibly get there before daylight. Good lord, if I could only swim."

"You'd what?" Maclain asked stiffly.

"I have a winch up forward. We could run up there and get that heroin. They wouldn't kill those kids if they couldn't find it, would they?"

"No. Two more murders for nothing. Saving that dope for Bar-ringer is all they're interested in. Go on, start the motors and let's get under way."

"Who will hook on to those containers?"

"I will," the Captain assured him. "I can see just as much as you can under water at night. I'm as good a diver as Cappo is with a face mask on, and believe me, I can swim."

"I think you're nuts, but I'll try it." The starter growled and the motors began to rumble. "I'll go out and cast off the lines."

"It's sort of a poetic justice," the Captain told him. "Customs have suspected Otis of using the *Kalua* for just this purpose: bringing heroin in."

TWENTY-FIVE

The wheelhouse was hotter and muggier than the night outside. Heat came seeping up from the Diesels just below as they began to warm to their work.

Jack cast off, stepped aboard, and backed her out from the slip without the warning blasts from her air-whistle. Maclain was grateful. He'd been waiting for that screech with every nerve in him stretched out like threads of glass ready to shatter at a touch.

He wondered if Dreist ever got the shakes, or knew the fear of anticipation. Probably not, thank heaven! Tell Dreist to 'guard' and he'd stay there until one of three voices, or the necessity of action, relieved him from duty. Unlike the Captain, or Spud, or Cappo, Dreist lacked that human weakness of trying to fathom the future. Neither bombs, earthquakes, nor sudden whistles would overcome training and cause a phlegmatic, protective police dog to jump out of his skin.

Perspiration had soaked the Captain's jacket and khaki slacks. He stood up and stripped down to the trunks he was wearing underneath. It was partly in an attempt to get cooler, partly for just something to do.

The wheelhouse had become a steam-heated mausoleum with Ronnie's body laid out on one lounge seat, on the other the body of Eileen Coles. They lay there, still and stark and so clear. Otis and Jack must have seen them, too. Tonight, at least, the water of the Gulf was glassy and the mausoleum was staying on an even keel.

A bell tolled once, gently and mournfully, rung by a long passing swell. They were a mile out now from Little Pass. The *Kalua* turned north around Bell Flasher One. Forty-five minutes and they'd be there.

At the sound of the bell he was lost again in that strange fog of fear that had enveloped him throughout the week. The knot in his belly drew tighter.

He listened to the engines, almost hoping for a break in their rhythm that would indicate a coming breakdown. He was enduring that moment of uncertainty that came at the wrap-up of every case. The same old routine. What had he forgotten? With Spud's keen eyes closed, perhaps forever, what details had he overlooked?

The mask and flippers? No. Jack had found those before they left.

Had he misjudged the cleverness of Otis Marble? Or the ruthlessness of Nick Papalekas? Or the boys, or Jack Manning? Without Spud's help, were the powerful forces of law and order sufficient to keep him alive? Would he finish like Ronnie, and that accountant, Norton, on the bottom of the Gulf with a fish-spear through him?

The answer was: "Undoubtedly!" if any one tiny fragment of his scheme should chance to go wrong. Now, at the very last moment he had a mad desire to cancel the trip; claim weariness, illness, anything to stop those irresistible Diesels from churning the two bronze screws that were shoving him on and on.

He only needed to say the word, refuse to dive, and Jack would turn back. Then, just as irresistibly as the Diesels, and far more destructively, Red Barringer's shrimpers would keep plowing the waves, and plowing more corpses under.

What had Cappo told him? "You never chickened out on anything!" Well, that was it! You could get hooked by a lot of other projects in life that were just as hard to shake as heroin or morphine.

Jack startled him with an inquiry: "Are you feeling okay?"

Somehow it had a familiar ring. Jack was showing too much concern about his, Maclain's, health. Or maybe it was two other fellows. Anyhow he'd been asked that same question either by Jack, or someone else, during the past week. Or was it tonight? Or yesterday? He was tired of lying about it to be polite.

"Right now I have a headache," the Captain said. "I'm pouring sweat. I have a cramp in my guts. My legs feel like water and the bump on my head hurts like hell."

"Are you sure you're up to that diving?" Jack asked solicitously.

"I can't think of anything better than a swim."

"Well, I hope so." He sounded doubtful. "I've got the beacon lined up with Anclote Key. Fifteen minutes now."

"Any sign of any other boats?"

"None. Of course they may be running with their lights out but that's not likely. Here's the plan—if you're sure you're going to try this."

"I'm sure. Go on."

"I'm going to put a belt on you and attach it to a Buddy Line, then make that fast to the cleat on the stern. The trouble is, it will have to be over fifty feet long so you can swim to the bow to—"

"That's out," Maclain said firmly. "You're putting no line on me. You'll pick up the buoy Cappo left with your spotlight. It's a red spar. You'll anchor so the boat will drift back until that spar is on one side of the bow. I'll go over in the stern by the boarding ladder. Then I'll swim alongside to the bow until I feel the grapple that you've lowered down to me." He paused. "You have a grapple, don't you?" he asked anxiously.

"Ice tongs," Jack said.

"Good. They'll do nicely. I'll hook the tongs in my belt. You can direct me how to swim to the spar buoy and when I've found it, I'll follow Cappo's line down. When I've hooked the tongs into the first container I'll give three tugs on the winch line. I'll come up with Cappo's line that leads to the next one and hang on to the boarding ladder in the stern out of your way. Yell when the container's on board in the bow. I'll swim to the bow, get the grapple and go down again. With no foul-ups we should have the six on board before midnight and be on our way."

"And just how do you expect to find the stern of this boat each time, Captain?"

"I can hear the motors idling while I'm under water, Jack. As a matter of fact under water I could hear an outboard coming a mile away. Maybe I'll come up underneath, or alongside and have to work my way to the stern. But I won't do it more than once, I'll guarantee."

"You must get more than money out of the chances you take," Jack said, thoughtfully. "What is it?"

"Life without blindness," Maclain told him simply. "Proof that if God has left you brains and courage, you don't need eyes to really see."

He pushed back from the boarding ladder, that Jack had

hung over the starboard side of the cockpit. There was a canvas tarpaulin under its hooks to protect the polished mahogany rail.

The feel of the milky warm water was silky against his hot skin, caressing him pleasantly. Jack yelled from the *Kalua's* bow. The Captain started his fifty-foot journey along the boat toward Jack's voice swimming his easy powerful crawl.

The ice tongs Jack was dangling overside touched his outflung hand. He hooked them in the belt at his waist, thinking that their weight of three of four pounds would make it easier to dive.

"The buoy's to your right," Jack yelled.

He found it without difficulty. Letting the line rest against his naked shoulder to guide him, he made a neat jack-knife and kicking his flippers began to swim down.

He didn't really become conscious of the immensity of his isolation until he was close to the bottom, ten or twelve feet down. Unseen tendrils brushed his skin with a slimy loathsome affection.

Overhead the Diesels throbbed reassuringly, but for the moment not even their sound seemed real. He thought of the Bible: "And the earth was without form or void. And darkness was upon the face of the deep."

Then his fingers probed through the grass and seaweed and touched the first heavy canister, and his brain flashed the words: "And God said: 'Let there be light!' And there was light." Instantly, with that message, his feeling of isolation was gone.

Of course, he couldn't very well have missed the canister. More than a hundred pounds, he guessed. Two feet by two feet of bolted stainless steel, and more than three feet long.

He didn't want to make a second trip down for that one, but he was battling for breath by the time he'd found the eyelets on one end. The ice tongs fitted as though they'd been made for that job, which they probably had been.

He shot to the top without waiting to tug on the winch line Jack was holding. He came up midway between the bow and stern of the *Kalua,* swam to the stern and clung to a rung of the boarding ladder, gratefully sucking in air.

"Thirty seconds," Jack yelled. "I don't suppose you got the tongs hooked on."

"Start your winch and see," Maclain yelled back. "I've got

the trick now. The others won't take so long."

The power winch clattered as Jack put it in gear. Five minutes later the first two kilos of the blood-money fortune in its waterproof casing had been lowered to the *Kalua's* deck by the small-sized swinging boom.

It was quarter past twelve when the sixth one with its trailing turtle started up after the Captain's tug on the line.

Maclain was closer to the point of exhaustion than he thought. He surfaced some distance forward of the bow this time, for the last of the canisters had been yards away, up against the tide which was running stronger.

"Come here and I'll give you a hand to get in! I'm waiting here in the stern!"

The Captain swam weakly, glad of the tide that was carrying him without any effort along the *Kalua* and toward Jack's voice. He clutched tightly at the boarding ladder, and finally got his feet on the bottom under-water rung.

"Give me both hands," he told Jack. "I've hardly got strength enough left to lift a leg over the rail. I'm about done in."

Assisted by the pull of both Jack's hands, he made it up a couple of steps. "I have to take a breather," he gasped, and doubled over forward. Both his arms were hanging inside the cockpit as Jack released his hands. Limply he hung resting, his stomach on the tarpaulin shielding the rail.

It was perfect.

Jack took the second of the two fish-spears that he'd filched from Chuck Lindsay's boat from where he'd placed it on the transom seat built across the stern. The first had done nicely with Ronnie, as the boy was slipping into the water. This one would do just as nicely, plunged into the exposed bare back of the incoming Duncan Maclain.

He clutched it tightly with his cotton fishing glove and raised it high for leverage.

That was an error.

Dreist, crouched on the cabin top in the shadow of the dinghy where Cappo had placed him while Jack was in the marina phoning, leaped six feet straight at the threatening figure with the upraised spear.

His seventy pounds of flying weight carried Jack and spear to the floor and sent the spear flying to the other side of the cockpit.

Jack screamed in pain and terror as he started to rise. The dog dove straight for his throat and, missing it, sank his frightful fangs into Jack's up-thrown protecting arm.

"Get him off, Maclain! Get the damned dog off! He's trying to kill me! Can't you see!"

Maclain snapped out a whiplash order. Dreist released Jack's bleeding forearm, and stood like a nemesis, his unmoving eyes fixed on his prostrate prey, his strong flanks trembling violently.

The Captain climbed wearily aboard and sat down on the transom seat.

"Get him away! Get him away!" Jack kept whining. "Can't you see he wants to kill me?"

"I thought you knew I couldn't see," Maclain said frostily. "I've decided to let him tear your throat out in a minute. It's most unpleasant, but you happen to be a type of gunsel that's most distasteful to me."

The calm assurance; the deep sincerity, and the almost fanatical hatred evident in every word of that dripping half-naked blind man were even more terrifying than the menacing jaws of Dreist.

"You've lost your mind, Maclain." Jack could scarcely speak for his trembling. "You couldn't turn a beast like this loose to murder a human being."

"It will be a pleasure, Mr. Manning. You're the murdering beast I intend to destroy. You killed my best friend seven years ago to steal his business, his wife and his fortune. You killed the comptroller, Norton, who could blast your Barringer alibi. That wasn't enough. Last Tuesday you killed Ronald's son as you tried to kill me just now. Still not enough. Night before last you spattered me with a woman's blood in another murder, and almost fatally shot the one man in the world I worship, my lifelong partner. But you're going to die before he does, Jack the Ripper. Pray if you can. I'm taking no chances that Barringer's lawyers can save you, as they've saved pour boss so many times."

"Why you mean it, you goddamn fool!" Jack lunged from the floor in a maniacal frenzy. Again he just managed to save his throat, but when the Captain snapped the order quieting Dreist, blood was flowing from a dozen gashes where fangs had torn Jack's other arm.

"I'll give you one chance to live, Manning," Maclain said in a voice that sounded to the torn man at his feet as brutal and insensitive as that of some mechanical robot. "You're no more of a human being than your boss, Red Barringer. Your only chance is to tell me the truth, unvarnished and from the beginning, from the day you started looting Dayland Fruits up to this minute. I'll let you live only if I find you have enough on Red to take him with you to face the law."

Jack broke at this faint glimmer of hope. Words poured out of him. After all, he thought, it was his word against a dog and a madman. Drooling in his eagerness he told the truth and told it all.

It was a miserable story: Losses at the races. Embezzlement from Dayland. Discovery by Norton, who'd agreed to play. Appeal to Barringer, whose financial help had sucked them both in. The building of respected Dayland Fruits into the nucleus of a dope distribution center. The poker party that he and Red had left together to get Dayland, the man who was stealing Red's woman and threatening to sell the Dayland groves, the hub of Red's great scheme.

The only murder Red had ever done himself, and Jack the only witness. How Red unmercifully beat Ronald to death after Jack had faked a breakdown, and Ronald Dayland recognizing him had obligingly stopped his car.

Then Norton had started blackmail, threatening to reveal that Jack and Red had left the poker party. Jack had killed him on Bar-ringer's orders. From then on he was Barringer's puppet. Kept alive only because Red had to have the *Kalua* and the Dayland groves to build his take to over a million a year.

Ronnie?

Barringer's orders. Ronnie had shown Jack the turtle and Jack had promptly given Red a call. Then everything had been done to throw suspicion on Paul Fraceti and Chuck Lindsay. News of the possible treasure find phoned around town so the boys would follow the *Kalua*. The .45 slug? Oh, Jack had ducked from the cocktail party to shoot it in the window, and later in the evening left the house to dig it from Ronnie's wall. The spears? Late that same night, he had substituted two of

Ronnie's for two he took from Chuck Lindsay's boat docked at Chuck's home just a short distance away. Red had sent out a phony deputy sheriff to substitute the *Casa ybel* coconut for the turtle the day that Ronnie was killed.

Eileen?

Barringer's orders again. Jack had been told to watch Maclain. Red had sent out another car. Jack had picked him up at Columbia Gardens, followed him to Chatham Springs and killed the girl before she blabbed it all. Spud he had to shoot. He'd barged in unexpectedly. He didn't know if Spud had seen his face between the curtains.

"And I was the last to be killed on Red's orders, is that it?" the Captain asked with disgust. "I suppose you got them when you went up to the marina and phoned him instead of the Coast Guard. He told you to get that heroin, and get rid of me. Papalekas would probably get the blame, except that the *Stingray* is an undercover Customs Boat, and Nick, the boys, Gerry Farkas and his mate, Tetter, all lured you out here with that *Stingray* to Donna S-to-S call. Anyhow, Riker bugged that booth in the marina today, so we'll have a tape of your call. You can get up now if you want to."

He snapped another order to Dreist and the dog lay down, his eyes following Jack as he got to his feet, wiping blood from his arms.

"So you've got all the truth, Maclain, and what are you going to do with it? Put the dog on the witness stand? Why half of this stuff I can hang on Otis. Everything, except Ronnie's murder, and that pooch is the only witness how I tried to get you. And suppose I refuse to take you back to Mandalay. What about that?"

Maclain stood up and stretched his arms. "I'm sick with your murderous drivel, Jack. You're going to the electric chair and Bar-ringer with you. You make me want to vomit. Ask Otis what we're going to do. He came aboard with Dreist. He's been standing right inside the screen of the owner's cabin ever since you started to squeal. He's had a gun on you, and a tape recorder. Not only has he seen everything, but both he and the tape recorder have certainly heard it all."

TWENTY-SIX

It was more than a month, the middle of May, before Spud Savage was out of the hospital. Ten days later, still weak and shaky, he was able to testify at Jack's trial. He had seen and recognized Jack at Eileen's just before Jack shot him. That fact, coupled with Jack's recorded confession, from which Otis had carefully eliminated all the Captain's threats to have Jack eaten alive by Dreist, which would certainly have constituted duress, eventually sent Jack to the chair.

Fighting to the last ditch to save himself, the three time killer finally did his best to convict the infallible Lewis (Red) Barringer and gave an eye-witness account of Ronald Dayland's brutal murder to which he had been both accomplice and accessory.

Lars Hanssen's colleague, Anson Stiles, defending Red, promptly jumped Jack and tore him up worse than Dreist. Jack had no corroborative witness. He was implicating Red in an attempt to save himself. Stiles then produced Barringer's shyster lawyer, Hanssen; the C.P.A., Walter Slazenger; and Captain Carlos O'Brien of the Eileen, who swore that Jack had left the poker game, alone, at eleven, on the night of Dayland's murder, but Barringer had been there all night long.

Hadn't Jack confessed to murdering Ted Norton? Why? Because Norton was blackmailing him by threatening to tell not only about Jack's embezzlements, but to expose the fact that Jack had no alibi. Jack had lied again and killed again. That was all.

To the press and public it looked like Red would walk out free to become a public benefactor once more.

It was at that point that the State produced a surprise voluntary witness in the person of a fragile, cowed elderly woman, who was sworn in as Margaret Barringer, Red's wife.

Answering every question in a quiet determined voice that the jury believed, Marge Barringer proceeded to blow her untouchable husband into the death house with more force than any H-bomb.

She knew Red had another woman, but she wanted protection from scandal until her two children were older. She had followed her husband and Jack on the night of the poker game. Trailed them on to the parkway with the lights off on her car. The gist of it was she was parked off the road a hundred feet away when Ronald Day-land was murdered and had seen the whole crime.

Every day for seven years she had lived in terror that this murderer would discover her secret and do away with her and the children. Every day she had hoped he would be picked up by the law, but no one had even suspected him.

Why hadn't she gone to the law herself?

Please! Her unsupported story, that Hanssen would call a frame-up of a jealous wife, against a murdering husband and the alibi of five ruthless men, three of whom had given false testimony just now?

Proof?

Yes, the State had proof. The jack handle used as a murder weapon had been recovered from the mud after seven years. Mrs. Barringer had shown the authorities the exact spot where Red had tossed it off the parkway into the shallow water of Old Tampa Bay.

"I wonder if old Nick brought it up," the Captain said.

They were talking the whole affair over again early in June as the Cadillac sped northward with Cappo at the wheel.

"Too shallow for Papalekas," Spud said. "He's a deep water diver like our buxom boy."

"It seems to me that Celeste is the one who got the short end of this deal," Sybella said. "She's lost two husbands and her boy. And Dayland Fruits is on the rocks from what I can hear. I think the risk of having to produce thirty-five thousand suddenly for that charter boat had a lot to do with Jack killing Ronnie."

Rena said: "Celeste and Dayland Fruits are both pretty hardy properties if you're asking me. My bet is Celeste will have a new husband-general-manager, named Arch Ransom, within a year."

"The tarpaulin cover that was stolen off of the *A-bomb!*" Maclain exclaimed suddenly sitting up straight.

"Don't be cryptic," Spud said. "That's what you keep telling me. What about it?"

"Jack took it before he woke Ronnie, wrapped the two spears in it, and put it in the back of his car. When he got to the *Kalua* he tossed it into the cockpit before they went on board."

"Just routine," Spud said. "Would you like to feel the two bullet holes in me?"

"He hung it over the rail to catch any blood there might be when he stabbed the boy. Then he tossed it over. If Otis had noticed it and missed it Jack could have claimed it was blown over in the storm. No tarpaulin missing from the *Kalua*, don't you see? Well, there'd have been one missing if he'd gotten me. He used the same precaution. Of course then he thought Otis had gone."

"He has now," Rena said.

"Where?"

"Maybe you think Celeste is broke and tight, but yesterday she gave the *Kalua* to the skipper for a charter boat. He's taking it to Miami."

"He earned it." The Captain sat back and opened a Braille book on his knee.

After a time Spud asked him: "What the devil are you reading?"

"It's a book called 'Tiger Man.' It's true. I sent north for it. Just before Jack killed her, Eileen Coles—"

"I heard her," Spud said. "What's it about?"

"A man who killed over two hundred tigers in the South American jungles without shooting one."

"Oh. Strangled them, hunh? Or used a dog."

"What Eileen was about to tell me was he stabbed them with a spear."

"Grisly!" Spud said. "Before I take a nap, isn't there any one of you who'd like to feel these two bullet holes in me?"

CPSIA information can be obtained
at www.ICGtesting.com
Printed in the USA
BVHW081710150920
588719BV00009B/1007